Praise for David Wagner

To Die in Tuscany
The Seventh Rick Montoya Italian Mystery

"It's a win-win for all involved, including the reader."
—*Kirkus Reviews*

"An armchair traveler's delight."
—*Publishers Weekly*

"Vivid, often lyrical descriptions of Italian towns with their architecture, food, and wine bring the setting to life. Art history and the portrayal and meaning of individual works of art are seamlessly incorporated."
—*Booklist*

Roman Count Down
The Sixth Rick Montoya Italian Mystery

"Wagner's solid sixth Rick Montoya Italian Mystery…explains how he evolved from translator to sleuth… This one will satisfy hungry travelers heading to Rome."
—*Publishers Weekly*

"The tour of Rome, the food and wine, the colorful characters, and the intriguing mystery will keep Montoya fans happy and may well interest those unfamiliar with the series to catch up on the adventures of this engaging translator and sleuth."
—*Booklist*

A Funeral in Mantova
The Fifth Rick Montoya Italian Mystery

"Following *Return to Umbria*, Wagner's fifth series outing features a likable amateur sleuth who carefully analyzes other people. Rich in details of the food and culture of Italy's Lombardy region, this atmospheric mystery will be appreciated by fans of Martin Walker's French-flavored 'Bruno' mysteries. Readers of Frances Mayes's *Under the Tuscan Sun* may enjoy the colorful descriptions."

—*Library Journal*

"Wagner's fifth series entry provides his usual deft mix of art, travel, and suspense."

—*Kirkus Reviews*

"The many details of meals that Rick enjoys on his trip are a highlight, as are the author's appended notes on the food and wines of the area."

—*Booklist*

"This is a book for armchair travelers as much as it is for mystery lovers."

—*Publishers Weekly*

Return to Umbria
The Fourth Rick Montoya Italian Mystery

"Translator Rick Montoya is in Orvieto to persuade his cousin to return home to Rome when he gets drawn into investigating the murder of American Rhonda Van Fleet. Did Rhonda's past in Orvieto, studying ceramics, lead to her death? The setting almost overwhelms the plot, but Rick is a charming and appealing amateur sleuth."

—Library Journal

"Wagner skillfully inserts nuggets of local culture without slowing down the narrative pace, and perhaps even more importantly, he gets Italy right. He understands the nuances of Italian manners and mentality as well as the glorious national preoccupation with food."

—Publishers Weekly

"With taut pacing and enough credible suspects to keep the reader guessing until the end, *Return to Umbria* makes for an engaging read."

—Shelf Awareness

Murder Most Unfortunate
The Third Rick Montoya Italian Mystery

"Returning in his third outing, Rick Montoya travels to Bassano del Grappa to work as a translator at an art seminar. When one of the attendees ends up dead, Rick can't keep himself from investigating, along with Betta Innocenti, the daughter of a local gallery owner. Rick, as always, is a charming sleuth."

—Library Journal

"Though he spent his childhood in Rome, Montoya proudly kicks around Italy in the cowboy boots he brought with him from the years he spent in New Mexico. He is an easygoing, empathetic protagonist—with just enough American irreverence to keep his Italian colleagues entertained."

—Booklist

Also by David P. Wagner

The Rick Montoya Italian Mysteries
Cold Tuscan Stone
Death in the Dolomites
Murder Most Unfortunate
Return to Umbria
A Funeral in Mantova
Roman Count Down
To Die in Tuscany

BEST SERVED COLD

BEST SERVED COLD

A RICK MONTOYA ITALIAN MYSTERY

DAVID P. WAGNER

Poisoned Pen
PRESS

Published by Poisoned Pen Press, an imprint of Sourcebooks
P.O. Box 4410, Naperville, Illinois 60567-4410
(630) 961-3900
sourcebooks.com

Library of Congress Cataloging-in-Publication Data

Names: Wagner, David P., author.
Title: Best served cold / David P. Wagner.
Description: Naperville, Illinois : Poisoned Pen Press, [2023] | Series:
  Rick Montoya Italian Mysteries ; book 8
Identifiers: LCCN 2022061971 (print) | LCCN 2022061972
(ebook) | (trade paperback) | (epub)
Subjects: LCGFT: Detective and mystery fiction. | Novels.
Classification: LCC PS3623.A35623 B47 2023 (print) | LCC PS3623.A35623
  (ebook) | DDC 813/.6--dc23/eng/20230113
LC record available at https://lccn.loc.gov/2022061971
LC ebook record available at https://lccn.loc.gov/2022061972

Printed and bound in the United States of America.
SB 10 9 8 7 6 5 4 3 2 1

For Mike Coleman

"If an injury has to be done to a man it should be so severe that his vengeance need not be feared."

—NICCOLÒ MACHIAVELLI

CHAPTER ONE

The room had but one window, high above the tile floor. One slat of the blinds covering its dirty panes was missing, letting in a few rays of Sicilian sunshine, though not enough for Rick to read the typewritten pages on the table. He had been given a small lamp that threw a harsh light on the paper. In one way the lack of sun was a blessing, since the heat of Palermo had already brought the inside temperature up to the point of discomfort. Without the blinds he would have been dripping in sweat. Of course the room had no air conditioning. He caught the faint smell of paint and wondered why a new coat had been needed on the walls. Regular maintenance, or were they covering up something?

In front of him sat a laptop, similar to the one he used in Rome when he worked on translations, but this one showed marks indicating it hadn't been well treated. That would be expected. To the left of the computer was the stack of papers, and on the other side, a video recorder was propped up so that Rick could see the screen. At the moment the recorder was set to pause, freezing an image of a man, shabbily dressed and sitting at a table. *It's probably the same table where I'm now sitting*, thought Rick, as he rubbed his eyes and looked around the room.

Unlike his Rome apartment, this workplace was austere, even barren. The only decoration on the walls was a calendar, which appeared to be from a year ago. He squinted in the weak light. Make that two years ago. A fluorescent light hung from the middle of the ceiling, but it had not been switched on when they'd brought him into the room, so Rick didn't know if it worked. A frayed extension cord connected the lamp, recorder, and laptop to a plug in the wall. The battered wastebasket under the table held the remnants of his lunch. Next to it sat Rick's overnight bag. Two other chairs rounded out the furniture inventory, both on the other side of the table.

He rubbed his hands on his jeans before returning to the keyboard to continue the translation but soon stopped when he came across a sentence in the transcript that wasn't clear. He turned on the recording and brought it up to where the man was speaking the words on the page. It was highly accented Italian, with the occasional word in dialect, but after running the tape back and forth twice, Rick was able to understand and typed in the English version.

The face on the screen showed signs of fatigue, even exhaustion. At least three days of stubble darkened the man's cheeks and crept down his neck toward an open collar. The eyes were hard to read. A tinge of fear? Or simply resignation? Rick had become as adept at reading Italians' body language as interpreting their words, but this was Sicily, and the body vocabulary was not the same as on the mainland. He took in a breath and returned to the task at hand, continuing to change the man's words into English.

The slats of the blinds clicked softly as a warm breeze pushed its way into the room, bringing with it rich scents from a nearby stove. A restaurant, or just the kitchen of a Palermitana housewife getting an early start on dinner? Either way, someone in the neighborhood would be having a considerably better meal than the panino and bottled water unceremoniously dropped on Rick's table earlier.

An hour later the creak of the door handle pulled his attention away from the keyboard. A man with coifed salt-and-pepper hair entered, closed the door behind him, and walked to the table. He pulled a handkerchief from his pocket and whisked off the chair seat before sitting down. His gray pinstripe trousers were perfectly creased and tailored in a cloth that said they belonged to a suit, perhaps a three-piece suit, though Rick couldn't be sure since the man wore no jacket. In the spot where a pocket would have been found on most American dress shirts was a small embroidered monogram: MC. The creamy white of the shirt and subdued color of the pants created a contrast to the bright stripes of a silk tie. When his suit jacket covered the leather straps of his shoulder holster, Rick imagined his visitor would cut an elegant figure on the streets of Palermo.

"Is everything going according to schedule, Riccardo?" The question was accompanied by a smile that tried to conceal the man's impatience. "You said originally that it would take you two days. Soon your first day will be complete." He stopped and awaited an answer.

Rick sniffed the air and avoided the question. "Couldn't you have taken me to a local trattoria instead of bringing me a stale sandwich?"

The man sighed. "You know that's impossible, Riccardo. But this evening, with the cover of darkness, you'll be taken to a place where you can sample some of our island's excellent cuisine. There is a restaurant where we have special connections, with private rooms, and two of my most trusted men will guide you around the menu. The swordfish is the best in the city."

"I look forward to that."

"And I will try to arrange a better lunch tomorrow."

"That would be very kind of you."

Satisfied, the man rose to his feet. "Is there anything you need now? Another bottle of mineral water, perhaps?"

"Yes, please. Chilled this time, if possible."

"I'll have one of my men bring it immediately." As he opened the door, he stopped and turned back to Rick. "You will have the transcript translated by tomorrow, won't you?"

"Of course. You can count on it."

———

Inspector Cribari was correct; the swordfish was indeed excellent, but not what Rick expected. It came as *involtini*; thin slices covered with a paste of sweet raisins, pine nuts, and caciocavallo cheese before being rolled up and lightly grilled. At the suggestion of his two police bodyguards, Rick started the meal with a dish of small gnocchi tossed lightly in a sauce of eggplant, tomato, and basil. Those three items, they assured him, were staples of Sicilian cuisine. Unstated, but in body language that even Rick understood, was the message that they would not be pleased if he ordered anything else.

The two had met him at the airport that morning and stayed close during the entire day, always just outside the room when Rick was working on the translations. Both of them, Cribari had told him, were sergeants, but neither wore a uniform. Given their duties on this day, and the next, it would be expected that they would not broadcast that they were police. Tonight both had the same first course, spaghetti with a tomato sauce, and grilled fish as the second. At their suggestion Rick had ordered a bottle of Bianco d'Alcamo, produced just south of Palermo, but they waved off more than a few sips for themselves when he tried to fill their glasses. They were on duty, after all.

"What hotel am I staying at tonight, Sergeant?" Rick directed the question to the thinner of the two men, who ate with more enthusiasm than his colleague.

"You'll be very comfortable, Riccardo. We have a good relationship with the owner, and he will see to it that you have excellent accommodations."

Rick was curious about this relationship, but didn't press it. Likely, it was the same kind the police had with the owner of the restaurant, and his meal was certainly satisfactory. The hotel should be the same. Suddenly the two men were startled by the sound of trumpets, and they instinctively reached for their weapons.

"It's all right," said Rick, reaching for the phone in his pocket. It would be too complicated to explain that his ring was the Lobo Fight Song from his beloved alma mater, so he didn't try. By coincidence, the number had the 505 area code of New Mexico, but it was not one he recognized.

"Hello?"

"Rick, you old scoundrel."

The low, rumbling voice was so distinctive there was no doubt who was calling. Zeke Campbell had been Rick's fraternity brother at the University of New Mexico and, as a defensive lineman on the football team, was feared by quarterbacks throughout the conference. His specialty move against opposing linemen, involving a hammering swing of the forearm, had been dubbed the Zeke Tweak by an Albuquerque sports writer.

"Zeke, how long has it been? Ten years? The last time I saw you was just after graduation when you were heading off to boot camp at Quantico."

"It's more like twelve years, Rick, but who's counting? I hope I haven't interrupted anything. Are you having dinner?"

Rick looked at the two policemen whose faces indicated they didn't speak any English. "Just finished. It's great to hear your voice. What's new in New Mexico?"

"Actually, I'm here in Rome, and darned if only today did I find out you're living here. Someone in my tour group—it's all New Mexicans—told me, and I made some calls and got your number. I thought maybe I could see you tomorrow morning for breakfast. We're leaving late morning."

"I'd really love to, Zeke, but unfortunately I'm…" He glanced again at his keepers. "I'm not in Rome right now and won't be back until tomorrow night. Are you flying back to the States in the morning?"

"No, no. The next stop is Assisi, tomorrow. We'll be there for five nights."

It sounded like a long time for a tour group to spend in Assisi, which wasn't that big a town. Perhaps they were using it as a base to visit other sights in Umbria.

"Zeke, my schedule is pretty open at the moment, so I'm going to do my best to get up there to see you, even if I just come up for the day."

"Is it that close to Rome?"

"About as far as Gallup is from Albuquerque. Didn't they teach you map reading in the Marine Corps?"

"I always had a sergeant to read maps. Listen, I've got to go. Give me a call on this number when you know when you'll be in Assisi. Can't wait to see you."

"We'll relive the good times in Albuquerque, Zeke."

"Maybe not all of them, Rick. What is it you say here? *Ciao?*"

"You're almost a native. *Ciao,* Zeke."

After he slipped the phone back in his pocket, Rick realized he hadn't asked Zeke what he had been up to since leaving the Marines. And his old friend just didn't seem like the kind of person to fit into a tour group. Perhaps it was an anniversary and his wife always wanted to visit Italy. Could he have married that girl who was about half the size of Zeke? Rick tried to recall her name but came up dry. He poured the last of the wine into his glass and took a swig. There would be quite a bit to catch up on.

———

Twenty-four hours after Rick's call from Zeke, a distant sun aimed the day's last rays across the Valle Umbra toward Assisi. From the top of the hill, just beyond the battlements of the ancient castle, the view was the best in town. The roofs of the city spread out below like terraced steps, broken only by winding streets and the occasional spire and dome. In contrast with the town, where humanity squeezed together surrounded by harsh stone, the valley that spread below it was sparsely peopled, flat, and fertile. The view extended into the hazy distance, and the dips between the hills darkened as the sun continued its descent.

It was not by chance that the *rocca* had been built on this hill hundreds of years earlier. The towers were silent now, but in their day, soldiers would have stood on them, watching for movement below. The view then was in some ways the same as now, in others very different. The first row of hills in the distance, where Bettona and other small villages perched, would not have changed, nor would that of the higher Monti Martani farther off. The farmland below Assisi, thanks to the Tiber River, was just as fertile now as in the fourteenth century. But today's view was dominated by shades of green and brown inside geometric plots, sliced by paved roads, and dotted with agricultural buildings and houses. What would shock those soldiers most was the town of Santa Maria degli Angeli, back then a bend in the road to Perugia, now spread over the surrounding land, with a monumental church towering over in its center.

The narrow road leading up to the castle ended in an open area covered with gravel and dirt. Thanks to car traffic, and an almost constant wind, nothing much grew except stubby weeds, and near the walls, stubborn grass. Birds perched on the railing at the edge of the parking lot, facing the wind so that their feathers wouldn't ruffle. The light wind brought with it the smell of pine sap from the distant woods. The olive trees below the railing gave off no scent, or if they did, the wind blew it downward toward the town. Their rustling leaves offered the only sound, had there been anyone there to hear it.

The sun's last rays climbed up Assisi's hill, pulling behind them the black blanket of night, while the wind slowed its moan and stopped completely. Between two olive trees, the man lay where he had fallen. In the silence, darkness covered the body like a shroud.

———

The next morning, his work in Sicily completed on schedule, Rick sat patiently in the chair across from his uncle's desk at the *questura* in downtown Rome. Commissario Piero Fontana looked up at the ceiling and moved his free hand in a circular motion to indicate that the person on the other end of the line was rattling on too long. Rick looked around the office once again. He had spent many minutes in the past waiting while his uncle took calls, so he'd nearly memorized the room's furnishings. The Italian flag and picture of the President of the Republic, almost a requirement for someone of Piero's rank, were displayed behind his desk. The work surface was free of clutter, which would be expected, given the man's obsession with efficiency. Files in one corner, a bookshelf, and a meeting table with six chairs completed the decor along with the more comfortable seating used for formal meetings. The single window looked out on the busy street that ran in front of the police station, but from where Rick sat, he could see only the building on the other side. He had politely declined the offer of a coffee, since he had just come from having his morning cappuccino and *cornetto*, but now he wished he had accepted. After the late flight from Punta Raisi to Fiumicino, and getting up early for his daily run, he was still a bit groggy.

"*Si, onorevole. Capisco, onorevole.*" With a thumbs-up to Rick, Piero indicated that the person on the line was getting close to making his point. He promised the man to do the needful, ending the call with a few courteous but brief phrases before putting the phone back in its cradle on the desk.

"Sorry about that, Riccardo. He is on a parliamentary committee that oversees our budget, so I have to be polite."

"Something about your budget allocations?"

"Of course not, his staff deals with such things. His son-in-law is in difficulty, but tax issues are something handled by the Guardia di Finanza. I'm not sure the *onorevole* understands that they are a different branch." He pushed himself away from the desk and leaned back. "I am anxious to hear about your adventure in Palermo. It was good of you to take on the assignment at short notice. Inspector Cribari was getting desperate."

"He didn't seem to me a policeman who would show desperation. Nobody ever explained to me why they couldn't find a translator locally."

Piero rubbed his chin before answering. "As you undoubtedly found out, it was a rather delicate topic. There was only one translator in the city they trusted, and she declined for reasons of health."

"She was worried about her own."

"Precisely. Your English transcript of the man's interrogation should already be on its way to the FBI in New York, and there are people in Palermo who will want to find what it contains. Only Cribari, who conducted the questioning, and his boss in Palermo know what's in that transcript. They are understandably concerned about leaks."

"And I'm the third."

"Well, the fourth. There's the *penitente* himself, but he's been removed to an undisclosed location for his own safety. That was part of the deal."

"Somewhere here in Italy?"

Piero shrugged to indicate that such details were not his responsibility.

"If I too must be sent to an undisclosed location for helping the police, Uncle, please make it somewhere that has good restaurants."

The *commissario* did not appreciate the humor in Rick's comment. "I was extremely careful to keep your identity a secret, Riccardo."

"Which is why you issued me an identity card with another name to show the airline. Where did you get that old picture of me?"

Piero didn't answer the question. "Not even the police in Palermo knew you by anything but your first name."

"I noticed that. But the Mafia knows about their turncoat?"

"They know he disappeared, and so might be suspecting the worst. What they don't know is what he might have told to police, nor that what he said will be used by the FBI to go after a member of their family in America."

"They will have to find out eventually."

"When charges are brought against the guy in New York, the family in Palermo will know, but that should not be for a few weeks. In the meantime, we have intelligence that another prominent crime syndicate has been attempting to take over their territory in Sicily. Dealing with a turf battle should be enough to keep them busy."

"Too busy to track down some anonymous translator?"

Piero waved his hand as if to push aside the negative thoughts going through both their heads. "Cribari treated you well, I trust? I didn't tell him you are my nephew, of course."

"I only saw him a couple times. He assigned two of his men to hold my hand while I was there, and from what you just said they probably didn't know what I was doing."

"And didn't want to know."

Rick chuckled. "I could not help wondering how one can tell the cops from the criminals in Sicily. I've thought the same thing here in Rome, but my sense is that the difference in appearance is even less pronounced in Palermo." He crossed his right leg over his left knee, exposing most of his boot.

"Perhaps we should issue white and black hats, like in your American cowboy movies."

"That would certainly be helpful."

The policeman stayed silent for a moment, as if he were actually toying with the idea, before turning his attention back to Rick. "What are your plans now? Any interpreting jobs coming up? It will take weeks before the police bureaucracy pays you for your excellent work in Palermo."

"In fact, Uncle, I was going to get on the train today for a quick trip to Assisi but not for work." In response to Piero's look of puzzlement, Rick told him about his phone call from Zeke Campbell. Months earlier he had attempted to explain American football to his uncle, with little success, so he didn't mention Zeke's involvement in that pastime, saying only that he was an old friend from the university.

Piero held up an index finger. "I have a suggestion, Riccardo."

"A hotel in Assisi? I was there years ago with my parents, but I don't remember where we stayed. I didn't ask Zeke where his group was being lodged."

The index finger waved. "No, no. A place to stay in Perugia, which as you know is minutes from Assisi. Have you ever stopped in to thank your great-aunt Filomena for renting you that wonderful apartment? She would love to see you, and since I haven't heard from her in a while, I have been wondering how she's doing. She usually calls me every month, but it's been several since we've talked. And I'm ashamed to admit that I've been too busy to call her myself."

Rick groaned inwardly. What could have been a relaxed reunion with an old college friend might suddenly become a tedious visit to an aging relative. He also knew that it would be difficult to say no to his uncle. His recollection of the woman was fuzzy, going back to his grandparents' funeral: just gray hair piled on a small head. He couldn't bring up a face, though he remembered her as tall. But he was a small boy back then, and everyone seemed tall.

Piero, perhaps sensing Rick wavering, pushed on. "The woman is getting on in years and would love to have a visit from her American great-nephew."

"I don't know, Uncle…"

He reached into his pocket, took out a ring of keys, and removed one from it. "You can use my car; the tank's full."

"The Spider?" He had been in his uncle's red Alfa Romeo 4C only once, an inaugural drive along the twisting roads of the Alban Hills. It had taken Rick an hour to catch his breath and get the blood back in his knuckles. He decided then that he would never have a car in Rome because the 4C was the one he wanted, and he could never afford it.

"It's the only car I have, and I don't drive it that often."

"You know, Uncle, you're absolutely right. It would be wonderful to see my aunt Filomena again."

Piero handed Rick the key and pulled out his *telefonino*. "Excellent, I'll call her now." He stopped after scrolling partway through his phone list. "Perhaps Betta can get some time off and go with you. Filomena would enjoy meeting her."

"Betta's working in Pisa at the moment."

"Her art theft cases are always fascinating. What's this one about?"

"She didn't tell me."

———

After her arrival in Pisa on the late train, Betta Innocenti had checked in to a hotel she'd been told by the ministry to use, since it gave a discount. The Hotel Barbarossa was a short cab ride from the station and only a few blocks from the Arno River. It seemed perfect for her needs; the room was clean, and the breakfast she'd just finished was adequate. Every hotel she'd stayed in recently, either with Rick or on assignment with the art fraud squad, had the same self-service spread of breads, sweet rolls, fruit, and yogurt. This one was no different. The clientele appeared to be a mixture of Italian businessmen and German tourists.

She folded the local newspaper and slipped it into her shoulder bag. A story about the theft had been on the second page, but it didn't give her anything different from what she'd been told in Rome. A pastel by a local artist from the eighteenth century had disappeared from a side chapel at the small Saint Ursula church on the edge of the city. The priest, Father Oresti, was beside himself with anguish, describing it as a masterpiece of inestimable value. It did have value, Betta knew, but said value could easily be estimated, since two by the same third-tier artist had recently sold in Milan. The newspaper had found a color photo of the work and published it next to the picture of the priest. It was a representation of Adam and Eve in the Garden of Eden, complete with serpent and strategically placed leaves. The colors had faded, or more likely it was just the dark style of the period. Definitely not something Betta would put among her favorite works that she'd been assigned to track down during her time in the art fraud squad. She again wondered why she'd been sent to Pisa for something that could have been handled, albeit clumsily and likely unsuccessfully, by the local constabulary. The reason had to be the confrontation she'd had the previous week with her boss when he'd made some not-too-subtle advances. The guy was a menace. Her good friend and mentor in the art police, Caterina Scuderi, had tried to cheer her up, saying it was a chance to get out of the office and do some work on her own. Betta was not convinced.

She finished her coffee, dropped the napkin on the table, and got to her feet. First a call on the local police, then Father Oresti. Perhaps she could squeeze in a visit to the cathedral. She dropped her key at the reception desk and pushed open the door to the street. Fortunately, the *questura* in Pisa was close enough to Betta's hotel for her to walk to it rather than getting a taxi. As in most Italian towns, a large part of the historic center was a pedestrian zone, with exceptions given to residents who had passes for their cars. That meant parking spaces were scarce but moving vehicles minimal, which was helpful due to the lack of sidewalks. She strolled along streets that appeared relatively straight compared to other Italian cities, likely thanks to the Romans, who had left their mark everywhere. She reached the police station and looked at the drab facade, its architecture stubbornly fascist but hoping nobody would notice. She entered through the doorway under the flags of Italy and the European Union, and walked through the reception area.

"Detective Pisano, please."

"Is he expecting you?" asked the uniformed policeman as he smiled and not too subtly checked her out.

"He should be. Dottoressa Innocenti from the ministry in Rome."

"Oh, yes." The cop became serious. "I'll tell him you are here." He picked up the phone while Betta turned and looked around the room, which could have been any of a hundred police department waiting rooms in the country. "He'll be right out, Dottoressa."

She thanked him and pulled her phone from her briefcase to see if Rick had texted or left a message. Nothing. He was probably poring over some translation since he hadn't mentioned any interpreting jobs. She returned the phone to its place just as a man burst through a door, spotted her, and rushed over.

"You must be Dottoressa Innocenti." He pumped her hand. "I am Luca Pisano. Despite my name, I'm not from Pisa. Nor from Lucca, for that matter." The quip was delivered with a grin, like he relished using it with people he met for the first time. It added a touch of mischievousness to what was already an elfin demeanor, since Betta, of average height, stood a half foot taller than the man. Despite the spring temperatures, he wore a three-piece suit, which, had it been green, would have completed the image of a leprechaun. "Won't you come into my office?" he said, as if requesting her help to search for a pot of gold.

The office was a few steps away and small, perhaps to match his stature. Betta took the only chair other than the one behind the desk, and Pisano hoisted himself into that one. Once seated, she realized that her chair was low and his high, resulting in their eyes meeting at the same level. After the required offer of coffee and her expected "*No, grazie,*" he got down to business. She figured he must have used up his repertoire with the "I'm not from Pisa" line.

"A terrible loss for Saint Ursula, Dottoressa, not to mention to the arts community of Pisa. We are grateful that your office has sent you to find it." He did not appear to be concerned about Rome sending someone to tread on his turf. On the contrary, his tone exuded relief.

"I hope I can be successful, but the percentage of these kinds of cases that end with the return of the artwork is, I'm afraid, quite low." She could have added that the work was likely a long way from Tuscany already, but she restrained herself. "Tell me what you know, if you would." She took a pad and pen from her shoulder bag.

Pisano settled back into his chair, the desk keeping Betta from seeing if his feet reached the floor. "The robbery was discovered last Monday morning after the priest, Father Oresti, finished celebrating mass on the main altar. One of the celebrants, an old woman, asked him if he had finally sent it out for a cleaning. He rushed to the side chapel where it had hung and discovered it gone." He raised his hands to indicate he was finished.

"That's it?" Betta asked. "Fingerprints? Signs of forced entry? A ransom note?"

Pisano shrugged. "The cleaning woman had been there earlier, and she was very efficient. And the church is left open most of the time, including the previous night."

"So anyone could have waltzed in and taken it off the wall of the chapel, without so much as a 'by your leave.' No alarm system, I assume?"

"It is a poor parish, Dottoressa."

"It's even poorer now."

CHAPTER TWO

Rick tried but could not recall ever seeing anyone stopped on the *autostrada* for speeding. That was a good thing, since he was keeping the Alfa at about ten kilometers over the speed limit. In New Mexico the locals considered speed limits as a suggestion, not an order, and that was the case on Italy's toll expressway system. If you're going to spend that much on tolls, went the reasoning, they shouldn't tell you how fast you can go. As he swung off the crowded Raccordo Anulare, Rome's ring road, onto A1 heading north, he had put the pedal down and kept it there. Climbing some hills and tunneling through others, the highway now stretched along the wide plain of the Tiber River Valley. As the Alfa shot past a tractor-trailer, it was itself overtaken by the high-speed train hurtling along the elevated track next to the highway. Beyond the train Rick got a blurred view of Orvieto. A skyline of low buildings, broken only by the city's famous cathedral, spread along the top of the steep hill.

His last visit to Orvieto had been with Betta, just after she'd started working for the art squad, when they had taken the train up from Rome. That trip turned out to be more exciting than they had expected, he recalled, but with Betta excitement was what you got. Uncle Piero was right, it would have been nice to have had her along on this trip. She was great with older people and would charm Filomena, taking off him some of the pressure to socialize. And she certainly would charm Zeke, whose head was always turned by beauty. Rick thought about trying to call her in Pisa, seeing if the car's Bluetooth would work with his phone, but he decided against it. She was probably busy with her work. Was her new boss in Pisa as well? It wouldn't surprise him. When the turbo kicked in as he roared past another semi, he decided it was just as well that she wasn't along. It would have been a constant battle to decide who should drive.

He paid his toll at the Val di Chiana exit and headed east on another stretch of *autostrada*, this one without a toll, that would take him to Perugia. Ten minutes later he crossed from Tuscany into Umbria. Through the trees on his right, the blue water of Lake Trasimeno appeared, its surface broken by a lone windsurfer having trouble picking up speed in a late-morning calm. The car rounded a bend and passed the site of the Battle of Trasimeno, where Hannibal ambushed and massacred the Roman legions commanded by Giaus Flaminius. Rick slowed only slightly as the highway took him past the resort town of Passignano, then picked up speed as he climbed into the hills before approaching the Umbrian capital. The Alfa's GPS directed him off the expressway and guided the car up the hill toward the center of the city. The route—an endless series of curves over mostly green hillsides—would have been tedious in any other car, but the constant shifting of gears was a pleasure in this one.

Due to its sylvan surroundings, Aunt Filomena's house qualified as a villa, even though from the road it appeared to be relatively modest. A metal fence formed a decorative barrier between the pavement and a small patch of grass made even smaller by a gravel parking area. As promised, the gate was open, and after driving in and parking, Rick walked back to close it. As it clicked shut, he heard a voice behind him.

"*Benvenuto*, Riccardo."

Great-Aunt Filomena was not what he remembered or expected. According to his calculations, she had to be in her eighties, but from her appearance he would have guessed at least a decade younger. Her gray hair was stylishly short, framing a tanned face with the kind of natural elegance that would never age. She was dressed in a silk blouse and linen pants that betrayed not a single extra pound. She stood with her arms folded over her chest and head slightly tilted, just as his mother always did. He embraced her, detecting a hint of a fragrance he couldn't identify. He would have to ask her later.

"Zia, how wonderful to finally see you. And how kind of you to invite me to be your guest."

She stood back and looked him over. "You have changed since the last time I saw you. How is it that some *Romana* has not gotten such a handsome young man as you in her clutches?"

"You are reminding me of my mother, Zia."

"And how is she, and your wonderful father? In Brazil, if I recall."

As they walked inside he brought her up-to-date on his parents, as well as his sister and her family back in Albuquerque. The front door led them into a room that took up most of the ground floor. To one side he could see into a kitchen where a woman worked at a counter, and on the other a stairway led downward. Between was an expansive living area. The room's decoration was unexpected—modern modular furniture set on colorful rugs over terra-cotta tiles. On the walls behind him and to the sides hung a few works of art, colorful and impressionist. Directly ahead was a series of sliding glass doors running the width of the room, exposing an even larger terrace. A teak table with matching chairs, under a canvas *ombrellone*, was set for two. Beyond the railing Umbria rolled off into the distance. Rick walked to the edge of the terrace and took in the view. Directly below were balconies of what Rick assumed were the bedrooms, each with a stairway leading down to an oval swimming pool. Beyond its paving stones, a grove of scraggly olive trees extended to a dirt road in the distance.

"This is magnificent, Zia. I hope you use the pool to get your exercise."

"And my tan. It's very private."

He let the comment pass. "How long have you lived here?"

"Goodness, decades. Enrico, my second husband, bought it just after we were married, though we had an apartment in town." She tilted her head in the direction of Perugia proper. "We found we were spending more and more time here, and when he passed away, I sold the apartment and moved here full-time. I can be in the heart of the city in minutes when I need excitement." She put her right hand to her forehead. "But where are my manners? You should have something to drink after that drive from Rome." She turned toward the smaller door that led to the kitchen. "Anna. *Il* Prosecco, *per favore.*"

"*Subito*, Signora," came the voice from inside.

Filomena took Rick's hand and led him to a set of cushioned chairs, placing him in the one with the better view. A woman dressed in a dark skirt and blouse hurried onto the terrace clutching a tray with two flutes and an ice bucket in which rested a bottle.

"Allow me," said Rick, getting to his feet and pulling the bottle from the ice water. After removing the foil and wire from the top, he twisted the cork carefully until it came off into his hand with a low pop. Filomena held up the glasses as he poured, waited for the bubbles to settle back, and finished filling. He put the bottle back in the bucket and took the flute given him by his great-aunt.

"To *famiglia*," she said and tapped his glass.

"To *famiglia*."

A few minutes later, when the bottle was half empty, they moved to the table where Anna had set out a bowl of pasta salad. The pasta was rigatoni, tossed in oil with the flesh of ripe tomatoes, capers, and basil. The olive oil, Filomena pointed out, was from the trees around the pool, cultivated by a neighbor who claimed it was the finest in Perugia. Rick could not but agree. After a few bites of pasta, the conversation continued.

"All the years you've lived here, Zia, you must almost consider yourself a Perugina."

She waved a finger with her non-fork hand. "Come now, Riccardo, you have lived in Italy long enough to know that Italians can never give up their native cities, even if they wanted to. Though I've lived here since I left Rome—except for a few years in Paris with my first husband—I am still a Romana."

"You do still have a slight Roman accent."

"Only slight? I work hard to maintain it. My friends here have always called me *la Romana*, and they always will. No doubt they still remember all the centuries of warfare between Perugia and the popes, and they find it important to keep up local traditions. I've reminded them that we were allies in the second Punic War, but it doesn't seem to help."

He laughed and poured her the last of the Prosecco. "How can one tell the difference between Romani and Perugini, aside from their accents?"

She put down her fork and leaned back from the plate. "The residents of this city have always had a reputation for irascibility. It probably goes back to the Etruscans, but during the Middle

Ages, this place was especially violent, even by the standards of that time. The Oddi and the Baglioni families famously spent decades murdering each other while battling for political control of the town. So Perugia became known for vendettas and treachery, and the stereotype has stuck. Many of my friends here are quite comfortable with it, I should add, even if they don't practice treachery themselves. At least not any treachery that I'm aware of, unless you include business or adultery."

They watched a tractor kicking up dust along a farm road in the distance, partly obscured by the olive trees. The distant sound of its engine was somehow mesmerizing in the relative silence of the terrace. Anna broke the spell when she appeared and gathered up their empty plates.

"Every city has its own personality, doesn't it? Almost like a person."

"Very definitely, Riccardo. Perugia is the cranky relative who's always looking for gossip to demonstrate his superiority over someone else in the family. Rome is the jaded and aging nobleman, the collar of his shirt frayed, for whom there is nothing new under the sun. He's seen it all." She took a sip of what was left of her Prosecco, warming to the topic. "Milan? Ah, Milan is the fastidious accountant, first into the office and last to leave, always aware of the bottom line. I am tempted to describe Naples as the street urchin, but it is the urchin grown to adulthood yet retaining the skills that kept him alive in his youth, always looking for a way to survive."

"What about Palermo?" asked Rick, without mentioning his recent visit there.

"Unfortunately, the image that most people have of the city is correct. Palermo is the black sheep uncle who is always in trouble, but defiantly proud of his reputation."

"All of those cities are male."

"This is Italy, Riccardo. But if it makes you feel better, Venice would be a woman, but not one of high repute."

Anna came back out with a platter that she set between them before handing Filomena a serving spoon pulled from her apron. "Should I bring the wine, Signora?"

"Yes, Anna. The pitcher in the refrigerator. And new glasses."

Anna collected the empty flutes and the ice bucket before returning to the kitchen.

"It's *vitello tonnato*, Riccardo; I hope you like it. We're not yet into the heat of summer, but it seemed like a good choice."

"It's one of my favorites, Zia."

She took his plate and spooned out a thin slice of cold veal covered with a sauce of tuna, mayonnaise, capers, and anchovies. She spooned some extra sauce over the meat and passed it to Rick. After serving herself she wished him another *buon appetito* and took a taste.

"I have been remiss," said Rick after taking a bite, "in not thanking you immediately for renting me that wonderful apartment in Rome."

"I'm glad you are enjoying it. My husband and I used it when we were in the capital, but I don't go there that often these days. Most of my friends from childhood are gone, so it's only Piero and you. And now you have come to visit me here. I hope it will be the first of many visits."

"Absolutely, Zia. I—" He was interrupted by the ring of his cell phone. Instinctively he pulled it out and checked the number. "It's from my American friend, but I can call him back."

"The one visiting Assisi? Piero told me about that. Please take it."

Rick hit the button and switched into English. "Zeke. I was going to call you after lunch. I should get to Assisi in about an hour."

"Sorry if I've interrupted your meal. We have a problem here that I thought you might help with. If you can."

Rick glanced at his aunt, who was sipping wine and studying the view as if seeing it for the first time. "What's the problem?"

"Well, our guide seems to have run out on us. He's an Italian who teaches at UNM, and we got him at the last minute when our original guide got sick. Perhaps you could help out until he turns up, you being the interpreter."

"Guiding tour groups is a bit out of my skill level, but if I can help, sure."

"Bless you, Rick. Where are you now?"

"I'm in Perugia, staying with my great-aunt."

"Perugia? That's near Assisi, isn't it?"

"Sounds like you've consulted a map since the last time we talked, Zeke. Yes, very close. I can almost see Assisi from where I'm sitting."

"Hmm, I wonder if I could ask another favor."

"An old friend would expect you to."

"Our guide, his name is Ettore Biraldo." He spelled it out. "He is originally from Perugia. Would it be too much to ask to go by the address we have for him to see if he's there?"

Rick always carried a pen and notepad, and he pulled them out of his pocket now. "I'm ready to write. Go ahead." Rick wrote down the information Zeke gave him.. "Let me check something, hold on." He put down the phone and showed the address to his aunt, returning to Italian. "Zia, do you know where this street is? Would it be hard for me to find it?"

She pulled reading glasses from somewhere in her clothing and put them on. "It's near San Bernardino and shouldn't be difficult."

He put the phone back to his ear. "My aunt says no problem. I can go by there on the way down to Assisi. I'm driving my uncle's car."

"Great. I can't thank you enough. So you'll be here in Assisi soon?"

"It's only about a half hour away, so it will depend on how long it takes me to tie up Biraldo and stuff him in the trunk of the car."

"Your sense of humor seems not to have changed, Rick."

"So where will I find you, Zeke?"

"I'll be in the lobby of our hotel, the Hotel Windsor Savoia. It's—"

"That's all I need. I just remembered that my uncle's car has GPS. I'll text you when I'm leaving town."

"Looking forward to seeing you Rick."

"Same here, buddy." He ended the call and put the phone back in his pocket just as Anna appeared with a new set of glasses and a ceramic pitcher of wine. Rick filled the two glasses. The wine had a slightly darker straw color than the bottle they had finished. "You will have to excuse me for the interruption, Zia. Zeke is an old college friend, and I haven't seen him since I left school."

"Is there a problem? My English isn't very good, but I could tell something from your tone of voice."

Rick finished the slice of veal that he had popped into his mouth. "He's in a tour group, and their guide, some guy from the university, has disappeared. That address is one Zeke had for him here in Perugia. So I'll stop by on my way down to Assisi."

"Do whatever you need to, to help your friend. You can come and go here as you please. I'll give you a key."

Rick was pleased with Aunt Filomena's reaction. On the drive up he had wondered if, as a widow living alone and starved for company, she would insist on monopolizing his time. To his great relief he'd found a relaxed and independent woman.

"This missing man is an Italian?" she asked.

"Apparently. I'll find out more about him when I see Zeke in Assisi, but let's hope that by then the man has reappeared. I don't really want to be a tour guide. That's too much like real work."

"I'm sure you would make a wonderful guide, Riccardo."

He took a drink of the wine and found it went down smoothly, as Italian whites were supposed to. "I went to Assisi with my parents when I was a kid, but I don't remember very much. A lot of stone, but of course you could say that about almost any town in Umbria. The old cathedral over the tomb of Francis I remember vividly. Narrow steps leading down to the crypt is an image that still sticks in my mind, as well as people kneeling on the stone floor in front of the saint. I don't remember much else. But that was a time when my parents were dragging me through so many Italian towns that they were starting to look alike. Walls. A big church. Small tourist shops. Lots of stone buildings. Much later I found how different they are, despite what is sometimes a superficial similarity."

"And you didn't realize then how fortunate you were to have seen all those places."

"You're right, that came later as well. When I started at the university in America, I went through a bit of culture shock. Nobody really understood what it was like to be a foreign service kid. When I'd tell them I'd lived in other countries they'd just say, 'That must have been interesting,' and change the subject. They couldn't get their heads around it. But that didn't bother me for long. I quickly got into enjoying the life of a college student, perhaps enjoying it too much."

She looked down at his cowboy boots. "Is that when you started wearing those, Riccardo?"

He laughed. "A friend of mine talked me into trying them, and I was surprised to find that they're very comfortable. A bit bulky when packing them in a suitcase, but that's the only downside."

"They set you apart in Italy. Italians, as you know, are very much into fashion, which includes shoes. I'm sure the Romane notice them."

"I have had some comments from Roman women."

Again she tilted her head in the way his mother did. "In that regard, Riccardo, you did not answer my question when you arrived, so I'll ask it again, but more directly. Are you seeing any woman on a regular basis? A handsome young man like you could not lack for female companionship. Especially with those boots."

She was probing into his private life, something he would have resented from anyone else, but somehow he had no problem with Zia Filomena doing it. He sensed that if he confided in her, she would never betray his trust to Piero, and certainly not to his mother. Maybe he needed a grandmother figure in his life. Even though she didn't have the typical image of one, at least age-wise she fit the bill, and if fate delivers a grandmother to you, why not take her? He took a drink of the wine.

"I have been regularly seeing a young lady; her name is Betta Innocenti. We met in Bassano del Grappa when I was working as an interpreter at a conference of art historians. She works in the art fraud section of the culture ministry." He pulled out his phone, scrolled through his pictures, and passed it to her.

"She's lovely. I like her hair."

"Betta keeps it short. It's easier to take care of with her job."

"But she can pull it off with such striking features. Now I am anxious to meet her. Perhaps I need to get down to Rome. To inspect the apartment I'm renting there." She patted Rick on the knee. "Riccardo, how serious is it between you and Betta?"

"You certainly come directly to the point."

"At my age I'm allowed to."

"Well, Zia, lately I've been asking myself that very question. When I have an answer you'll be the first to know. After Betta, of course. We've had our ups and downs in the relationship since she moved to Rome to start her job. Right now it's…" He shrugged.

"What is Piero's opinion of the young lady? I trust he's met her."

"He's one of her biggest fans."

"Ah. That is important. Your uncle is an astute judge of character. I think it comes with being a policeman." She looked at his plate. "Finish that last bit of veal and be on your way. It appears that you will be busy for the rest of the day, so you'd better get to it. I'll give you a key, and you can let yourself in if it's late."

Rick cut the last slice of veal and spread it with sauce. "You earlier described the personality of other cities, Zia. What about Assisi?"

She looked out over the hills in the direction of the home of Saint Francis. "It is not what you would expect for a town that still draws as many pilgrims as tourists. But there is more to it than meets the eye. How would I characterize Assisi?" She thought for several seconds before answering the question. "Assisi is the pious priest, member of a venerable religious order, who carries inside him a secret blacker than his own cassock."

———

Looking from the street, the age of Saint Ursula church was not easy for Betta to estimate. Its facade was plain except for a small and very dark rose window over the single door at the center. The sloped roof came to a point above the window, and a small cross topped it. The church was wedged between stone residential buildings that were easier to date, probably from the sixteenth or seventeenth century, so perhaps the church was the same. She thought the tall wood door would creak when pushed open, but the noise was even louder than expected. Maybe the parishioners were all old and hard of hearing, so it didn't bother them. She entered and was engulfed in darkness and the faint sweet scent of incense. The rose window behind her let in little light; the only other illumination was from the rows of candles, set at intervals, and another dark stained-glass window above the main altar. She waited a moment to let her eyes adjust to the darkness, and slowly the shadows cleared so she could see the outline of the space.

With the exception of a single small chapel on each side, the church was an open plan, and narrow enough not to need columns. High above the tile floor, wooden crossbeams held the walls apart and supported the roof. Four rows of empty pews were arranged directly in front of the main altar, which was covered with a white cloth. Above it hung a painted wood crucifix, which Betta estimated to be older than the church, though she was still unable to guess the age of the structure. The bare walls inside hadn't helped. She walked toward the altar, the sound of her heels bouncing off the walls, but stopped when she was between the two chapels. The one on the right side looked to be the one she had come to see, since the space above its small altar was bare. She walked to it, noticed a small metal box on the wall, and opened her bag to find a coin. When her euro was inserted into the slot on the box, a single spotlight popped on with a click, shining on a lighter square of brown in the midst of a darker brown wall. A single rusted nail caught some of the light's beam. As she got closer for a better look, she heard quick footsteps and then a voice.

"If you've come to see our masterpiece, I'm afraid you'll be disappointed."

She turned to see a round priest, dressed in a cassock buttoned from neck to hem. In contrast with his black garb was a rosy face and a few wisps of gray hair above each ear. Lines in his cheeks and forehead indicated a longtime smoker, and his voice confirmed it. He clasped his hands together and held them to his chest.

"You must be Father Oresti."

"Yes, my child, and this is my humble church." His eyes moved to the ceiling and back to Betta. "Did you come here to see the *Garden of Eden*?"

"Not exactly. My name is Betta Innocenti. I was sent from Rome to see if we could find it."

Oresti's face lit up. "Of course. Detective Pisano told me they were sending someone. But I didn't expect..." He stopped himself.

"Someone as young as me, Father?"

"Yes. That's it exactly." He wiped his brow with his hand. "You must be very good at what you do. What can I tell you about this terrible theft? I'm sure you want to get right down to business."

"Just begin by telling me what happened." She took the pen and paper out of her bag and was about to lean it against the chapel wall when he stopped her.

"You'd better not put it there, Signorina; it could be damp. One of the leaks in the roof is directly above us." He took the bag from her and placed it on the altar like an offering. After stepping back, he began. "I had just finished the early mass. It was celebrated by the usual group, mostly old women and a few old men. Young people just don't want to get up early. I was chatting with one of the women after the benediction when Signora Lupara came back and asked me what had happened to the *Garden of Eden* pastel. I rushed over and found this." He raised both hands in the direction of the rectangle of lighter paint above the altar. "I was beside myself."

"When was the last time you'd seen it in place?"

"Oh, my. That's hard to say. I walk past it every day, of course, though I usually don't stop to look at it. But since our cleaning woman worked the day before, in the morning, I'm sure she would have noticed if it was gone. She cleans both the chapels, including the altars, so she would have told me immediately."

"Which means it was taken sometime between when she finished and the next morning, when you were celebrating mass. What time does she normally finish?"

"It takes her a few hours, from midmorning until about one. She has to go home to make lunch for her husband."

Betta tapped her pen on the pad. She had written down nothing since she had learned nothing new. She knew the answer to her next question but asked it anyway. "Is the church locked when not in use?"

The priest was ready with an answer. "The Lord's house is always in use, Signorina. We leave it open for anyone who feels the need for solace or prayer."

"I see." She didn't bother asking about security cameras. "I don't suppose you had noticed anyone suspicious hanging around the church in the last few weeks?"

It apparently was not a question he'd gotten from Detective Pisano, and it elicited a rub of his chin while he thought. "No, I don't recall anyone, and I keep an eye out for visitors. You never know when someone might become a regular. Of course someone could have—"

"Come in when you weren't here, since it is not locked."

"Precisely. We do occasionally get tourists in to see the *Garden of Eden*, of course. But it has been quite sparse lately, and they tend to drop by during the afternoon, when I'm not here."

Betta thanked the priest, told him she would do her best, and left the church. Outside on the street, she looked back at the facade and took quick stock of the situation. It was not good. She had hoped for something to grasp onto, some tiny clue, but there was nothing. How could anyone be surprised that Father Oresti's precious *Garden of Eden* had disappeared? He might as well have posted a sign outside announcing "Free Artwork, No Waiting."

She pulled out her phone and started scrolling through the contacts list. Yes, he was there.

———

Thanks to the GPS, Rick drove to the street Zeke had given him over the phone. The faceless Italian voice had cleverly avoided areas where traffic was restricted to residents or official vehicles, and instead skirted him around the edges of Perugia's historic center. The neighborhood looked like it had sprung up in the last years of the twentieth century, its streets winding around brick and cement apartment houses built on various levels of incline. There was just enough difference in design to make each building appear unique, but the style was the same, as was, likely, the builder. Small balconies jutted out from each apartment, but only upper floors facing downhill had a view of something other than the neighbors across the street.

As he slowed down to check the address, a delivery van pulled out of a space, and Rick ducked in before anyone else could claim it. He got out, click-locked the Alfa, and found a street number next to a doorway. The address he wanted was the next one up the hill, and he got to it by squeezing between the building and the cars. There was no sidewalk, nor was there much of an entrance to the building. What he stepped into was a slightly recessed doorway off the street with a row of mail-boxes built into one side and an equal number of buttons on the other. Most of the buttons had names, but under the one that went with the address Zeke had given him, the space was blank. He pushed it anyway and waited. Just as he pushed it a second time, a woman came out of the door, stopped, and looked at him.

"Who are you?" the woman asked. The tone was something between curiosity and annoyance.

"I'm looking for Ettore Biraldo."

"You and everyone else."

"Doesn't he live here?"

"Last I heard he moved to America." She walked away and scuttled up the street.

So Rick was not the only one looking for Biraldo, and from the way she'd said it, those others did not include Biraldo's friends. What kind of a person was this guy, and how did he get selected to lead a tour group? Rick would have lots of questions for Zeke when he got to Assisi. He walked back down the hill, got into the car, and set the GPS for the Hotel Windsor Savoia. After checking his side mirror, he pulled out into the one-way street and was just starting to speed up when he passed the apartment building. A man in a blue blazer and open-collar shirt was stopped in front and looking up and down the street. Just as the car passed the entrance to the building, the man ducked into the shadowed entrance. Could it be Biraldo? Rick was tempted to stop, but someone was right on his back bumper, and he had nowhere to pull over on the narrow street lined with cars. He hit the gas pedal and shot up the hill.

———

Rick's final half-dozen kilometers to Assisi, after getting off the highway and passing near Bastia Umbra, were on a straight two-lane road lined by flat fields. He mostly saw dark, churned-up soil, which would be ready for planting sometime later in the spring. Some vineyards appeared as well, gnarled trees connected by thin wires ready to hold future clusters of grapes. After a bend in the road, a square structure, sitting on the edge of the hill looking down on the flat land like a fortress, became visible in the distance. It was the Sacro Convento, built out over the hill, an extension of the Basilica of Saint Francis. As he got closer, the outline of the church bell tower appeared, with Assisi spread out behind it. Above it all were the stone ruins of the castle, and towering beyond that the green hump of Monte Subasio.

Minutes later the flatland he'd been on ended, and the road began to climb. After a few cutbacks and traffic circles, the Alfa arrived at the imposing San Pietro gate, its rough stone contrasting with the regular pavement of a large bus terminal and parking area next to it. The GPS ordered Rick to continue past the signs indicating limited access, and he wondered if the voice in the dashboard would talk a policeman out of giving him a ticket if he were stopped. Fortunately, the hotel immediately appeared on the right. Rick made a sharp turn through the gate and found a space in front of the entrance.

The hotel's age, like that of so many buildings in Italy, was not easy to guess. It was built to blend in with the stone of the rest of Assisi, but being outside the city's walls, it couldn't be that old. The name—Windsor Savoia—was more of hint. The use of Italy's royal house would put its founding somewhere between the nineteenth-century unification of Italy under the monarchy and the postwar national referendum by which the king was banished. Rick decided on the early part of the twentieth century, and he turned out to be correct. Adding the name of another royal house had to be a shameless ploy to attract British tourists.

He stepped under a portico and into the hotel lobby, which was immaculate but as dated as the building's exterior. His boot heels clicked on the marble floor as he walked toward a long wood reception desk that was at the moment unattended. He was about to ring the bell on the counter—another vestige of the past—when he glanced toward the opposite end of the lobby where a few stuffed chairs competed for space with large potted plants. Sitting in one of the chairs intently reading a book was Zeke Campbell.

Rick paused and studied his old friend, trying to decide if the guy had changed any since their days at the university. He was still large, as would be expected, but it didn't appear that he'd put on any extra weight, as often happened with football players once they stopped working out. Hair? Definitely shorter than the modified Afro he'd remembered, but that might be left over from Zeke's days with the Marine Corps. There were the glasses, but they looked like reading glasses. Even Rick was starting to think he might need them himself. Was there some salt along with the pepper in his hair? Hard to tell from a distance. There was, however, one obvious change that was clear from the way his friend was dressed.

Zeke was now a priest.

CHAPTER THREE

"When we talked, you didn't mention your, uh, calling," Rick said after being crushed in a bear hug. "What does one say? Congratulations?"

Zeke beamed. "Whatever you'd like. I'm still somewhat surprised myself. The Lord works in strange ways. In my case it was through a Marine Corps chaplain, but that's a story for another day."

"Well, I'm relieved that it all worked out. As I recall, after graduation you kind of dropped off the map. Your friends knew you were in the Marines, and several of us tried to contact you, but you never got back to us. We finally gave up."

"There was quite a bit going on in my life, and especially in my head. You'll have to find it in your hearts to forgive me. But what about you? Tell me about what you've been doing. I'm sure you are the finest translator in Italy and turning down offers."

"I wouldn't exactly say that, but it pays the bills, and I like the flexibility of my schedule. If I worked nine to five, I wouldn't have been able to come up here to see you."

"Very true." Zeke nodded and slapped his knee. "Goodness, what a pleasure to see you, Rick. I'm sorry that it had to happen under these circumstances."

"Tell me about this tour group and how you are involved. I wondered why you were going to spend so much time here in Assisi, but now I can understand. This is probably not one's typical group of tourists."

"No, not at all. It was organized by the diocese of Santa Fe, where I have been assigned temporarily." He looked up to see if anyone else was nearby and lowered his voice. "All the participants are prominent supporters of the diocese."

"Fat cats?"

"I would not have used that term, Rick, but let's say they have been very generous in what they have done, and continue to do, for the church. It was the bishop's idea to organize this pilgrimage. As you will recall, the cathedral basilica in Santa Fe is dedicated to Saint Francis, so it made sense to bring them here to Assisi. We are visiting other places where Francis preached, of course, and doing some regular tourism, but it is very much centered around the life of the saint. And just before we return to New Mexico, we are scheduled for an audience with the Holy Father." Unintentionally, he held up his hands in a very papal gesture. "It hadn't occurred to me, but of course, you will have to join us."

"It would be an honor. Assuming I don't have to work that day. But tell me about this group. Everyone is from New Mexico, I assume. I may know someone."

"I never thought of that, but perhaps you do. But other than Chris, our driver, and me, there are only six. We wanted to keep the numbers down so we could travel by a small van. Easier to navigate narrow streets."

"That is indeed a small tour group. I trust these people are paying premium prices for the exclusivity of the tour."

"Let's just say they were not bothered by the price."

"Which I assume included another generous donation to the church."

"But they get their own resident priest to minister to their spiritual needs while traveling."

"Such a deal. Who are these people?"

"They have a free afternoon and are out and about, so I can't introduce them to you until this evening at dinner here at the hotel. This morning we celebrated mass at the cathedral and then heard a talk by one of the priests about the life of Francis. We were going to cancel it when I realized that Biraldo had gone missing, but the old guy insisted he could do it in English. I'm not sure when he learned his English, but I suspect it was before he entered the seminary, and he hasn't used it much since then. We could have used you, but thankfully, everyone was polite to him, even though they didn't get half of what he was saying."

"By the way, Zeke, I drove by that address you gave me, and nobody answered when I rang the bell for the apartment." He didn't mention the suspicious-looking man.

"Thank you for that; I hope it wasn't too much trouble." Again he glanced around the lobby, which was still empty. "Just between us, Rick, Biraldo wasn't my choice for a guide, but we were desperate, and he was recommended by one of the members of our tour group, so I couldn't protest too much. And now I'm beginning to be concerned."

"Did he just disappear?"

"Not exactly. When we got to the hotel yesterday afternoon he seemed to be quite agitated. Everyone was checking in, and he told me he had an appointment on a personal matter and would not join the group for dinner at the hotel. Then he walked out."

"Did he leave his ID at the desk when he checked in?"

"He never registered. He left his suitcase with the desk clerk and told her he would be back in the evening to check in. The bag is still there."

"Perhaps the personal business was very personal, Zeke, since he spent the night somewhere else."

Zeke frowned and shook his head. "He does consider himself quite a ladies' man. I may be a priest, but I could see the way he talks with women, especially attractive ones." He inclined his head toward the woman behind the reception desk. "By the way, I've got another address here in Assisi where he might be found. I was going to try and find it this afternoon, but it would be very helpful if you could go with me, in case there is a language issue with someone. The hotel clerk said it's relatively close by, but from the looks of the town everything is close by."

"Let's go right now. We can catch up some more while we're walking."

"Great." Zeke got to his feet. "Let me go up to my room and drop off this jacket. It's warm enough out that I don't need it, and I've found that the black shirt really picks up the heat in the sun. You can check in while I do that."

"Check in?"

"Yes, of course. I can't offer to pay you for your services, but we can certainly provide you a room in the hotel. I've already arranged for it; they have your name at the reception desk. I'll be waiting for you back here." Zeke walked to the elevator and pressed the button.

Fortunately, Rick had not taken his suitcase out of the car at Aunt Filomena's villa. He retrieved it, came back inside, and was greeted by the young woman at the reception desk. She wore a blue blazer, white shirt, and blue tie, the unisex uniform of her profession. He couldn't see if she wore a skirt or slacks, and decided he shouldn't lean over the counter to find out. Since he was now with a priest, he had to be on his best behavior. She flashed a welcoming smile. Yes, they were expecting him, and yes, he could leave his car where it was. He filled out the registration form, turned over his identification document, and was pleased that the key she gave him was not a plastic card but rather a real key, hanging from a heavy tassel.

His room was on the third floor on the side of the building that faced the valley. He went in, dropped his bag on the bed, and opened the window and shutters, letting light stream into the room. He stood for a few minutes taking in a view that was even better than that from Aunt Filomena's terrace, though he wouldn't tell her that. For a moment he thought of taking a picture with his phone and sending it off to Betta, but he remembered that Zeke was waiting downstairs. He would get a picture later—the vista begged to be photographed.

When he emerged from the elevator, he found Zeke talking with an imposing woman who wore loose jeans and a white blouse, both cinched by a belt of silver and turquoise. Strands of gray hair were visible under a dark wide-brimmed hat, and she held a carved walking stick topped by more silver and turquoise. For footwear it was high-end hiking shoes. Zeke looked up as Rick approached and the woman turned to appraise him.

"Adelaide, this is Rick Montoya, whom I was just telling you about. Rick, Adelaide Chaffee."

She was still checking him out when Rick shook her hand. "Ms. Chaffee, it is my pleasure."

"I hope you don't think I look so aged that you can't call me Adelaide." She pressed on before Rick could react. "Father Zeke tells me you will be stepping in to take the place of that bounder Biraldo. I never should have recommended him. So we'll have a New Mexican rather than an Italian guiding us in Italy. Somewhat ironic, I'd say. Well, I'm off to walk around the town before dinner. Not as healthy as hiking the Sandias, but it will give me my needed exercise. I like your boots, Rick. See you both later." She took the first of her long strides toward the door.

"Nice to meet you, Adelaide," Rick called after her. When she was outside, he turned back to Zeke. "Is everyone in your group like her?"

"No one is like Adelaide."

"I felt like I was back on the Plaza in Santa Fe. All she was missing were pastel cowboy boots and a squash blossom necklace."

"She'll be wearing those at dinner."

"Is there a Mr. Chaffee?"

"No, and I don't think Adelaide ever married. She is accompanying her niece on this trip. She thought a spiritual experience might knock some sense into the girl, to use Adelaide's phrase, so she talked her brother into sending Jessica along. She's keeping the girl on a tight rein."

"How old is Jessica?"

"She's a sophomore at UNM. Photography major, so she's always got her camera with her."

"There's a lot to photograph in Assisi, including the view from my room. Shall we go find our missing guide?"

"Absolutely. The desk clerk said the address was easy to find. Perhaps she can give us exact directions." They walked to the reception desk.

"Yes, Padre?"

Zeke took a sheet of paper from his pocket and spread it on the counter. "You said this address was easy to find. Can you give us some specific instructions?"

"I can do better than that, Padre. Let me show you on a map." She reached behind her and brought back a map of Assisi, which she unfolded in front of the two men. "The hotel is here." She pointed with a pen and then made a mark while explaining the route. Her English was smooth but heavily accented.

"That should be easy," said Rick. "How long will it take to get there?"

"Ten minutes. Perhaps fifteen."

Rick took the map, folded it, and put it in his pocket. "Thank you very much."

They got outside and Zeke said, "Why didn't you talk to her in Italian?"

"First, so that you could understand what we were saying. But more importantly, when someone makes an effort to use a language other than their own, you have to encourage it."

They stepped onto the street, which, like those of all ancient towns in Italy, had no sidewalk. It climbed sharply before they walked through the double arches of the Porta San Francesco. A set of tall wooden doors, held by massive hinges and studded with iron rivets, was pushed to the side, ready to slam closed with a crash if marauders were spotted in the distance. Today the invading hordes were not barbarians but tourists, and they were welcome. Assisi, as much as any city in Italy, was accustomed to this constant invasion. Since the thirteenth century, when word of the deeds of Francis began to spread, those who came were pilgrims wanting to walk and pray where the saint had walked and prayed. The city had its share of ancient ruins and famous art, but over the years it continued to be the saint that brought visitors. As if aware of the seriousness of its spiritual reputation, Assisi maintained an air of spirituality, helped by the number of religious institutions it hosted. Priests and nuns mixed with the tourists, and dressed as he was, Zeke fit right in.

As they walked, the two men updated each other on their lives since they'd parted ways more than a decade earlier. For Zeke it was the Marine Corps, seminary, a short stint in a parish in southern Arizona, and his recent assignment to the diocese of Santa Fe due to his college connection with New Mexico. He was hoping to be sent to a church in downtown Chicago.

"I think a Black priest could do some good work among the young people."

"And being a very large and athletic Black priest certainly wouldn't hurt," Rick said. "I hope you get the assignment." Rick recounted his odd jobs after getting a master's degree and then starting his translation business in Albuquerque. The big leap had been when he decided that he could do better out of Rome, including branching into interpreting.

"What's the difference?" Zeke asked.

"Translating involves the written word, interpreting the spoken. Two different skills, and I enjoy doing both things. One I do in my apartment with my laptop, and for the other I work at conferences or small group meetings. Like what I'll be doing here."

At the address Zeke had been given was a narrow two-story stone structure wedged between other buildings of the same height. Rick estimated its construction to be from the fifteenth century, but like so many adobe buildings in Santa Fe, it could have been built in the twentieth and made to appear old. It had a narrow door on one side, which he assumed opened to a stairway to a second-floor apartment. Most of the street level was given over to a small store with only a metal-and-glass display case to alert pedestrians as to what was on sale inside. The shop, which sold paper supplies, was just far enough from the cathedral and other sites that it catered to the locals rather than tourists. Zeke stood back while Rick pressed the button next to the smaller door. When there was no response, he rapped on the wood, in case someone upstairs might hear it. Zeke was lifting his large fist to give it a try when they heard a voice from the door of the shop.

"Rucola's not there." The woman wore a long gray apron which matched long gray hair done up in a bun. Reading glasses hung from a cord around her neck. She eyed Rick and Zeke as if they were attempting a break-in.

"We were actually looking for Ettore Biraldo," said Rick in Italian.

"He lives in America."

"In fact he is here in Assisi, or at least he arrived here yesterday."

Rick's comment elicited a scowl. The phone rang inside the store, and she gestured toward the door before turning and going back inside. Rick told Zeke what she'd said, and they went in after her. The shop was a combination stationery and toy store, its shelves behind the counter and under the glass case filled with pens, pencils, workbooks, greeting cards, backpacks, and games. A metal rack hanging just inside the door held post-cards to tempt any lost tourists who might wander by. The woman was behind the counter now, but kept her eyes on Rick and Zeke as she talked on the phone.

Rick looked around the tiny space and said to Zeke, "There was a *cartolaio* like this near where we lived when I was a kid, and I loved going in. I still have some of the notepads from the place that I keep for sentimental reasons without using them. For my interpreting gigs, I always carry a pen and notebook, but now I get them at Vertecchi, a huge store in Rome. I can't walk past their pen selection without buying one." He pulled a pen from his pocket and was clicking it when the woman ended her conversation.

"If Biraldo is here in Assisi," she said to Rick, "he might have been the one I heard yesterday afternoon. He owns the building."

That got Rick's attention. "So he stays upstairs when he's in Assisi?"

"No, no. He rents it to Agostino Rucola. Maybe Rucola hadn't paid his rent. That wouldn't surprise me." She glanced at Zeke who was perusing the postcards. "Doesn't the padre talk?"

"He doesn't speak Italian. He's leading a group of American

pilgrims on a trip to Italy. Biraldo was part of it, and he's gone missing."

She snorted. "That doesn't surprise me either. Probably ran off with some woman. But I am surprised that a priest would allow the man to be part of his group."

"You said you may have heard him yesterday?"

"Yes, there was a commotion upstairs just before I closed for the day, and I could hear Rucola shouting at someone." She pointed toward the ceiling that was crisscrossed with dark wood beams. "At least I think it was Rucola, since I couldn't make out the voices. The other person must have been Biraldo. He didn't stop in here to see me, but of course I pay my rent regularly to the agency."

Two boys, both about ten years old, came through the door and went to the glass counter, passing Rick and Zeke as if the two men were invisible. The kids stooped down, eyed a row of matchbox cars on the middle shelf, and began a whispered conversation. The woman shook her head. "They've been in here every other day for the last week, trying to decide which one of the cars to ask for as a birthday present."

Rick bent over and looked past their heads at the cars. "Forget the Ferrari, take the Topolino," he said, before turning back to the woman. "Thank you very much, Signora, we'll leave you to take care of your customers."

She held up her index finger. "I am not a gossip. I would not have said anything, but since you are with a priest, I trusted you. Do you understand?"

"I understand."

"What did she say?" Zeke asked when they got back to the street.

"Your man owns the building, and she rents the store. The apartment above it is rented to a guy named Rucola, and she thinks she heard him and Biraldo arguing up there in the late afternoon yesterday. She did not seem to think much of Biraldo. She confirmed what you said about him being a ladies' man. When I said he had gone missing, she thought he could be with a woman."

Zeke sighed deeply. "I never should have allowed him on this trip."

Rick didn't mention that the woman had said that very thing. They started walking back to the hotel. In Assisi, one walked either up a hill or down; now they were going back down.

"She also said she wouldn't have told me anything if I hadn't been with a man of the cloth."

"Really?"

"Yup. When did you start to exude that aura of spiritual authority? They didn't teach that in Marine boot camp, did they?"

"At seminary. Spiritual Authority 101. Required course."

Back at his room in the hotel, Rick hung up the few items from his duffel that needed hanging and extracted his laptop from its bag. The room's furnishings could have been original, including a small writing desk that had the standard notebook of hotel services, a notepad, and pen, and now he set up his computer on it. He turned it on, typed in the hotel password, and signed in to his website email. There was only one new message since he'd checked it that morning in Rome, a request by a Milanese biology professor to translate a paper to be read at a conference in Warsaw. He had heard about Rick's services from a colleague in another department at his university. Science was not a subject Rick enjoyed working with, but he could do it, and the deadline wasn't until the end of the month. He typed in a quick reply. Then he called Aunt Filomena.

"It's not a problem," she said after he explained what was going on in Assisi and that he would be staying at the hotel that night. "I'm having dinner with a someone in town and was going to invite you along, but it is better that you are with your friend."

He pictured a doting blue-haired woman, not nearly as sharp as Filomena, who would try to pry into his private life while calling him a dear. He had dodged a bullet.

"You can meet Eduardo another time," she continued. "He's a busy man, what with the bank and his real estate, but we see each other often." Her phone buzzed. "That's him calling now. *Ciao*, Riccardo."

So much for the lonely maiden aunt. He got up and walked to the window while punching in another number. His uncle answered on the second ring.

"I trust you are enjoying Perugia, Riccardo."

"After a lovely lunch with Filomena, very much so. But it turns out I'm now in Assisi and may be here for a while." He gave Piero a brief rundown of the situation. "As a result, I've checked in to the hotel here and am at this moment looking out on a beautiful view of the upper Tiber River Valley. I'll be meeting Padre Zeke downstairs in the bar so he can tell me about the people in the group."

"Padre?"

"Didn't I mention that my friend has become a priest?"

"A minor detail. But I thought all your *compagni* from the university were debauched and dissolute."

"I thought so too. Zeke is quite a disappointment."

Piero laughed. "I have to go. Give my love to Filomena when you next see her."

Rick stowed his phone in his pocket and took another look at the view from his window. The sun was beginning to drop toward the horizon, and soon it would be shining directly into the room. He closed the louvered shutters but left the window open to allow outside air to circulate. No use turning on the room's air-conditioning if it could be avoided. He picked up his room key and headed for the door.

Zeke was waiting for him in the hotel bar, a long rectangular room with tables lined up along the wall across from the counter. Two women sat at a far table sipping tea. Probably Brits.

"I just got here," said Zeke. "What can I get for you?"

"No, this is on me. I think a cold beer would be in order, just like old times."

"That sounds perfect. I've heard that Italian beer is good, and I haven't had any yet. That walk up the hill worked up my thirst."

Rick ordered from the bar and returned to take his seat. "It will be fun to be with a group of New Mexicans again. Tell me about them."

Zeke sat back in his chair, clasped his hands together, and held them over his stomach. It struck Rick as a very priest-like gesture, and he wondered if his friend had picked it up at the seminary.

"Rick, I will try to be as subjective and nonjudgmental as I can. They are all essentially good human beings, but there have already been some clashes of personalities. Nothing serious, of course, but as you would imagine, these people are used to getting their way. I suppose that comes with wealth."

"You can count on me to be discreet."

The waiter arrived with two bottles of Peroni and two glasses, as well as a small dish of peanuts. He poured half of each bottle into each glass and departed.

"Here's to old times," said Rick, raising his glass.

"To old times. But it does seem strange that we're not drinking directly from the bottle." They tapped the glasses and took their first drinks. "And I do appreciate your discretion, Rick. In fact, I've been thinking how good it will be for me to have someone to talk to who is not part of the tour group. Even a priest has to be able to confide in someone occasionally."

"I can't hear your confession, Zeke, but I'll be glad to listen to your gripes."

"No gripes, really." He took another sip. "This is quite good. I'll have to order it at meals. Not that the wine is not excellent, of course, and someone in the group always orders some fancy bottle. But there's nothing like a good cold beer. All right, our fellow New Mexicans. Let me start with Leon and Vicki Alameda. He has been very successful in construction and real estate in Santa Fe, both residential and commercial, including some buildings near the Plaza. They live in Las Campanas, and he plays golf there. He's told me he is very interested in history, and has urged us to include some historical places on the itinerary along with the religious ones. Not that he isn't a very pious man."

"And his wife."

"Vicki is somewhat different. Much younger than her husband and somewhat—how shall I say it?—somewhat flashy. Opposites attract, they say. No children."

"Sounds like a trophy wife."

"I would not want to characterize her in that way."

"You being a priest."

Zeke shrugged and had another swig of the Peroni. "The other married couple in the group are the Raels, Peter and Lillian. He's an Albuquerque businessman, owns a research firm in the tech park near Sandia Labs. He doesn't talk about what his company does, but of course it's defense related like most of them in the tech park. He's originally from Texas, and proud of it. Lillian is also from Texas and will tell you that she gave up a career to become a mother. I have not decided yet if she's bitter about the decision or proud of it. Their kids are grown up and living on both coasts. They live in Tanoan."

"That's the gated community in the center of town with the golf course. So he must play golf, like Alameda."

Zeke shook his head. "No, he's a tennis player, and he and Leon have argued over that. Peter says golf is just a game for old men, while tennis is a real sport, for athletes. Leon points out that Tiger Woods has more muscles than most tennis players."

"Perhaps the two just like to argue."

"There may be something to that. It's never become heated; they always pull back before it gets to that point."

"Because there is a priest present?"

"That could be part of it." He took a peanut. "Adelaide you met. She owns an art gallery and is a member of an old Santa Fe Anglo family that was in ranching for generations. The Chafees used their cattle money in the middle of the twentieth century to buy up property in Santa Fe. Very prescient on their parts, given what it is worth today."

"And she's the one who recommended Biraldo."

Zeke nodded. "And as you heard from her, she now regrets it. Biraldo apparently talked her into importing some art from Italy to feature in her gallery. Perhaps it didn't sell, or maybe there is some other reason the relationship soured. I don't know and don't want to ask."

"What about her niece?"

"Yes, Jessica. A very pretty girl, but possibly spoiled too much by her father. Adelaide may have been correct in thinking that a spiritual experience would do her good, but the girl is suffering from withdrawal."

"From drugs?"

"No, her cell phone. Her aunt insisted that she could not bring it on the trip. Adelaide didn't want the girl constantly texting and staring at the small screen when she should be seeing great works of sacred art. Jessica's father, who apparently makes all major decisions for his daughter, agreed. The poor girl was close to tears on the flight and the first day in Italy, but she's starting to get used to it. She takes a lot of pictures with the fancy digital camera her father gave her for the trip."

"It must also be difficult to be the only young person in the group."

"Well, there is Chris Carson. He's what you might call my administrative assistant, but his main job is driving the bus and getting the luggage on and off. Chris was an exchange student in Italy for a semester, so he speaks some Italian and has driven here before. Also, he is the son of a couple who have been very generous to the church. He's just a few years older than Jessica."

"Are they...?"

"Chris seems very interested, but she not so much, as far as I can tell." Zeke drank the last beer from his glass. "So that's the lot of them. I'm sure you will get along well with everyone." He checked his watch. "The hotel will be serving our dinner at seven. That seemed a bit late to me, but the manager said they normally don't open until seven thirty."

"You'll get used to it, Zeke."

The priest looked over Rick's shoulder toward the door. "You won't have to wait until dinner, to meet Vicki Alameda. I can introduce you to her now."

Rick sniffed the air, catching the unmistakable scent of Shalimar. *Could it be?*

He got up and turned around. *Yes, it could.*

CHAPTER FOUR

Zeke watched as Rick and Vicki Alameda embraced, giving him the clear sense that they had been more than just friends. "I didn't realize that you two knew each other."

Vicki extracted Rick from her arms and brushed back an errant lock of blond hair. "You could say that, Father Zeke. I had heard that Rick was in Italy, but I didn't expect to see him here."

"Zeke drafted me after your guide went missing."

She made a face. "That creep. Excuse me, Father, but I say good riddance. Especially so, given his replacement." She squeezed Rick's arm.

"Perhaps I should let you two catch up. Rick, thanks for the beer." He walked hurriedly toward the lobby.

Vicki took the priest's place, and Rick sat down across from her. For a few moments neither said anything until Rick broke the silence. "You're still wearing the same perfume."

"Leave it to Rick Montoya to notice." She glanced down toward the floor. "Cowboy boots? You always wore Italian loafers in Albuquerque, and here in Italy you're wearing cowboy boots?"

"They're comfortable. Can I get you something? A coffee?"

She looked over to the bar. "Do they have anything stronger than coffee here?"

"If I remember correctly, you like red wine. I'll get you some." He went to the counter, ordered, and looked back at Vicki while the bartender poured a glass from an open bottle. Her style was casual, a running suit and sneakers, but it looked like she was now shopping at Neiman Marcus instead of using her employee discount at Dillard's. He brought the glass to the table and set it in front of her. She picked it up, tapped it on his half-full beer glass, and studied his face.

"What's happened in your life since I saw you last, Vicki?" He immediately regretted mentioning their last encounter. "And tell me you're happy."

"Am I happy? Why shouldn't I be? Leon is a good husband and wonderful provider. We live in a beautiful house on a golf course. I have many friends, even a few still from the old days."

Rick was not convinced but didn't press it. "How did you meet your husband?"

She took another sip of the wine, its dark color matching her lipstick. "He came into the store to buy something, and walked through the perfume department. I guess I caught his eye."

"You've always had a way of catching a man's eye, Vicki. Who's idea was this tour?"

She laughed. "Certainly not mine. If I had chosen a trip to Italy, it would have been to a villa on the Amalfi Coast. But Leon is a very pious man, so when our priest mentioned this to him, he jumped at it." She smiled. "Now I'm glad we're here and not on the coast. What about you, Rick?" She drank what was left in the glass. "Are you happy? Do you miss New Mexico?"

"I've settled in well, my business is now established, I have many friends."

"Any special friends?" She put an emphasis on the second word.

"There's a woman I have been seeing regularly."

"Is she here? Will I meet her?"

"No. She's in Rome."

"We'll be back in Rome at the end of the tour. Perhaps I can meet her then."

"Her work schedule is kind of crazy, Vicki, and she doesn't speak English."

"You're a professional interpreter, aren't you?"

He remembered that even one glass of wine always had an immediate effect on her. "That's true. Which reminds me that I really should go up to my room and work on a translation. We'll see each other at dinner, and you can introduce me to your husband. It's been great catching up, Vicki." He stood.

She got up from the chair and brushed his cheek with her hand. "We've got much more catching up to do." The hand lingered at his arm. "Rick, did you ever think that maybe we—"

"Let's not go over that again, Vicki. It's all ancient history."

Zeke's voice at the door snapped them back to the present. "Rick. Sorry to interrupt. I need you urgently to translate. Or interpret. Whatever it is."

"Of course, Zeke." He waved a hand at Vicki and walked quickly to his friend. "What's going on?"

"I don't know. There's a policeman here who I think needs me for something."

In the lobby a uniformed cop stood at the reception desk, talking and gesturing to the woman behind it. Rick walked to him. "I'm the father's interpreter. How can I help you?"

A look of relief spread over the man's face. "I was not told that the padre didn't speak Italian. Inspector Berti told me to bring him to her."

"Is this about Signor Biraldo?"

The young policeman, already uncomfortable, now became defensive. "I have only been told to bring him. The car is outside."

"I'll come as well."

The cop nodded and gestured toward the door.

"Zeke, your presence has been requested by a certain Inspector Berti. Our friend here is not aware of the issue, or if he is, he won't say, but I would suspect it involves your missing man."

"We'd better do what he says." They started toward the door, following the policeman. "It will be like old times, Rick. Remember when we had to go down to the police station and bail out Hector after they took him in for disorderly conduct?"

"I had forgotten that one."

"I wonder what ever happened to Hector."

"Last I heard he became a rocket scientist."

A few minutes into their ride in the police car, Rick had the distinct impression that they were not going to the police station. The car had made a circle around the walls of the city and begun climbing through its eastern streets. He knew from experience with his uncle that police drivers were incapable of going slow, even through traffic, and this driver was no exception, frequently using bursts of his siren to move cars or people out of his way. Sitting in the back seat, Rick and Zeke were thrown from one side to the other as the car made sharp turns. When the street straightened out and narrowed, they could see the roofs of the city on the left side of the car, and the valley beyond it. Finally the car slowed and burst over the hill onto a flat, open area in front of Assisi's castle.

There was enough space to park every vehicle in the city, but only a few were lined up near the railing that ran along the top of an embankment. All were police cars except one ambulance. Two of the cars had their emergency flashers going, sending red rays bouncing off the stone of the castle. Below the railing, the tops of olive trees were visible, and beyond them the city and valley. The view was similar to the one from Rick's room, but much higher, and so even more spectacular. Most of the policemen on the scene were standing at the railing, and most of those were peering below toward the olive trees. Rick counted ten, most of them in uniform. The car swung around and stopped a distance from the other cars.

"Wait here," the driver ordered. He got out and walked toward three people looking over the railing. One was in uniform, and of the two in civilian clothes, one was a woman. Their driver waited while she spoke to the other two, a clear indication that she was in charge. Must be Inspector Berti. Rick turned his head to check out another group: two uniformed cops facing a man in a dark suit who leaned against a patrol car. Rick squinted through the car window for a better look. Yes, it was definitely the guy he'd seen in front of Biraldo's apartment house in Perugia.

"We may have found your man, Zeke."

Zeke leaned forward to look, but before he could focus, the driver returned and rapped on the window. They opened their car doors, got out, and followed him to the three people standing at the railing. As they approached, Inspector Berti looked up, and her eyes went from Rick to Zeke and back to Rick. Dressed in a dark blouse and slacks, she had her blond hair pulled back as if she'd just come from the gym, and her figure indicated that a workout was part of her daily routine. The fit of her outfit showed off her figure, though her expression seemed to dare any man to take notice. She wore little makeup except for a splash of red on her lips. Rick introduced himself and Zeke, and she identified herself as Inspector Chiara Berti. They shook hands.

"Do most American priests travel with their own

interpreters?" she said, her eyes continuing to size up Rick. Her accent was Roman, and proud of it.

"I'm helping out with his tour group since the original guide departed rather suddenly." His eyes moved to the man still standing next to one of the cars, but Zeke was focused on the policewoman and didn't notice.

"We know about your guide. We had been trying to talk with him, but Detective Rossi was unable to track him down this morning." Her chin pointed to the man standing next to the car.

"That's Detective Rossi?"

"What's going on?" Zeke asked, frustrated at not understanding their exchange.

"Sorry, Zeke. I thought that guy was Biraldo. Let me see if I can find out why we've been brought up here." He turned back to the inspector. "What can the father do to help you, Inspector? He is just as anxious to find Biraldo as you are."

"We've found him. His body is down there."

"He's dead?" As soon as he said it he realized what a stupid question it was. "Did he fall? Suicide?"

She shook her head. "If he wanted to take his own life, he likely would have picked a fall of more than three meters. And aren't I supposed to be the one asking questions?"

"What's going on?" Zeke repeated.

"Sorry again, Zeke. Biraldo is dead; his body is down there where they're all looking."

"Oh, my Lord. I must go to him." He crossed himself as he rushed to the railing.

"If he wants to go to the body," Berti said, "the easiest way is by those steps down there." She pointed to a break in the railing near where the ambulance was parked. "He shouldn't get too close." Zeke somehow understood, ran down to it, and disappeared over the edge. Rick and Berti walked to the railing.

Facedown between the trees lay the crumpled corpse of Ettore Biraldo, dressed in jeans, a dark shirt, and a leather jacket. He was surrounded by a three-person forensic team. One took pictures, another examined the body, and a third wrote on a notepad. The group was partially hidden from their view by the branches of an olive tree, and Rick noticed that one had been snapped off. Rick pointed it out to Berti. "He has to have fallen from up here."

"Which is why we've already checked the railing for fingerprints and taken pictures of the dirt you're standing on." She looked at his cowboy boots and a slight smile creased her red lips. "Very observant. Are you some kind of deputy sheriff?"

"My uncle is a cop."

"In Texas? He must ride a horse to work."

"No, Inspector, in Rome. Perhaps you've encountered him. Commissario Piero Fontana." He didn't usually drop his uncle's name, but the woman was starting to get on his nerves. He looked down and saw that Zeke was on his knees in prayer, a discreet distance from the forensics team. Was he performing extreme unction? Rick wasn't familiar enough with the sacraments to know. One of the team carefully rolled the body over, and even from high above through the leaves, a gash on the forehead was visible. Rick thought it too large to have been caused by hitting the tree, but he wasn't going to say that to Berti. Let her figure it out for herself. And she was busy talking on her cell phone.

Zeke had gotten to his feet and stood several yards away, watching as the team took their time studying the ground around the body. It was as if he felt the need to stand vigil or was somehow protecting the body of Biraldo, which made Rick wonder if his friend had been in this situation before. He felt a tap on his shoulder and turned to see Inspector Berti holding up her phone.

"He wants to talk to you."

"Who?"

"Your uncle."

Rick frowned and put the phone to his ear. "Zio?"

"Riccardo, you seem to have found yourself involved in a murder investigation again. You're like the protagonist in a crime series." Inspector Berti, apparently not interested in overhearing the conversation, walked over to a group of officers and started giving orders. "The inspector told me you've already been of assistance."

Had she been referring to his observation about the broken branch or his interpreting for Zeke? "Not really, at least not yet. What's the story on her?" His uncle knew everyone in the police, either from personal experience or by reputation.

"I thought you'd ask. She was in my investigative training class a few years ago. It was immediately clear to me that she would be a good detective if she could overcome an attitude problem. Being a tough boss usually works with your subordinates, but you can't deal with the public the same way. I expect that you have already experienced her manner."

"Correct. Might that change now that she knows you are my uncle?"

Piero thought for a moment before answering. "A good question. Somehow I doubt it. There is also another issue with Chiara. How shall I say it without sounding like a gossip? She has a certain reputation."

"Regarding the opposite sex?"

"Very perceptive, nephew. And you've only just met her. But I hope that won't get in the way of your helping out in the case."

He glanced at the policewoman, whose back was now facing him. "Is there anything new regarding my last job, Zio?"

The answer did not come immediately. "Thankfully, no.

I have to go, Riccardo. Keep me posted on what's going on in Assisi. I'll read the reports, but your insights will help me put them in perspective. *Ciao.*"

Rick said goodbye and walked to the inspector, who was standing next to one of the cars talking to Detective Rossi, the man he'd thought was Biraldo. He handed her her phone and she introduced Rick. After shaking hands, Rick turned to Berti. "How did you know to send for Father Zeke?"

"I wondered if you'd ask." She reached through the window of the police car and pulled out two plastic evidence cases. Each contained a sheet of paper with crease marks indicating it had been folded. She handed them to Rick. " We didn't find a wallet or cell phone on him, so it could have been a robbery, or at least the murderer wants us to think that. But they didn't take these, which were in his pocket."

He scanned the papers quickly. One sheet was the itinerary of the group, with the hotels and contact information, probably so that people could leave a copy with family back in New Mexico. The second listed everyone on the tour, including Zeke, who was identified as its leader, and Biraldo as guide/interpreter. Both sheets were on Archdiocese of Santa Fe stationery.

"I'll need to talk with each of them, of course. Which is where your interpreting skills will come into play. Your uncle said you would be willing to help."

"Of course, Inspector."

"Since we're going to be working together, Riccardo, you can call me Chiara."

"Of course, Chiara."

Detective Rossi had kept his eyes on the ground during the exchange. Now he said to his boss, "What would you like me to do when the team concludes its work?"

"You don't need to wait. Take the padre and Riccardo back

to the hotel and get a statement from both of them. Although…
Riccardo, how long have you been here in Assisi?"

"I got here about two hours ago. I drove up from Rome this
morning and was in Perugia visiting a relative."

She checked the itinerary inside the evidence bag. "They
all got here yesterday afternoon. The preliminary estimate on
time of death is last night, so we only need a statement from the
priest. I don't think he would be a credible suspect, but he will
have to tell us where he's been since arriving in town. Riccardo
can translate."

"Interpret," Rick corrected.

"Whatever you want to call it. Also, Rossi, search Biraldo's
room at the hotel."

"He never checked in," Rick interjected. "He left his suitcase
at the front desk and took off."

She listened and turned back to the detective. "Then get that
suitcase and take it back to the *questura*. There may be something in it of interest. Okay, I'll interview all the others in the
group later at the hotel. Tell the priest not to let them wander."
She paused, in thought. "On second thought I'd better interview
the priest as well. Then I can compare it with what the others
say. I'll finish up here and come right down."

"You don't think any of the Americans could be involved in
this, do you?" said Rick.

She gave him an annoyed look, but it disappeared immediately. "If you've helped your uncle at all, you know we have to
cover all possibilities."

"Inspector…excuse me, Chiara…you said you had been
looking for Biraldo. Why did you want to find him? Couldn't
some Italian he was involved with have killed him? Was he
doing something that would have put him in danger?"

"Those are a lot of questions, Riccardo. Without getting into details, there was an official complaint from his former wife. It was enough to put him on the radar of a local police force that normally doesn't have murders to deal with and therefore had time to investigate. But it wasn't that serious; he wasn't the local Mafia don on another crime family's hit list."

The comment caused Rossi to chuckle, and the inspector pointed at him with her thumb. "Rossi here knows all about the Mafia, he was just transferred here from Palermo." She looked at her watch and started to walk back to the railing. After two steps she turned back to Rick. "I'll see you at the hotel."

Rick watched as she yelled questions down to the crime-scene crew; then he turned to Rossi. "I was recently in Palermo myself. Lovely city, though I didn't get a chance to see much of it. Shall we be on our way back to the hotel, Detective?"

The detective nodded. "We can take the same car you came up in, Signor Montoya. Here comes the padre." The priest climbed the stairs slowly, and his face was somber. He stopped and looked up at the stone walls of the castle, then out toward the valley.

"Are you all right, Zeke?"

"Yes, Rick. I'm thinking about how to break this news to the group. And I'll have to call the archbishop back in Albuquerque. Do you think they'll want to cancel the tour and fly back to Albuquerque?"

"I wouldn't think so. And they will have to be here any-way. The police will need to talk to everyone as part of their investigation."

"They don't believe—"

"No, no. Of course not. It will be just a formality. The inspec-tor in charge thinks the murder will likely have something to do with shady dealings he had here in Italy." It wasn't exactly true, but it would keep Zeke from worrying. "I'll be helping her out, interpreting when she interviews everyone."

"Your presence will be a good thing."

They watched as the sheet-covered body was brought up on a stretcher and put in the ambulance. Its door was shut with a soft thump, and the driver got in to start the engine. He would have no need for a siren or speed on the way down the hill.

———

The group had already gathered for the pre-dinner wine tasting, a daily ritual that had been a major selling point for the tour. Tonight it was a red and two whites from Montefalco, a town just to the south east of Assisi. A table had been set up against the wall of their private room just off the main dining room of the hotel, and the waiter was filling glasses, but not too full. The two older men, Leon Alameda and Peter Rael, were similarly dressed in New Mexico casual: loafers, summer-weight slacks, and short-sleeved polo shirts. Rael was in the better shape of the two, perhaps due to his tennis playing, but Alameda was taller and heavier. Rael also had a full head of hair compared with the almost disappearing hairline of the other man. Their wives could not have been more different. Lillian Rael wore a print dress and comfortable flats, with a gold necklace and matching earrings, giving the impression she was at an afternoon tea. Vicki Alameda, twenty years younger, had changed out of her sweats into linen pants and a clingy silk blouse with just enough cleavage showing to attract the attention of every man in the room. The two married couples, glasses in hand, formed a rigid conversational rectangle. Adelaide Chaffee, as Zeke had predicted, was in full Santa Fe regalia, from the pastel boots to the squash blossom necklace, and more turquoise and silver in between. Next to her was niece Jessica Chaffee in jeans with a silk tee, and a camera hanging from her shoulder like a purse. The final member of the tour group was Chris Carson, who stared blankly at Jessica. His outfit ran the risk of having him mistaken for a waiter: dark pants and shoes, a white shirt, and a thin blue tie. When Rick and Zeke entered the room, conversation stopped, and they all looked at Rick.

"I have some news for everyone," said Zeke, his hands clasped over his chest. "But let me first introduce Rick Montoya, an old friend of mine from UNM, who lives in Rome and has agreed to act as our guide and interpreter."

"A good change from Biraldo." It was Leon Alameda, and others nodded in agreement.

Zeke ignored the remark and introduced everyone to Rick before holding up a hand. "But I also have some tragic news to report. Rick and I just came from a meeting with the local police. Ettore Biraldo was found dead a few hours ago among the trees above the city."

Rick watched as the meaning of the words sunk in with the group. Several crossed themselves, Jessica Chaffee gasped, the two couples clasped the hands of their spouses, Adelaide Chaffee slumped into a nearby chair, and Chris Carson stood rigid while looking protectively at Jessica. None of them moved while Zeke led them in a short prayer. When he looked up at the end of his words, everyone remained silent. The priest went on: "The police are treating the death as suspicious."

"He must have had a few enemies here," said Adelaide, having regained her composure after sitting down. "I never got the full story from him on why he left Italy, but my impression was that it was a rather hurried departure."

"Some father with a shotgun after him?" Peter Rael might have intended to lighten the atmosphere with the wisecrack, but it had the opposite effect.

"I'd wager it had something to do with money," said Adelaide.

Zeke held up his hands to stop the comments. "As a formality, the police will need to speak to each of us. The inspector in charge of the case will be here soon to do that. Rick has been kind enough to volunteer to interpret, since she speaks no English."

"A woman cop?" It was again Peter Rael. Rick was beginning to get a sense of the man.

"I've helped police in these situations before," said Rick. "She will want to speak to each of you individually and will probably ask you about your contact with Biraldo."

Lillian Rael had taken a long drink from her wineglass. "That's the way they do it on the cop shows on TV."

"Father Zeke?" It was Leon Alameda, still clutching Vicki's hand. "You must advise the archdiocese. Perhaps even speak with the Archbishop directly. This could get into the papers back home, and he should be made aware."

"I was planning on doing that, Leon." There was a touch of annoyance in Zeke's reply.

Rick could hear the sound of a police siren outside. Was it Inspector Berti making a statement, showing her authority even before arriving? The sound arrived in front of the hotel, made a final beep, and stopped. He nodded to Zeke and left the room. When he got to the lobby, Berti was talking to the hotel manager, who could not disguise his discomfort. A uniformed sergeant stood nearby.

"...and I'll need a room to interview these people. Doesn't have to be large, just a table and a few chairs." The manager said there was a small meeting room just off the lobby that she could use and he would have water sent in. "Excellent." She noticed Rick. "Ah, Riccardo. Is everyone here? Let's start with your priest."

"Why don't we sit down and you can tell me how you want

to do this, Chiara? Also the group was about to have dinner, so how long do you think it will take? We could ask the restaurant to delay serving, which I don't think everyone would mind too terribly." He didn't think he needed mention that they were sipping wine and might welcome a delay to help them get their heads around what happened. Berti looked at him, and he thought she was trying to decide how to reply. Play tough and show who's running the show? Or be flexible to gain Rick's respect? He was expecting the former and instead got the latter.

"Sure. I have a call to make anyway. You talk to the manager about the meal, and I'll be waiting for you inside." She hurried off. The sergeant followed close behind.

The manager said it would be no problem to delay the meal, and he would be sure that the group was well supplied with wine, making Rick wonder if it might have been a mistake. As he was finishing at the counter, Zeke walked quickly up to him.

"Is the inspector here?"

There was a visible change in the priest. His muscular body was tense, and the tension showed in his face. It reminded Rick of game days back at the university, when Zeke headed off to the locker room, already in the mindset for a confrontation. His friends had learned to steer clear.

"She's making a phone call, but I'm going to talk with her first and then come and get you one by one. I asked the manager if they could hold the dinner until we're ready, and he agreed. I hope that's all right."

Rick's words seemed to relax the priest. He took a breath. "Yes, that's fine. They may all be sloshed by the time we eat, but that way they'll be relaxed. I may be as well."

"She wants to start with you, since you're the group leader." Rick patted him on the shoulder. "We'll talk to you all as quickly as possible so she can investigate some real suspects." Zeke walked away, and Rick noticed that the black shirt made him look even larger.

Inspector Berti was sitting as she talked on her *telefonino*, legs stretched out under the small table. The sergeant stood at a window that looked out at the alley behind the hotel. The room was about the same size as the one in which Rick had spent two days on his Palermo trip, but the similarity stopped there. This one was tidy and well lit, the table fitted with six comfortable chairs, the walls decorated with semiabstract paintings that added color to their clean surface without detracting from the room's businesslike atmosphere. A credenza against one wall already had a bottle of mineral water and six glasses. The manager had worked fast.

The inspector ended her call abruptly. "Let's get this over with, Riccardo."

Rick sat at the desk. "How do you want to do it, Chiara? I would assume you need to know where they all were last evening, and if they can recall something that might be helpful."

"That's it. You sound like you've been through this before. Just be sure you translate everything they say, even if you don't think it's important. I'll decide that."

"Of course." He stood. "You want Father Zeke first?" She nodded, and he left, returning a few moments later with the priest. The sergeant was now sitting at the table, notepad open and pen ready. The inspector also had a pen, but with a smaller pad. The water and glasses had been moved to the table.

"This is Father Zeke Campbell, resident of Albuquerque, New Mexico, United States," said Rick in Italian after they took their seats. The sergeant dutifully took down the information, but had to ask Rick to spell out the city name. Rick then asked Zeke where he was yesterday, interpreted the question, and explained that he would periodically interrupt to interpret the answer.

opeot

"The group arrived at the hotel yesterday at about four in the afternoon. We all checked in to our rooms, all except Biraldo. He told me that he needed to see someone, would check in later, and not to expect him at dinner. He seemed rather agitated about something. I was a bit annoyed, but since we didn't have any formal program where we needed a translator, it didn't matter. And we didn't need him for dinner here at the hotel. I think some of them had walked around town a bit before we ate, but I stayed in my room, checked my emails, and had a nap. The jet lag for me is worse than I'd expected. After dinner everyone went to their rooms, at least I assumed they did."

While Rick put his words into Italian, Zeke poured water into a glass and drank it.

"I woke up at about ten o'clock, wide awake still on New Mexico time. I got dressed and went outside since it was a pleasant night. There were a few people on the streets, but not many, and they seemed to be mostly Italians. But I did see two members of our group walking ahead of me, though I didn't talk with them."

When Rick interpreted, the inspector asked who the two were.

"Leon Alameda and Peter Rael," Zeke replied. "They must have had the same problem sleeping that I did. They didn't see me, and I didn't try to catch up with them. I was enjoying being by myself after spending the day with the group." He looked at Rick. "I hope that doesn't sound bad?"

After hearing the question in Italian, Berti assured him it did not, and asked what he meant by Biraldo being agitated. "What did he say?"

"He didn't say anything about what was bothering him, but I just had the sense he was preoccupied about something, and that's why he wanted to leave immediately, so he could deal with it." He continued after Rick interpreted. "I got back to my room at about midnight, tossed and turned for another hour before finally getting to sleep."

Berti had no more questions, at least for the moment. "Any preference as to who you'd like next, Chiara?"

"If I remember correctly there are four men, including the padre here, and four women. Let's start with the married couples, one at a time. First the woman, then her husband."

"Without any overlap so they can't coordinate their answers."

She didn't answer, instead scribbling something on her pad. Rick asked Zeke to send in Vicki first, and sent him on his way. While they waited, Rick asked, "Did you get anything out of that?"

"Other than the padre's problem with sleeping? Well, if he's correct, Biraldo was rushing off to meet someone, and from the way he was acting, it was a meeting of some importance to him. We will have to find out where he was going."

The door was pushed open and Vicki Alameda strode in, her heels clicking on the tile floor.

———

Just a block from Saint Ursula church, on the way back to her hotel, Betta came to a small art gallery wedged between a drugstore and a shoe repair shop. Having grown up working in her father's gallery in Bassano, she always made a point of going into such shops to chat with the owner and find out about the local art market. The lamentations of the shopkeepers were always the same: how slow business was, how people don't appreciate art anymore, how difficult it was to find good pieces to sell. Her father said the same thing whenever she called him from Rome. This gallery was far enough from the leaning tower not to be oriented toward the tourist trade, and if what she saw in the window was any indication, the inventory tended toward religious art. A sign on the door, with the hands of a clock, indicated that whoever normally ran the shop would return later. After a panino and glass of mineral water, as well as braving the crowds of tourists at the Piazza del Duomo, she was back. The sign had been replaced by one that said that Galleria Galilei was open, and the public was welcome to enter at no charge. A bell over the door tinkled when Betta walked in.

The religious art in the window continued throughout the large room. On one wall hung paintings of saints in various points of agony and joy, very much Italian, mostly oils on canvas. Along a smaller wall was a row of Eastern Orthodox icons, their tiny faces staring out blankly from the panels. It was not a genre she knew much about. The total effect gave Betta the feeling she was in the museum of the local diocese rather than a commercial gallery.

Detracting from the religious atmosphere, however, was the person sitting behind the small counter, a woman who looked to be in her very early twenties. "Let me know if you need any help," she said, looking up briefly from her cell phone. Betta tried to decide which was the more striking feature, the nose ring or the hair dyed to a color unknown in nature. There were also the elaborate tattoos, which, along with the hair, displayed some color. Everything else was black, including her lipstick.

"This is an interesting inventory," said Betta. "Are most of your clientele locals, or visitors like me?"

The woman reluctantly put down her phone. "It's a mixture. There are certain artists that we have frequently, and dealers around the country follow the collection on our website and contact us when they see something of interest." The nose ring twitched as she talked, and Betta had to work to keep from staring at it. "So we do a lot of business online. I take the pictures and post them."

"You'll pardon me for saying this, but you don't seem like someone interested in sacred art."

The woman laughed. "I'm not. It's my grandfather who does all the buying. This is his shop."

"I see. Is he here today?"

"No. He only comes in mornings. Early mornings. After lunch he takes a nap, and then goes and plays cards with his friends." She put her elbows on the counter and looked at Betta. "So you're visiting Pisa. You don't look like a tourist with that shoulder bag and business outfit."

"I'm here to help the police investigate the theft of a work of art." She gestured in the direction of Saint Ursula's. "It was taken from a church near here."

Her eyes widened, their irises competing for attention with the black eyeliner. "I know about that. It totally freaked out my grandfather. He's a parishioner there."

Betta fished in her bag and came up with a card. "Here is my cell phone number; please give it to your grandfather and ask him to give me a call. We'll need to talk."

CHAPTER FIVE

Inspector Berti had arched an eyebrow when Vicki Alameda made her entrance, and the sergeant also took notice before quickly dropping his eyes back to his notepad. Rick spelled out the name, gave the address again as Albuquerque, and introduced her to the policewoman.

"Ask her if she knew Biraldo before the trip."

Rick had an idea what Berti was getting at and had to admit that he was curious about the answer as well, since womanizing was one of the man's vices. But he covered himself by prefacing the question with "The inspector would like to know..."

"The first time I met him was when we were all getting on the plane in Albuquerque. He gave me the creeps."

Rick interpreted her second sentence as if Vicki had said "He made me uncomfortable."

Berti nodded and waved her hand to indicate he should go on with the other questions, which he did, starting with her activities the day before.

"When we got to the hotel yesterday," she answered, "we checked in to the room and both took a short nap. Then we came down to the dining room for the wine tasting, if that's what you call it, and after that had dinner. I came back to the room and watched TV. They have CNN here, but it's not the same as at home. Lots of British people on it who I don't recognize."

"Your husband?"

"Leon came up a couple hours later. I think he was in the hotel bar."

"So you didn't go out at all last night?"

"No, and I actually slept pretty well. Leon told me this morning that he couldn't sleep and went out for a walk. I didn't wake up when he went out or when he came back."

Rick almost said that he remembered her being a sound sleeper, but he caught himself. "Did you see Biraldo much that day? Did he seem different?"

"On the bus ride from Rome, I was sitting with my husband. He was behind us, with Adelaide, I think. Or maybe he was by himself. I can't remember. I don't remember seeing him get off the bus, or in the hotel lobby."

When he finished interpreting, with the sergeant taking it all down, Berti shrugged, which he took to mean that Vicki could go. "Could you ask your husband to come in, please?"

She stood up. "Sure. Am I going to see you later, Rick?"

"At dinner, I guess."

"I sense that you two know each other," Berti said after Vicki had gone.

"We were acquainted back in America. Albuquerque is a small town."

Berti smiled and shook her head. "From the way she was dressed, I gather her husband must be well off."

"Everyone in this group is well off, except for Chris Carson, the driver. And Father Zeke."

Leon Alameda tapped on the open door. Rick waved him in and pointed to the chair his wife had just vacated.

"He is married to her? He must have more money than I would have thought."

Rick ignored Berti's comment, introduced her to Alameda, gave the sergeant the full name and residence. "Leon, please tell the inspector what you did yesterday. It's a routine question."

"No need to say that, Montoya, I understand what's going on." The edge in his voice remained as he continued, making Rick wonder if he knew about his wife's previous relationship. "We left the hotel in Rome yesterday morning in the rental van. Lunch on the way, and we got to the hotel midafternoon. After we checked in, my wife and I rested before dinner. We're still recovering from the flight. It was just one stop, in Atlanta, but it took forever. After dinner she went up to the room, and I stayed in the bar and had a drink."

"Were you alone?"

His eyes narrowed. "No, I was not. Adelaide Chaffe was there having a coffee. Decaf. We chatted for quite a while about the real estate market in Santa Fe. I shouldn't have been talking shop, it drives my wife crazy, but it's impossible for me not to. Eventually I excused myself and went to the room."

"You slept well?" It was a setup question, after what his wife and Zeke had said.

"At first. But I woke up and couldn't get back to sleep, so I got dressed and went out for a walk. After a few blocks, I ran into Peter." He looked at the sergeant, who was scribbling notes when Rick interpreted. "That's Mr. Rael. We walked together for a block or so before he broke off and returned to the hotel. I walked a bit longer and then came back myself."

"When was the last time you saw Biraldo?"

Alameda put in some thought. "I guess it must have been on the bus. When it stopped for lunch, he sat at another table."

"Do you remember who he was sitting with?"

"Let me think. I believe it was Adelaide, Jessica, and Chris."

Inspector Berti broke in after Rick interpreted. "Ask him if he knew Biraldo before the trip."

Alameda listened to the question and hesitated before answering. "By reputation. I checked up on all the people in the group when I got the list, and called a few of my contacts in the university about him. To say that Biraldo's reputation was mixed would be an understatement. But you should ask Adelaide, since she was the one who recommended him in the first place. He did some business with her in Santa Fe." After hearing the Italian, the inspector tapped the pen on her pad and signaled that was enough.

Rick thanked Alameda and asked him to send in Lillian Rael.

When the door closed, Berti said: "The two men met each other on the street last night. Either of them could have found their way up to the murder scene, but why would Biraldo meet them up there? Or they both could have met him there. Neither scenario makes sense. I have to think Biraldo drove up there with one of his local contacts to talk, and things got rough."

"I agree. I haven't heard anyone yet say anything good about Biraldo, but it's hard to picture any of these people murdering the man, no matter what they thought of him."

A knock on the door was followed by Lillian Rael pushing it open and looking inside. Rick got up and went to her. "Please come in, Mrs. Rael. This is Inspector Berti, who would like to ask you a few questions." He noticed that she had brought her wineglass, which she now put down on the table. It held a ruby red.

"I didn't like him, but I didn't kill him."

"What did she say?"

Rick held up his hands to hold off more comments before interpreting Lillian's statement. "No one has accused you of anything, Mrs. Rael. Why don't you just tell us about what you remember from yesterday, and I'll tell the inspector what you said?"

She grasped her wineglass but didn't drink. "Yes, of course, Rick. Can I call you Rick? And please call me Lillian. Everyone does, even the young people. I mean Jessica and Chris, who are young enough to be my children. But you asked about yesterday." Now she paused and took a sip. "We left the hotel in Rome after breakfast, drove here on the bus, stopping for lunch at a charming place just off the highway. Chris can tell you where it was, since he does the driving. We got here in the afternoon and checked in to the hotel. Peter and I washed up and it was time for the wine tasting." She held up her glass to illustrate the point. "Then dinner. I don't know why any of this will help her."

Rick could not but agree. He interpreted and then asked: "Did you sleep well?"

"Goodness, I was out like a light. This jet lag stuff doesn't seem to affect me at all. Though I did doze off on the drive up, despite the beautiful scenery. Peter told me this morning that he couldn't sleep, but I was fine."

At least that confirmed something Leon Alameda had said. "What do you remember about Biraldo yesterday? Did you talk to him at all?"

"I didn't talk to him, no. He was on the bus, of course, but was sitting in front of us, with Adelaide. I don't recall seeing him when we got to the hotel, but it was a bit confusing, with the checking in and getting our bags from the bus inside and up to our rooms."

More pen-tapping by Inspector Berti. "She's got nothing more, Riccardo. Let's get her husband in here."

Rick stood up. "Thank you, Lillian. Please send in your husband."

Mrs. Rael looked around like she was hoping for more questions, then got up and walked to the door, glass in hand. After she was gone, Berti tapped again on her notepad. She had written down nothing during the interview. "Everyone is saying the same thing so far. They got on the bus in Rome, drove here with a stop for lunch, and none of them talked with our victim except the priest when they got here. Let's hope somebody exchanged a few words with him, like the woman who was sitting with him on the bus. Who was it?"

"Adelaide Chaffee. An older woman, as you'll see. She's traveling with her niece."

"Somebody said she had done business with Biraldo."

"That was Leon Alameda. Also, she told me earlier that she had recommended Biraldo for this job but later regretted it."

"Hmm. Well, let's see what she has to say. Is she next?"

"No, it's the husband of the woman we just interviewed, Peter Rael."

On cue, Rael appeared at the doorway. "Where do you want me to sit?"

Rick pointed to the chair. "Right there. This is Inspector Berti, and I'll be interpreting her questions and what you say to her."

"I know. Leon told me how it works. Let's get this over with; we're all getting hungry."

Rick decided that Rael was more worried about the amount of wine his wife was consuming while waiting for dinner. After giving the sergeant the man's name and address, Rick started in, asking what he remembered from yesterday, especially any contact with Biraldo.

"The only contact I had with him was as we came out of the hotel in Rome. He was so engrossed in a conversation on his cell phone that he ran into me, almost knocking me down."

"Was he speaking in Italian?"

"He was gesturing as if the person on the other end could see him, so it must have been Italian. He didn't even say excuse me. The guy was a jerk, if you'll pardon my saying so. I'll never understand why Adelaide suggested he be our guide, but I guess they were desperate. No offense against you, Rick."

"None taken. Your wife said he was sitting in front of you on the bus. You didn't talk to him during the trip up here?"

"No reason to."

"And after you got here?"

"I saw him talking with Father Zeke, and then he left. But I didn't speak with him."

"What about the rest of the evening? How did you spend it?"

"How do you think I spent it? Like everyone else. Wine before dinner, dinner here at the hotel, then off to the room." He suddenly pointed a finger at Berti. "Wait, I know what she wants to know. If I sneaked out and killed the guy. Well, I fell asleep early but woke up a few hours later and was wide awake, so I got dressed and went out for a walk. I could have killed Biraldo, I suppose. But Leon could have killed him as well, because I ran into Leon on the street. We walked for a bit together before I left him and came back to the hotel. My wife was still out cold when I got to the room."

After he left, Berti noted that they got at least one new detail. Biraldo was talking distractedly on the phone as they left the hotel in Rome. It had to be someone here in Italy he was talking with. "Likely the same one he went off to meet when he got here to Assisi," she said. "Which again reinforces the likelihood that it was an Italian who did him in, not one of you Americans."

"I have Italian citizenship as well as American, Chiara."

"That's good. Now I don't have to call the Guardia di Finanza to report an American doing business without a work permit."

She poured some water into a glass and took a drink. "Three more, by my count. Who's next?"

"It should be Adelaide Chaffee." He saw the sergeant write down the name, with the address as New Mexico, without being asked. "She's the one who recommended that Biraldo be hired, and she also sat with him on the bus ride. So maybe we'll get something of interest from her."

The sound of Adelaide's walking stick reached the room before she did. Rick walked to the door and opened it to let her enter. If Berti, dressed entirely in black, was taken aback by the glitz of the woman's outfit, she hid it well. Perhaps she just expected foreign women to dress exotically. "Please sit down there, Adelaide. This is Inspector Berti. I'll interrupt you at times to put your words into Italian for her. There's water if you need it."

"If I thought this was going to take long, Rick, I would have brought my wineglass." She carefully leaned her walking stick against the arm of the chair. "Well, have at me."

"Please tell the inspector your movements yesterday, and especially when you encountered Ettore Biraldo."

She stared at the wall for a moment while putting her thoughts together. "I didn't see him at breakfast at the hotel in Rome. But on the trip up here on the bus, we sat together. He was also at my table at lunch, along with...let me see...along with Jessica, my niece, and Chris Carson."

"You talked on the bus?"

"Not very much. I napped for a while. I think he texted someone at one point, or perhaps he was just playing with his phone, like people do these days. That's why I forbade Jessica from bringing her phone along. She would have been staring at that little screen all the time rather than seeing what Italy has to offer."

"What did you and Biraldo talk about?"

"He pointed out some towns on the road and gave me a bit of history about them. I don't know if he was making it up to impress me or not. Ettore was all about impressing people, then drawing them in. He did that to me in Santa Fe."

Berti looked up from her pad when Rick interpreted. He anticipated her question: "What did he do to you in Santa Fe?"

"I have an art gallery. It's mostly local art and artists, since that's what the tourists from out of state buy, but I have some other pieces, things that interest me. Ettore came into my gallery one day and, with his charming Italian accent, told me that he was an art history professor at UNM but also represented Italian sculptors as a sideline. Would I be interested in something Italian? At the time it sounded perfect, and the catalog he showed me was impressive. So I ordered a few pieces of sculpture and paid him up front."

Rick interpreted and then asked: "They didn't sell well?"

"That would be an understatement. We had to mark them down, to make room for other pieces, and ended up selling them under what I'd paid Ettore for them. So I lost money."

"You talked at all about this on the bus?"

"I was tired of talking to him about it, and no doubt he was as well."

"And at lunch?"

"Again, Ettore dominated the conversation, talking about Italian art and history. My niece was enthralled, though she's easily impressed. Chris didn't say much, but he seems quite shy. That's my early impression only, since the lunch was the first time I'd spent any time with the boy."

"Adelaide, if you'd had a bad experience with Biraldo, why did you recommend he be hired as the guide?"

She frowned and shook her head. "I asked myself that more

than once. He had read in the paper about the tour group and that the diocese was going to hire a new guide after the first one dropped out. When he found out I was going to be on it, he asked me to put in a good word for him. He said he'd lived in Assisi and so he knew the town well, and since the church was sponsoring the tour, he would ask only that his expenses be covered, no fee. It would be his own donation to the church. That was typical of Ettore to make it seem like he was doing you a favor. Despite the problems with the art shipment, his offer made sense, and the diocese agreed. I have a personal relationship with the archbishop."

"Did Biraldo seem at all agitated? You are the only person in the group who knew him at all before the trip, so you would be the one to notice a difference."

Adelaide gripped the walking stick and tapped it on the floor, as if it would help her remember. "When we got on the bus, I could see something was bothering him. Then he relaxed during the ride, and at lunch he was effusive, as I said, trying to impress the kids. But that could have just been a front. When we got close to Assisi, the nervousness returned, and I remember him looking at his phone a few times, either checking the time or looking for a message. I don't remember seeing him when we got off the bus."

"What did you do the rest of the evening?"

"Oh, this is where I have to present my alibi, I suppose. I rested my eyes the rest of the afternoon, and had wine and dinner with the group. Ettore was not at dinner, which I'm sure you already know. Then I had a coffee in the bar. Oh, and I ran into Leon Alameda there, so he can vouch for me. Then I went up to my room. I have a very understanding doctor back in Santa Fe, and he made sure I was armed with something to get me to sleep, so I had a good night's rest."

Rick interpreted the words, but Berti did not appear to pay any attention. She studied her small notepad and made checkmarks next to some of what she'd written. When he'd finished, she signaled to bring in the next person. Rick thanked Adelaide and asked her to send in her niece.

"We got a bit more out of her than the others so far," Rick said when the door closed.

"More confirmation that Biraldo was nervous about something. Which again makes it less likely that anyone in this group was involved in the murder. But we have to talk to all of them. Who's next?"

"The niece of the woman we just interviewed." He turned to the sergeant. "Her name is Jessica Chaffee. A college student who is interested in photography."

The door opened and Jessica stood in the doorway holding her camera. As she raised it to her eye Berti raised a hand and called out: "No, no. Tell her no photographs, Riccardo." Jessica understood without the interpretation and let the camera down. It hung from a strap from her shoulder.

"Jessica, this is Inspector Berti. I'll interpret her questions for you and your answers for her. Please sit down."

She sat, keeping her grip on the camera like a security blanket. Rick expected nervousness in someone her age, but learning of a murder and now having to deal with the police in a foreign country appeared to be more than she could handle. He would try his best to put her at ease, but could see it wouldn't be easy, especially with someone like Berti staring at her.

"This shouldn't take long, Jessica. You're a student at UNM, if I remember."

"I'm a sophomore."

"I'm a Lobo myself, perhaps Zeke mentioned that. Do you have a major yet?"

"Sort of. I'm taking classes in the arts. I enjoy photography."

Berti glanced at her watch and then at Rick. He was not moved by her impatience.

"There's water here if you need it. We're going to ask you the same thing that we've asked everyone else; it's pretty much routine. I'm sure you are as anxious to find the person who did this as all of us."

The girl swallowed hard and nodded.

"We'd like to know about yesterday. Tell us what you remember. What you did, who you saw, that kind of thing. Take your time."

She stared at Rick for a few seconds. "Oh. I'm supposed to answer. Sorry. Yesterday I had breakfast with my aunt, we got on the bus and came here. The bus stopped on the way up for lunch. We arrived in Assisi in the afternoon and checked in." She looked at the water bottle and back at Rick. When he nodded she poured a glass and took a sip. "We had dinner here." Her voice was steadier after taking the drink. "After dinner I went for a walk with Chris. We almost got lost and thought we were going to have to ask directions, but luckily we spotted a sign for our hotel, and that led us back here." She shrugged to indicate she was finished.

Rick put her words into Italian, then asked: "You said you had breakfast with your aunt. Did you sit with her on the bus? And at lunch?"

She took a moment to answer. "On the bus I sat in the back, with Father Zeke. When we stopped for lunch, there were four of us at the table; besides me it was my aunt, Chris, and Ettore."

"Had you met Ettore before? He taught at the university, as you know."

"No, I only met him in the airport when we were waiting for the flight."

"What did you talk about at lunch?"

"He did most of the talking, about Italy, what we had seen so far on the bus ride, and what we were going to see. It was interesting, the way he tied in the history of the area with towns. He told me what we would be passing in the afternoon so that I'd be ready to get a picture from the window. And when we were approaching Assisi, he insisted that Chris stop the bus so I could get a shot from a distance." She pulled her camera from her lap. "I can show it to you."

"Perhaps later, I'd like to see it." He looked at Berti who shook her head. "Thank you, Jessica, that was very helpful. Could you ask Chris to come in, please?"

She got up without looking at Berti and made her retreat, clutching the camera and forgetting to close the door on the way out.

"Let's hope this last one is a bit more interesting than she was," said Berti. "And with more maturity." *Maturità* was what Italian students were awarded when they passed their final secondary school exam, something Rick always found curious. By passing the exam, a kid was officially mature?

"She's just a kid, Chiara. Carson is a bit older, but not by much."

Chris Carson stuck his head through the open doorway. His hair was disheveled, and he had loosened his tie.

"I see what you mean," said the inspector. "Let's get this over with."

Rick switched to English. "Chris, come in and take a seat. We just have a couple questions for you, and then you can get back to the group and your dinner."

"That's good, because there is a lot of wine flowing in that room. They just opened a couple more bottles." He sat stiffly in the chair and looked back and forth between the three faces.

Rick again made the introductions and decided to try something different, hoping that Chiara wouldn't mind. "Why do you think someone would want to kill Biraldo?" She didn't seem to mind, and fortunately the boy didn't notice her smile, since he was stunned by the question.

"I…I don't know. I didn't know him at all until this trip, and the longest conversation I had with him was at lunch yesterday. But Jessica and her aunt were at the table too, so he wasn't just talking with me. He sure knew a lot about Italy, but I suppose that would be expected."

"How did you get involved in this tour group?"

"My parish priest found out they were looking for a driver and suggested me. I have a commercial license and work part-time driving a bus for a retirement home in Albuquerque. It's not that different from the bus we rented on this trip. Also, I'd spent a summer in high school here as an exchange student."

"Allora parli Italiano."

Chris stuck with English. "Not very much. The Italian kids all wanted to practice their English."

"Tell us your movements yesterday."

He acted like he'd been expecting the question. Perhaps the people back in the dining room had been talking about their interviews. "I was up early to pick up the rental bus and drive it to the hotel. After breakfast I loaded up all the luggage and we left almost on time. After that I was driving, except for lunch, and I mentioned that. When we got here, I got the bags off with the help of the hotel people, and then moved the bus to a space on the side of the building."

Rick interpreted. "That evening?"

"I stayed in my room until dinner. After that Jessica and I went out for a walk. It was the first she'd been out of the hotel, and I suggested it. After that I went to my room. I slept well. Driving the bus is not that difficult, especially on the *autostrada*, but it does take some concentration, and I was tired."

After the sergeant had taken notes from Rick's Italian interpreting, the inspector signaled that it was enough. Rick thanked Chris and sent him on his way.

"If you don't need me for anything else, Chiara, I'll go join the group for dinner."

She put away her pen and folded her arms across her chest. "You'll have to put off joining the group, Riccardo. I need to go over with you what we just learned from these people, getting your impressions, and we can do it over dinner. I have an excellent restaurant in mind."

The sergeant had stopped writing when she'd begun speaking, and now he was staring blankly at his boss. Rick broke the few moments of silence, but it was not in Italian.

"I don't detect much of an accent, Chiara. Where did you learn your English?"

CHAPTER SIX

When Rick appeared at the door of the dining room, the noise level was higher than before the interviews with Inspector Berti. The shock of Biraldo's death had worn off, helped by an ample flow of wine. Zeke walked quickly to Rick. "You're in time for one quick glass of wine, Rick; they are about to serve dinner. How did it all go? I couldn't tell from the look on the face of the inspector; she must be a good poker player."

"I think it went as well as could be expected, and everyone was very cooperative. Please thank them on behalf of Inspector Berti." She had not asked him to thank them, but she wouldn't mind him saying she did. "Listen, I'm going to pass on dinner with the group. She wants to go over the case with me."

Zeke put his hands together in what Rick thought was a very priestly gesture. "Are you sure that's all she wants to go over? Excuse my skepticism, Rick, but I recall how you were in college with the ladies. Your reunion with Vicki Alameda reminded me."

Rick took it as more of a ribbing than a rebuke. "I'll find out at dinner. Don't worry, Zeke, I can take care of myself." A waiter appeared with a tray and Rick took a glass of red wine. "Back in college, did I ever mention that my Italian uncle is a cop?"

The waiter was starting to walk away when Zeke reached out to take a glass himself. "You did not. At least I don't remember you telling me that. Cheers." He tapped Rick's glass with his.

"It's been a kind of running joke with my uncle Piero that I should become a policeman as well. I've helped the police a few times, usually like this situation, with interpreting. I talked to him when you were down with Biraldo's body, and he encouraged me to help out Inspector Berti."

"Ah, now I understand. You're having an intimate dinner with the comely inspector to please your uncle." He smiled.

"I'm glad to observe that even with your collar turned around, Zeke, you have not lost your rapier wit." He drained his glass. "I've got to go. I'll try to remember to call you when I get back so you won't worry."

"I won't stay up."

As Rick left the room, everyone was in animated conversation, thanks to the events of the afternoon. Only Vicki noticed him leave.

After a quick visit to his room, Rick came back to the lobby to drop off his key at the reception desk. When he approached it he saw a woman in an animated argument with the desk clerk. On closer examination, he saw that the woman was doing the arguing and the clerk was cowering behind the counter. Her outfit was flashy—the skirt a bit too short and the blouse a bit too fitted. For an instant Rick wondered if a pious town like Assisi could have...no, probably not. And certainly not in an upscale hotel like this one. The clerk saw Rick and gave him the look of a drowning man spotting a lifeguard on the beach. The woman turned, transferring her glare from the clerk to Rick.

"Signor Montoya, could you please help me with this woman?"

He didn't see how he could, but said: "If I can, of course."

"She says—"

"I'm looking for Ettore Biraldo," she interrupted. "Are you connected with this tour group?"

Rick gestured to the clerk that he would deal with the problem, and the man quickly retreated to the other end of the counter. "Yes, I am." He assumed his most soothing manner, and she relaxed, though only somewhat. "Signor Biraldo is not here at the moment; perhaps you could give me a message for him."

"He was supposed to meet me. He called yesterday morning, and I made arrangement to come to Assisi. Then, not a word. And I was going to give him some important news. Well, now it's his problem. I shouldn't have trusted him."

"Are you staying at this hotel?"

"No, no. I always use the Capri. He knows that. Tell him I'm not happy." She began walking to the door.

"And your name?"

She stopped and turned. "Letizia Gallo."

Fifteen minutes later Rick stood on a corner half a block from the Hotel Capri. The sky was dark, bringing the streetlamps to life, and the few people who were out and about appeared to be heading to dinner, which was what Rick was thinking about. The light lunch at Aunt Filomena's had worn off long before, and with all the excitement and then his interpreting, he had worked up an appetite. But first was the small matter of Letizia Gallo. He pulled out his phone and checked the time. Was the inspector busy at the police station or was she arriving late to make another statement, like she did by using the siren while driving up to the hotel? There was a certain drama with this woman, no doubt about it. He turned to see her coming up the street on foot. She hadn't changed from her work outfit, but of course this was still work. He did notice a splash more of color on her cheeks as she walked toward him.

"This is going to work out well, Riccardo. The restaurant is just a short distance away." Having made her linguistic point back at the hotel, she'd returned to Italian. "This hotel is not as posh as the one where you are staying. In fact it has the reputation as a place for trysts. Which gives us a hint as to why she was staying here."

They started walking, and Rick wondered how Chiara knew about the hotel's reputation. He decided not to ask. "Letizia Gallo told me she always uses the Capri."

"Perhaps Biraldo wasn't the only person she's been meeting up with here. What is the woman like?"

Rick described Letizia as accurately as he could without seeming too judgmental, but Chiara got the picture. "She sounds like—what's the word in English?—a floozy."

"I was thinking *hussy*."

"That's a good one too. What was it again? I mean what did she say?"

They were almost to the door of the hotel. "That she had some important news for Biraldo."

"Right. Well, she can just pass whatever it is on to me."

The hotel lobby was smaller than that of the Windsor Savoia, but because of its location in the heart of the city, the building itself was considerably older. The interior, however, had been brightened with buckets of stucco and white paint. The marble floor and walls reflected light from a large chandelier hanging between the small reception area and a slightly larger sitting room that held three chairs, an end table, and a sofa. A tiny unattended bar took up the corner. The inspector surveyed the room quickly before marching up to the woman behind the counter.

"Please tell Letizia Gallo that her visitor has arrived." She put on a charming smile. "Don't tell her anything else; we'd like it to be a surprise."

They had only been sitting for a few seconds when the woman came down the stairs and stormed into the reception area. Her face changed instantly from anger to puzzlement when she saw Rick and the inspector.

"What is…? Who are you? Where is Ettore?"

Chiara got up and motioned for her to sit down across from them. She held up her identification. "I'm Inspector Berti, and you have already met Signor Montoya. I have some questions for you about Ettore Biraldo."

She slowly sank into the sofa. "It doesn't surprise me that he's in trouble with the police. That's probably why he didn't show up today. Well, I don't know where he is, I can tell you that immediately." Her eyes darted between Rick and Chiara. He remained silent, watching the inspector work. Uncle Piero would be interested.

"He was in trouble with the police, but now he has troubles of his own. He's been murdered."

Not the smoothest way to start an interview, Rick thought, but if its purpose was to get the woman's attention, it worked.

"Oh my God, Ettore dead? Who would have done it?"

"Probably not you, Signora Gallo, or you would not have come looking for him at the hotel. When did you expect to see him? You'd made some arrangements to meet?"

She took several deep breaths to compose herself before answering. Her hand, shaking slightly, flitted up to her face. "He called me yesterday morning from his hotel in Rome and said he'd be in touch when he got to Assisi, either last night or this morning. When I didn't hear from him all day today, I came to his hotel."

"You're not from Assisi."

"No. I live in Perugia. I drove down this morning."

"Where were you last night?"

She swallowed hard. "Can I get some water?" Without waiting for an answer, she walked to the bar, found a bottle of mineral water, and poured some in a glass. When she got back to the sofa, she took a long drink and put the glass on the table. "Last night I was at home."

"You're married?"

"Yes."

"So your husband can confirm that."

"He worked late and didn't get home until about eleven. But he can confirm that I was there when he got home."

"Where does your husband work?"

"He manages a chocolate company, Dolce Vita. Perhaps you've seen their products. He also produces wine, same name."

Rick was more impressed by the chocolate than the wine, being a big fan of Dolce Vita's hazelnut-flavored bars.

"We'll need your husband's address and phone number."

The inspector's request made Letizia Gallo fidget. She clenched and unclenched her hands in her lap. "I suppose you'll have to." She pulled her skirt down over her leg, though there was not much of it to pull. Inspector Berti didn't appear to notice; she kept her eyes on the woman's face.

"Your husband was not aware that you were coming here today, Signora?"

"He doesn't give me his work schedule, and I don't tell him about what I do every day." A touch of defiance had crept into her voice and face, but it disappeared with Berti's next question.

"You told Signor Montoya that you had some important news to give to Biraldo. What was it?"

Signora Gallo glared at Rick and then took another sip of the water. "Who is this guy, anyway? Is he a cop as well? He led me to believe that he was with the tour group."

"He is with the tour group. He will be taking Ettore Biraldo's place as guide. Can you answer my question, Signora?"

"I was going to tell him that if my husband heard he was back in Italy, it could be a problem."

Rick thought he knew why it would be a problem, but he was glad when Chiara asked. They both waited while the woman thought about her answer.

"Ettore owed my husband money, and not a small sum, apparently. They had been childhood friends, and Ettore came to Cesare and asked him to back a business deal he was involved with. That was over a year ago. Apparently, the deal fell through, and then Ettore left for America. Cesare was furious." She looked at the frown on the inspector's face and realized what she'd said. "But Cesare wouldn't have killed him. Don't you see? It wouldn't make sense." She looked from Berti's face to Rick's, and pleaded, "With Ettore dead, he won't get the money back. And all my husband is interested in is money."

The inspector had said that the restaurant was nearby, which in a town as small as Assisi meant it would be a few minutes' walk from the hotel. Signora Gallo said she would be staying at the Capri that night and returning home to Perugia in the morning. By the time they'd left her, she appeared to have gotten over any grief from the loss. It was unlikely, Rick decided, that she had been spending her days without male companionship after Biraldo had escaped to America. She would get through this.

They passed a window almost at pavement level, its opening crisscrossed with iron bars. The street was already too narrow for even the smallest car, and now it became even narrower.

Just ahead a windowed passageway joined two buildings at the second-floor level. They went under its arch, through medieval darkness, before coming out into the light of a streetlamp.

"Does she really think," said Chiara, "that money would be the only motive her husband could have to murder someone?"

"Are you insinuating that her husband could have suspected a relationship between the two of them?"

She gave him a puzzled look that then turned into a smile. "I forgot that I am with an American who has one of those ironic American senses of humor."

"You never told me how you learned your English, Chiara. Obviously in the States."

"My father was a journalist, and he was sent to Washington by his paper to be their correspondent there. My mother insisted my brother and I go to public school where we lived, in northern Virginia. I was about ten and had already studied some English, but when they dropped me into a class where nobody spoke Italian, I was forced to learn quickly. By the time we left four years later, I could have been taken for a local."

"Kids can soak up languages pretty fast, especially at that age. But you didn't learn words like *floozy* and *hussy* in middle school."

"I read novels in English now; it helps my vocabulary. What about you, Riccardo? If Commissario Fontana is your uncle, your mother must be Italian or your name would be Fontana."

"*Brava.* I can see why you're a police detective. Yes, I learned Italian and English at home. When my sister and I were alone with Mama, she always spoke Italian. When dad was there, we went into English. With my friends we switched back and forth."

"What did your father do?"

"Diplomat. Still is. He's the consul general in Rio at the moment."

"But you grew up in Italy?"

"I'm still growing up."

"There's that humor again. And here's the restaurant."

He would have missed it; there was only a small lamp that threw light over an even smaller sign. The door had a few glass panes covered from the inside by someone leaning against it. When Rick pulled open the door, a man stumbled to one side and apologized. Chiara squeezed past him, followed closely by Rick. At least ten people milled around the entrance, and the dining room—which was likely the only room in the place—was crowded with diners. A waiter walking by them carrying a bottle of wine and two glasses looked up and spotted the inspector. He stopped, looked around the room, and gestured to her.

"Your table is ready, Chiara," he called over the din. "The one in the corner."

"Grazie, Baldo," she answered, pulling Rick along by the arm, while getting the evil eye from the people waiting. They worked their way around elbows and heads before arriving at their table, somewhat quieter than the middle of the room they had just passed through. The chairs squeaked as they pulled them out to sit down.

"Good thing you called to make a reservation."

"I didn't."

Rick smiled and spread the napkin on his lap. "I'm impressed, Inspector." Menus were dropped in front of them by an unseen hand. Rick picked up his. "I suppose you have the menu memorized."

"Not quite." Without looking she said, "I would suggest the *spaghetti con pasta di olive* followed by the *pollo all'arrabbiata*, if they haven't already run out of it."

"I'll put myself in your hands," he said, immediately regretting his choice of words.

"The chicken is pretty spicy. Do you think you can handle it?"

Rick gave her a derisive laugh. "You forget that I spent many years in New Mexico. Now what about a wine to go with this piquant dish?"

"We'll see what Baldo suggests."

Rick looked around the room and concluded that the darkened entrance off an alley was part of the plan to keep the place a local secret. Everyone appeared to be a regular. There was not a tourist to be found, and he heard only Italian being spoken. He recalled a dark day several months earlier when an article about a favorite restaurant of his in Rome had appeared in the *New York Times* travel section. Nobody he knew went there after that because the quality declined and it was always too crowded. Fortunately, this place was still under wraps. The proof would be in the eating, of course, but every dish he noticed while working their way to the table looked quite toothsome.

Baldo returned, took their order, and suggested a Torgiano cabernet sauvignon to go with both courses. They agreed and he scurried off.

"How long have you been here, Chiara?"

"Almost two years."

"You're Romana, if I have your accent correct."

"One hundred percent. My mother was not happy that I was leaving Rome but pleased that I was coming here since I was named after Santa Chiara."

"The famous Saint Clare, the right hand of Saint Francis and founder of one of the more famous orders of nuns. Somehow I have trouble picturing you locked up in a monastery as a member of the Poor Clares."

"But I am dressed in black."

"Yes, but it's not a habit."

The wine arrived and Baldo filled their glasses before leaving the bottle and departing. They toasted and sipped. "Chiara, aren't we supposed to be discussing your murder investigation?"

"Yes," she said, "I suppose we must." She rubbed the back of her neck, as if fatigue had suddenly overtaken her. "What did you take from the interviews of your compatriots?"

"Not much. Their alibis for the time of the murder were weak, but none of them had any strong motive for getting rid of Biraldo either. The only one with a motive may have been Leon Alameda, and that would only be if Biraldo had been trying something with his wife."

"The lovely Vicki Alameda, your former acquaintance."

He ignored the comment. "Leon Alameda and Peter Rael confirmed each other's stories about being out late for a walk. But either of them could have met up with and killed Biraldo after they separated. Or they could have been in on it together. As far as their wives, I have trouble picturing either of them murdering the man. Vicki could have slipped out while her husband was in the bar talking with Adelaide Chaffee, but that may be a stretch. Lillian Rael, forget it."

"Adelaide could have met Biraldo and struck him with that cane of hers."

"Walking stick. I can't picture it, but I suppose it's possible." He opened a packet of breadsticks and broke one in two. "The two kids? Too young and innocent, and they did corroborate each other's stories, at least for the time they were out walking. But either of them could have gone out later and committed the murder." He bit off a piece of the breadstick. "So what do you take from what they all said? There must be something, since you heard it twice, in English and then Italian."

She picked up her glass and turned it slowly. "I agree with your analysis. Your uncle must have taught you well."

The pasta arrived and was placed in front of each of them. As he always did, Rick studied the dish before picking up his fork. The spaghetti had been darkened by a paste of olives and mushrooms with which it had been tossed in the frying pan. Pieces of both were scattered among the strands of pasta, and flakes of parsley added a touch of green. Impressed, he wished Chiara a *buon appetito* and twirled his first bite on the fork. The olives dominated both smell and taste.

"The best dishes are the simplest ones."

"Very true, Riccardo. Here in Umbria they are very proud of their black olives, and of course mushrooms are a local specialty as well. Sometimes they shave truffles over this dish, but to me that's a bit much."

"I agree. Truffles should be used sparingly, and for me, only with cheese dishes."

They spent a few moments in silence, enjoying the spaghetti, before Rick returned to the subject at hand. "If the Americans, as you call them, are unlikely to be involved, it brings you back to those Italians who had dealings with Biraldo."

Chiara patted her lips with the napkin. "*Dealings* is an interesting way to put it. Clearly, I will have to have a chat with Cesare Gallo, the chocolate man. But there are others Detective Rossi was going to talk to about Biraldo before he met his end. One is a man named Rucola. Agostino Rucola."

"The one who lives above a store."

She put down her fork. "How did you know that?"

"Father Zeke had the address, and we went there looking for Biraldo this afternoon. We talked to the woman who owns the store."

She shook her head. "Rossi went there and didn't find Rucola. He didn't tell me about any store under the apartment."

"She thought Biraldo was there in the late afternoon and was arguing with Rucola. She could hear the voices but couldn't make out what they were arguing about."

"We'll have to pay a visit to Signor Rucola." She picked up

another forkful of spaghetti. "But not until after dinner. This pasta is excellent; the chef here is one of the best in Umbria."

Did she really mean both of them when she said "we"? No, she had to be talking about Detective Rossi. He had to admit that he was enjoying his involvement in the investigation and would not mind going with her to see Rucola. Perhaps his uncle was correct about him needing to join the police force. He used a bit of bread to dip into the dark olive sauce left on the side of his plate. "You never told me what Biraldo had done to have you looking for him."

She placed her fork on an almost empty plate, a signal to Baldo that she was done. "We were asked by our colleagues in Trieste to track him down. His ex-wife, who apparently is prominent in Triestini circles, claims that the last time they were together, just before he departed for America, he absconded with some of her jewelry. They had heard a rumor that he was back in Italy."

"So he was a jewel thief along with his other misdeeds? Quite a guy, this Biraldo."

"Well, she admits that he gave her the jewelry when they were married, but her lawyer has pointed out that legally it belonged to her. There was nothing in their divorce settlement that said he would get it back."

"Where was she last night?"

"I called Trieste and they checked. She was at some society event. Ironclad alibi."

"She could have hired a hit man."

"I doubt it. This isn't Palermo."

"Which is why I didn't see any swordfish on the menu." The comment earned him a puzzled look. He went on without explaining. "Let me try to understand what you have so far on Biraldo. He stole his wife's jewelry. He was paid to import artwork to Adelaide Chaffee's gallery in Santa Fe, but she lost money on the deal. He borrowed money from Signor Gallo, an old friend, and not only hasn't paid it back but was carrying on with Gallo's wife. Does he have any outstanding parking tickets?"

A waiter arrived to whisk away their empty pasta dishes, and Baldo followed him immediately with their *secondo*. The chicken pieces had been simmered in a tomato sauce with a dash of chili pepper to give it heat. Just from the smell wafting off the dish, Rick could tell that it would be considered mild back in Albuquerque. The chef had been generous in the sauce poured over the chicken, and Baldo, knowing what would be needed to enjoy it, replaced their almost empty bread basket with a full one. Rick took the bottle and filled their glasses before Chiara took the new fork that Baldo had given her and speared a piece of chicken that had fallen from the bone. Rick did the same.

"Melts in your mouth," she said in English.

"And not in your hand?"

"M&Ms. I loved those things. Why don't we stay in English? I don't get to practice speaking it that often."

"You don't really need the practice, Chiara, but sure, whatever you want."

They kept the conversation in English for the rest of the meal, including a discussion of growing up in a culture other than one's own. Rick noticed that the brash defensive shell that had surrounded Inspector Chiara Berti at the murder scene had almost disappeared. Was it the wine? Or could it simply be part of her plan for Rick Montoya? Whatever it was, he was enjoying it. The conversation was interrupted by the ring of Chiara's cell phone.

While she took the call, speaking in a low voice, his thoughts went to Betta. She was probably having dinner with some art police colleague in Lucca, or maybe a local contact in the investigation. Did she have any old friends in Lucca? He hoped she wasn't eating alone at her hotel. He would give her a call when he got to his hotel if it wasn't too late. Or perhaps not, since she would ask about his dinner. *I'm involved in a murder investigation and had dinner with the police inspector. Really, what's he like?* No, better to call her tomorrow.

Chiara finished her call and stuffed the phone back into her purse. "That was Rossi. He should have called me earlier. I'm wondering how good a cop he really is." It was a curious comment to make, and perhaps without realizing, she had made it in Italian. She took her fork and cut a piece of the chicken, pushed on some of the sauce, and put it in her mouth. Rick waited while she chewed, and when she started cutting another piece he spoke, also in Italian.

"Well? Anything of interest from Rossi?"

"A couple things," she said, the words muffled from chewing the *pollo.* She swallowed, took a drink of the wine, and got down to business. "The autopsy report says that he had a wound on his head caused by a blunt object. Nothing new there. But the actual cause of death was the fall. You'll recall that the drop was only about three meters, but he must have fallen in a way that broke his neck."

"He hit the blunt object when he fell?"

"Unlikely, and we didn't find anything near his head, or even near the body, which could have caused that wound. Plus the ground was quite soft. No, he was struck on the head and then either fell or was pushed over the railing. It was not a very high railing, you'll recall. If he had hit some of the thicker branches of a tree, that might have saved him, and he would have ended with only a gash on the head and perhaps a broken leg."

"And if he hadn't been stunned by the blow, he might have cushioned the fall himself."

"Correct. Instead, he dropped awkwardly."

Rick nodded. "I noticed something just now that I don't think you did."

She frowned. "Oh, really? What's that?"

"I was having dinner with Chiara, when suddenly Police Inspector Berti arrived at the table."

She laughed loud enough to get the attention of the next table. "That's good, Riccardo. But listen, there was more from Rossi. He searched Biraldo's suitcase."

"I hope he found the name of the person Biraldo was going to meet up with at the castle."

"Not exactly. But he did find something we will have to follow up on."

There was that *we* again, he noticed. "And that was?"

"A business card of a sculptor here in Assisi named Arnoldo Fillipo."

"He could be the one whose work Biraldo was selling to Adelaide Chaffee's gallery. I could ask her tomorrow."

"If it is the same person, I would not be surprised if Biraldo hadn't paid him." She looked at her watch before spearing the last piece of chicken on her plate. "We can get a coffee on the street, Riccardo. Do you think you can find the place where this guy Rucola lives?"

"I thought meals in Italy were supposed to be relaxed and not hurried. Something sacred. Now you want to hustle me off to interview someone?" He picked up his wineglass, slowly and deliberately, and took a sip.

"I'll get the check," she said, signaling to Baldo with a wave. "You're working for the police, so I'll find a way to write your dinner off."

"You're a good Romana, Chiara, so why don't we do this *a la Romana*?" Her expression turned serious and she closed her eyes in thought.

"What's the matter? Something about the murder?"

She shook her head. "No, I was trying to remember what that expression is in English."

"Dutch treat."

"Of course. I guess that's why they pay you the big money as an interpreter."

Baldo was able to point them in the direction of Rucola's street, and they set out on foot. Rick wondered if Chiara had dismissed her driver for the evening, and if so, what that meant. Of course she could summon a police car instantly if it was needed, but still....

The route took them through Assisi's main square, the Piazza del Comune, where a few tourists still sat at outdoor tables with their drinks, soaking up the atmosphere. What would have been a rectangular shape was thrown off kilter by the streets coming into it at either end from different levels, irregular building facades, and an awkwardly placed fountain. The early-fourteenth-century Palazzo dei Priori, which now served as the seat of *comunal* government, dominated the south side of the square. Across from the Comune, the tall columns of the former Temple of Minerva were a reminder that this space was once a forum built by earlier inhabitants of the city, who called it Assisium.

While Chiara waited, Rick climbed a few steps up to the fountain and scooped some water from its bowl. He patted his face to cool himself down and wash away any effects of the wine. The temperature had dropped from its late afternoon high, but the city's stone still held firmly to the heat. They continued through the square, stopping for a moment in front of the ionic columns of the temple, bathed in light from a hidden lamp.

"Santa Maria sopra Minerva, the same name as one of my favorite churches in Rome," said Chiara. "I've always been impressed by how Christians built churches on top of pagan temples. The symbolism is about a subtle as a sledgehammer. Usually they tore down what the pagans had built, but here, fortunately, they kept the facade."

"What's the interior like?"

She shook her head. "Nothing like its namesake in Rome, that's for sure. Obviously much smaller, and of course no Michelangelo sculpture."

"And no elephant statue out front either."

"You're making me homesick, Riccardo."

They left the openness of the square and reentered the labyrinth of streets before reaching Rucola's building. Other than a black cat that ambled along without paying any attention to the two humans, the street was deserted. The store under the apartment was dark and protected by a sliding metal gate. A faint light came from one of the windows above.

"He's here," said the inspector. She walked to the door, pressed the button, and held it down.

They heard a faint buzzer followed by a shuffling of curtains from the window above, then the noise of someone coming down the stairs and the clicking of the lock. The door was pulled open revealing a towering Agostino Rucola, who became less imposing when Rick realized the man was standing a few steps above them. His clothes—shorts, a T-shirt, and flip-flops—diminished the menacing first impression, but an unkempt beard and piercing eyes added to it. The inspector identified herself and introduced Rick. The man didn't move, but only looked from one face to the other.

"What's this about?"

"We need to ask you some questions about Ettore Biraldo."

The reaction was quick, but almost imperceptible. "What about him?"

"We've been looking for him. Perhaps we could talk inside?"

He considered the question, shrugged, and without answering started walking up the stairs.

Rick thought about the interview with Letizia Gallo in the hotel. Would this one be different since Gallo had not been a strong suspect but Rucola could be? He suspected that the inspector's interrogation style was the same even if the offense was jaywalking, but he'd soon find out. Before climbing the stairs she turned to Rick and said in a low voice, in English: "You play good cop."

"Anything you say, Inspector."

At the top they entered what appeared at first to be one large room, but a door just off the stairwell indicated at least a closet, but more likely a bathroom. If there had been a system to separate the various sections of the living space, it had been abandoned, and they were now blurred. A bed—really more of a cot—was pushed against one wall and strewn with papers. The room's one table had become a desk, and was stacked with books and more papers, though one corner of it held a dirty bowl, a fork still inside. The papers on the table were mostly drawings of figures. Pans hung from hooks over the tiny sink where more dishes were stacked and canned goods lined the top of the small refrigerator. A dresser near the bed was the only place in the room that could hold clothing except for a set of hooks near the bed that were covered by items of apparel. Only one decorative item hung on the walls, between the two windows: a photograph of a fountain.

Without being asked, Chiara walked to one of the two chairs

at the table. Rick wondered if she would brush it off before sitting down, but she did not. He took the other chair while Rucola stood in silence before realizing there was nowhere for him to sit except the bed. He moved a few papers to make room and sat down. The springs creaked under his weight, which was considerable.

"When did you last see Biraldo?"

Rucola seemed startled by her question, even though it was the most obvious one to begin things. "It was yesterday. Late afternoon. He was here."

"Why did he come here? An old friend stopping to say hello?" The way she said it indicated that she was taking seriously her role of bad cop, but it didn't appear to faze Rucola.

"I was expecting him to want to see me, since I owe him some money. I was starting a new line of pieces and had talked him into backing the idea. So far it hasn't panned out, so I haven't been able to pay him back."

Chiara glanced at Rick, who took the cue to play good cop. "From the drawings on the table, it appears that you are an artist." He picked up one of the sheets, which had a sketch of a fountain similar to the one on the wall. "This is quite good." Was he overdoing it?

"Those are sketches for garden statuary I create in my studio down the street."

"Part of the new line that Biraldo was investing in?"

"Yes, exactly. They will be larger than the ones I usually make; I think they'll sell better."

The bad cop spoke. "But so far they haven't, and Biraldo was not happy when he came here to see you yesterday. Was there an argument?"

Rucola rubbed his hands together and stared at the floor. "Not really. He wasn't happy that I couldn't pay him. He said he needed it badly. But we didn't really argue."

Chiara jabbed a finger at the floor. "That's not what the woman downstairs remembers. She said it sounded like two people were going at each other tooth and nail. Or did you have a fight with someone else here yesterday afternoon?"

"She's an old busybody."

"That doesn't answer my question, Signor Rucola."

"He shouted at me. But I am a calm person."

"Most artists have an even temperament," Rick said. "How did you leave it? I'm sure you are as anxious to pay him the money as he was to get it."

The man was relieved to be able to address Rick rather than the inspector. "He knows I'm good for the repayment, with interest. He'll have it as soon as I sell a few of these pieces. There's a shop here in town that's interested, and it's in a good location. Lots of tourists."

Rick took from his answers that he either didn't kill Biraldo or was very good a pretending that the guy was still alive. How long would it take for Chiara to bring up the murder?

"What did you do for the rest of the evening, after Biraldo left?"

His reaction to her question was puzzlement. "I kept on working, made my dinner, and worked some more." He held up his hands and shrugged. "Look, I assume you are looking for him because of some issue other than what I owe him. It's a lot of money for me, but certainly not enough to get the police involved. I didn't meet him later, and I have no idea where he went after he left here."

"He was murdered last night," said Chiara. "Can anyone vouch for you being here?"

Rucola looked at Rick as if needing a confirmation of what he'd just heard. When Rick kept silent, the man pushed a hand through his unkempt hair and worked himself up to an answer. It took a full minute. His voice was lower, and he spoke slowly while looking from one face to the other. "Ettore was an unsavory character, but he didn't deserve to die. And I didn't kill him. I live alone and can't afford to eat out very often. Unlike Ettore. So you have only my word that I was here all evening."

"If you didn't do it, who do you think would have had a motive to murder Biraldo?" Rick asked.

A trace of a smile crossed Rucola's face. "A girl's outraged father or brother? Someone he cheated in business? A cuckolded husband? Take your pick. The small sum of money I owed him was likely the most minor of motives."

"Names?" The question was barked out by Chiara.

"I don't know the names of his female conquests, but on the business side, you should talk to Arnoldo Fillipo. He's a sculptor but does individual pieces that he sells in his own gallery." He waved a finger at the papers on the table. "Not like my work that gets sold to Eastern European tourists." The smile widened. "Arnoldo is a brilliant artist—just ask him and he'll tell you."

Chiara stood up. "We will do that. Don't leave town."

CHAPTER SEVEN

Rick easily found his way back to the hotel. He had always been a map person, and the layout of Assisi was already firmly set after he had studied it in the hotel. When he was a kid and his father came home to announce where they were to be sent next, he always brought with him a map of the new city. Father and son would go over the country map in the atlas, and then Rick would huddle with his new city map. By the time the family arrived in their new diplomatic posting, Rick had done his research and was familiar with all the landmarks. It was a running joke among his school friends that Montoya was like a compass: he always knew where north was.

More difficult than finding the hotel was separating himself from Inspector Berti. Chiara had suggested getting a coffee, or perhaps an after-dinner drink, to talk about the two interviews and what to do next. Rick begged off, claiming fatigue after the long drive from Rome and all the day's excitement. But he did feel the need for a *caffè*. He picked up his key at the front desk and walked to the bar, where a bored attendant stood behind the counter.

"Hi, Rick." The voice was that of Lillian Rael. She sat by

herself, a glass of red wine on the table next to her, and a magazine on her lap. She was dressed as she had been before dinner, when she was also nursing a glass of wine. "Come sit."

Rick ordered his coffee, gave the barman his room number, and walked to the table. "How are you, Lillian?"

"Couldn't be better." She pronounced the words slowly and deliberately before fortifying herself with a drink of wine. "We missed you at dinner."

"How was it?"

"I always thought Italian food was spaghetti with tomato sauce. Not tonight. First they served rice with mushrooms, then steaks. I didn't know Italians ate steaks. It was quite good, but a bit on the rare side for me."

Rick's coffee arrived at the table and he stirred in sugar. "What else has surprised you about Italy so far?" It was something that he always found interesting: people's impressions when arriving for the first time in a country other than their own.

"How old everything is. Of course I knew about that, but it is different when you actually see something that was built before Columbus discovered America. We consider New Mexico to be old by American standards, but there's no comparison."

"That is a common reaction I've heard from people visiting Italy for the first time. You get a completely different sense of history when you experience a more ancient culture. It puts things in perspective."

"Do you miss being home in New Mexico, Rick?"

He downed his espresso in one gulp and thought about how to answer. It was a question he got often from visiting Americans, especially proud New Mexicans. There was the long answer, explaining that, as a foreign service brat, "home" was a relative concept, usually defined as where the pictures were presently hung. And if "home" wasn't where they were living at that moment, then whose home would be home? Was it the Rome of his mother or the New Mexico of his father? It had been that way during most of his youth, and even when he went off to college, when UNM became his home. He ran all that through his mind and decided to go with the short answer, which accepted her premise that he considered New Mexico his home. "Some things I miss. Friends, obviously, but with the internet it's easy to keep in touch with them. There are New Mexican dishes I can't get here in Italy, like chiles rellenos. I miss those sometimes." She nodded, and the slowness of the nod made him wonder how much of what he said was getting through. "I will say it's been a pleasure seeing Zeke again, and meeting such a nice group of New Mexicans reminds me what a great place my home state is."

Lillian took another drink from her wineglass and carefully set it back down. "There's more to this group than meets the eye, Rick." A sly smile turned up the sides of her mouth.

The comment took him by surprise. "Everyone seems to get along well. What am I not seeing?"

"I really shouldn't say anything."

Rick held up his hand as if swearing an oath. "I can give you a reverse Miranda and assure you that nothing you say will be held against you."

She laughed. "Just so it doesn't get back to anyone in the group." Rick waited while she took another sip of wine. "First of all, Father Zeke is a darling. We all love him to death. But after that, there are some personalities that just naturally don't get along, though thankfully nothing has burst into the open yet. Adelaide, with her little niece in tow, acts like the tour was her idea, and is always telling us how tight she is with the archbishop. Yet she's to blame for having that terrible Biraldo along, and look what's happened to him now. It's a disgrace. And her little Jessica? I wouldn't trust her as far as I could throw her. Always snapping pictures like she's some famous photographer. It's starting to get on everyone's nerves. I'm not being a gossip, am I Rick?"

"No, certainly not. You're just giving your honest opinion."

"Good. I need someone to talk to. Peter doesn't like me going on about people, and there is something about you that makes me feel that I can trust you." She blinked her eyes, which was more from the wine than flirtation. "Has anyone told you that before?"

He had indeed heard it before, and was still undecided if it was a curse or a blessing. "What about Father Zeke? I'm sure you can go to him if you have any concerns."

"Oh, no concerns. I'm just giving you my take on people."

Rick considered excusing himself and going to his room, claiming fatigue as he'd done with Chiara Berti, but he was fascinated by the gossipy Mrs. Rael. In addition, he could not help wondering what she was going to say about Vicki Alameda. Probably saving her for last. "Chris Carson seems like a nice kid," he said as neutrally as possible.

"I suppose. But how did he manage to get this job? A free trip to Italy, and all he has to do is drive a bus and carry a few suitcases? The bellhops did most of the work when we got here to the hotel."

"It would have cost quite a bit to hire a local driver."

"With what we're paying, I'm sure it could have been covered. All Chris does is make goo-goo eyes at Jessica, even sometimes when he's driving."

Rick could not avoid immediately pondering what would be a good translation of "goo-goo eyes" into Italian. It was the curse of the professional interpreter. Fortunately, the term had not surfaced yet in any of the conferences where he did much of his interpreting, but he would try to remember later to think of just the right Italian phrase. If some American economist ever used it in a scholarly paper, he would be ready. He put the thought in the back of his mind and returned his full attention to Lillian. She was just hitting her stride and needed only a nudge to get her to the finish line. "You appear to be enjoying the company of Leon and Vicki Alameda. Did you know each other before the trip?"

"My husband, Peter, knew Leon from the chamber of commerce and some activities in the church. But I'd never met either of them, certainly not Mrs. Alameda." The "Mrs." was carefully enunciated. "She did not seem to me to be the kind of person to go on a religious tour organized by the archdiocese. Not that the rest of us are that pious, but still…"

Rick was relieved that Lillian did not appear to know about his past relationship with Mrs. Alameda, and he wasn't about to tell her. "She is a bit younger than her husband."

Lillian snorted. "A bit? The classic case of a gold digger going after an older man. And Leon Alameda doesn't seem to have a clue about what kind of woman she really is."

"What kind is she?"

Lillian looked left and right, more for dramatic effect than to confirm that they were alone. "Well, you should have seen the way she carried on with Biraldo the night we spent in Rome. The group went out for dinner at a restaurant near our hotel, and you would have thought Leon Alameda wasn't at the table. She was shameless."

"She does appear to be a very outgoing woman."

"That's one way to describe her. Not that her husband, Leon, is an angel himself, mind you." She looked at her almost empty wineglass, and Rick feared that she was about to order a refill. She didn't. "He's a bit of a blowhard and a bully, even trying to provoke my husband with some scurrilous insinuations."

Was Lillian upset that someone else had been allowed to engage in gossip? "What did he say?"

"I don't even want to repeat it, but it had to do with Peter's faith. Imagine, a devout Catholic all his life and strong supporter of the archdiocese, and Leon Alameda comes along and questions my husband's commitment to the church. The Raels were one of the first Spanish families to settle in the territory. They brought the church into New Mexico."

Lillian Rael was in high dudgeon and breathing hard. It appeared that her previous observations on the members of the group had been innocent gossip compared to whatever Alameda had said about her husband. She drained her glass and brought it down on the table with a bang, getting the attention of the waiter. It startled her as well, and she blinked and stiffened. "I'd better be getting up to the room. Peter was already dozing off, so I'll have to sneak in quietly. It was so nice chatting with you Rick, and remember, this was all just between us."

Rick got to his feet. "Of course, Lillian. See you tomorrow." She walked unsteadily out of the room, and Rick sat back down before pulling out his cell phone to check the time. He noticed a text message and realized that he had not turned his ringer back on after silencing it for the interview with Letizia Gallo. He hit the button to read it.

Call me if you're still up.

It was from Betta and had come in twenty minutes earlier. His finger hesitated over her number before finally hitting it. After three rings she answered.

"*Ciao*, Rick. Are you working on a translation? When you didn't reply, I assumed you were asleep."

Was there something in her voice, or was it the connection?

"*Ciao*, Betta. Actually, I'm in Assisi; I drove up this morning. Piero was kind enough to let me use his car."

"A last-minute job?"

"No, no. An old college friend is leading a religious tour group that's going to be in Assisi for a few days, so I wanted to come up to see him. Piero suggested I stay in Perugia with my aunt Filomena, the one who owns my apartment. You remember hearing about her?"

"I do, but I'm trying to get my head around a college friend of yours leading a religious tour group. From what you've told me about your days at the university, I would not have expected that."

Rick recalled that his uncle had said the same thing. "He's actually a priest."

"This is a joke, right?"

"It gets even stranger." Rick went on to describe the events of the day, and how at Piero's request he had been drawn into the investigation. He carefully avoided any mention of Inspector Chiara Berti, using the collective noun *the police* when he described how he was cooperating with the local authorities. "The murderer has got to be someone involved with Biraldo locally, since he was into some shady activities. It's difficult for me to believe that someone involved in a religious pilgrimage could be a suspect."

"But you're not ruling them out."

"Of course not. We both know from experience that nobody should be ruled out unless they have an ironclad alibi. And what have you been up to in Pisa? I assume you are still there and not calling from Rome."

Her sigh was audible. "Yes, I'm here. This case is the classic story of a precious work of art stolen out of a church that didn't have proper security. It's a small color pastel of the Garden of Eden, and the congregants have been praying to it for centuries. It also brings in the occasional tourist that puts coins in to light it up. The museum of the diocese had tried for years to put it in its collection, which has excellent security, but the priest always resisted."

Rick had always been fascinated by Betta's work with the art fraud squad, but he knew that too many of these cases ended without the recovery of the stolen art. When that happened, Betta remained depressed for days, despite his reassurances that it was not her fault. Her love of art had gotten her into the job, but it also made the loss of any precious work almost personal. As a result, her next comment was a bit of a surprise.

"It's an ugly little work, in my opinion, but it has some value. There's no accounting for taste."

"Sufficient value to send their crack investigator to track it down."

"I don't think that's what happened. Normally we would not have sent anyone, but I think Carlo wanted to send me up here so I could fall on my face. There's not much of a chance of recovering the pastel."

The mention of Carlo Melozzo got Rick's attention. Betta had told him several stories about the man, and none of them flattering. Melozzo was infamous both for his vicious office politics and his reputation as a womanizer. "Now that you've spent a day there, do you still think it's a lost cause?"

She took a few seconds to answer. "I'm not sure. But one thing that is certain, I'm going to take advantage of the time to see a bit of Pisa. The last time I was here was with a school trip from the *liceo*, and all I remember is taking staged photographs of us holding up the tower. Carlo doesn't want me back any time soon, so why not? Once you get a couple blocks away from the tower, the tourists disappear and there's a lot to see."

"I wish I were there to see it with you."

"Me too."

"So you had dinner alone?"

"No. I looked up an old college friend who works in a museum here, and we had dinner."

"Is she involved in the case as well?"

"He, actually. His name is Elio Piombo."

"Suddenly I don't feel bad for you."

"Tomorrow he's going to give me a VIP tour of his museum. It's the best one in Pisa."

"Doesn't he have to work? Don't you have to work on your case?"

"He'll take some time off."

Rick didn't like where this was going. "Perhaps he can help you break open your case."

"I haven't told him anything about it, only that I'm here with my work. You never know. He could be a suspect in the theft. Fortunately he didn't push me for details, and we mostly talked about old times." She coughed softly. "Did I mention that he's very good-looking?"

"Oh, great. Thanks for telling me that."

"He's also gay."

He laughed. "Betta, you could have drawn that out a bit more and had some real fun at my expense."

"You're right. I guess I'm tired."

"I'll let you get some sleep. Good luck finding your pastel."

"And to you on finding your murderer. Your investigation sounds much more interesting than mine. Keep notes so you can give me all the details when we're back in Rome."

When they'd said their good nights and he'd slipped the phone in his pocket, he realized that they had talked about her dinner, but she hadn't asked about his. Perhaps that was for the best. He thanked the bartender and walked to the elevator.

———

The streetlights were still throwing a dim light over the pavement the next morning when Rick got off the elevator and trotted toward the door of the hotel. The clerk on duty glanced at him from behind the desk, apparently not surprised that a guest would be up and about before the dining room was open for breakfast. Rick had opened the window of his room to check the temperature and decided that a T-shirt and shorts would be all he'd need for his run. Some stretching would be required before heading out, and when he pushed open the door, he was surprised to see someone on the hotel steps doing just that.

"Good morning, Padre."

"Well, well. I didn't expect to see you up at this hour, Rick." Zeke wore loose-fitting shorts and a gray tee with the letters USMC. "I don't remember you as a runner." He kept stretching as he talked, and Rick began his own routine as he answered.

"I started a couple years after graduation when I noticed that I was putting on some weight. What about you?"

"I can thank the Marine Corps. Runs were a part of our daily routine. What's funny is that I remember how I looked forward to leaving runs behind when I became a civilian." He grunted as he stretched one calf, then the other. "But when I got into the seminary, I realized that getting out for a run was not just important physically—like what you said about gaining weight—but also spiritually. Do you find that's the case with you, Rick?"

"I use the run to clear my mind for the day's activities. And in the early morning, the streets of Rome are delightful. It is a different city around dawn, with different people." He pulled his knee to his chest. "You must have run yesterday morning, Zeke. Do you want to take the same route?"

"Yesterday I ran up into town; I thought today I would head

down to the plain. You'll be glad to know I checked a map last night on my computer." He pointed toward the green farmland that spread out below them. The sun was starting to peek over the hill behind them, sending streaks of sunlight west. "We'll go down to Santa Maria degli Angeli, then run parallel to the highway before turning to come back to Assisi."

"Lead the way, Captain."

They started down the street below the hotel, ran past the parking lot that was starting to come to life with early day-trippers, and quickly dropped to the flat farmland. It had rained during the night, and they avoided the few puddles on the road that the day's heat would soon evaporate. The air was fresh with agricultural smells, enhanced by the moisture. Every field they passed had a different crop or animal, each more pungent than the last, but always the aromas of nature. It was very different from what Rick's nostrils picked up during his morning runs in Rome.

"I had an interesting conversation with Lillian Rael last night in the hotel bar," said Rick. With the level road, they were barely breathing heavily, so conversation was possible. That would not be the case at the end of the run, especially the last few kilometers up Assisi's foothill. "She's quite a talker."

"That's one way to put it," Zeke answered, dropping back to run parallel with his friend. "Did she say anything of interest?"

"Her opinion of each of the people in the group. Nothing but praise for Father Zeke, of course."

"She didn't want to say anything about me that she'd have to unburden in confession."

"There was something she said about Leon Alameda that I found curious." They came to a crossroad, turned left, and started toward the town of Santa Maria degli Angeli. A tractor passed them going in the opposite direction. "Since she wasn't in the confessional, I can tell you."

"She didn't say she thought Leon killed Biraldo, I hope."

"No, it was more oblique and nothing to do with the murder. Something about Leon's scurrilous insinuations regarding her husband's faith. Not something I would have expected, given the religious nature of your group."

Zeke did not answer for a full minute, and Rick could almost hear the gears grinding. "I think I know what she was referring to. It's nothing I heard in confessional, so I have no constraints in that sense, though normally I wouldn't talk to anyone about it. But as I said to you yesterday, I need someone to talk to about these people, so I'm glad to have your ear. Now that this terrible thing has happened, I appreciate having it even more."

The houses of the town were starting to take the place of open fields, and they passed the occasional resident working in the garden before the day's heat made it uncomfortable. More trees and hedges lined the road, casting irregular shadows.

"Lillian," Zeke continued, "was probably referring to the accusation that her husband's distant ancestors were *conversos*. Are you familiar with the term?"

"It rings a bell, but I can't place it."

With the dome of the basilica looming in the distance, they jogged left and started along a street parallel to the railroad line. The Assisi station appeared on their right, but with no trains expected any time soon, the square in front was empty. Their running shoes slapped the pavement as they passed through it and Zeke continued.

"In the fourteenth and fifteenth centuries, in Spain, Jews were forced to convert to Christianity, faced with exile or worse if they did not. Many of the converts, called *conversos*, came to the Americas, including to New Spain, which became Mexico. The number of them who truly converted is impossible to know, but there were those who practiced their Judaism in secret while professing to be Christians. When the inquisition came to Mexico City, one target was these people. Many *conversos*, even though they were practicing Catholics by then, moved north into the wild country of New Mexico, out of the inquisition's reach. Over the centuries they intermarried and any family recollection was mostly forgotten. But with the recent interest in genealogy, some New Mexican Catholics have discovered that dozens of generations earlier someone in their family tree may have been a *converso.*"

"Fascinating, but why would it matter?"

"Apparently it matters to Peter and Lillian Rael."

They were out of the town and back in the countryside. It was not difficult to keep their bearings since Assisi and the higher hills behind it could be seen off in the distance. With a left turn onto a narrow road they entered the third side of what was a rectangular route through the flatlands and hills of central Umbria. It stayed level for another ten minutes, by which time the two runners were concentrating on their pace and not conversing. Slowly the road lifted and turned. They passed through groves of olive trees, then vineyards, then more olives like the ones where Biraldo's body was found. The hill on either side of the road became overgrown with bushes and small trees until they reached the wider paved street that ran along the lower wall of the city. There was the occasional car now, and they ran on the left, facing the oncoming traffic. Their route twisted left and right, passing two large parking areas, before the final climb up the hill to the hotel. They bounced in place in front of the entrance, letting their muscles return to normal.

"We are celebrating mass at Santa Chiara church right after breakfast, Rick. We have reserved a side chapel. Can I count on you being there?"

"With my old friend officiating, I wouldn't miss it for all the pizza in Naples."

"See you at breakfast. After church we get in the van to see Santa Maria degli Angeli. Didn't we go near there just now?"

"We saw the dome in the distance."

Once inside they got their room keys and walked to the elevator where a man and woman were waiting. When the doors opened, Rick gestured for the two to go up without them. The woman looked at their sweaty T-shirts, smiled stiffly, and accepted. When Rick got to his room, he checked his phone, found a missed call from Inspector Berti, and decided to call her back before showering.

"What's up, Chiara?"

"We're interviewing that sculptor Fillipo this morning; I'll pick you up at the hotel."

"I was going to mass at Santa Chiara with the group."

"You'll have to settle for a less saintly Chiara. I'll see you in forty-five minutes." She hung up.

Rick peeled off his T-shirt and walked to the window. Scattered clouds sprinkled shadows across the plain, changing the view from what he had seen that morning. It reminded him of the Sandia Peak seen from below in Albuquerque, never the same even one hour to the next. Sometimes the changes were dramatic, like when the aspens high on the crest turned bright orange in the fall. Other times it was more subtle: the western sun peeking from a cloud and playing light on the rocks, or wind doing the wave through the evergreens.

Forty-five minutes later, after a shower and quick breakfast, Rick walked through the lobby and out to the street. Inspector Berti was standing next to the open rear door of the police car talking with a man with three days of stubble on his face, wearing jeans and a loose-fitting white shirt. In his hands were a pen and pad. Chiara looked annoyed. She spotted Rick and jerked a thumb toward the car door.

"Is this someone helping with the investigation?" The man sized up Rick while scratching his long hair with the pen.

"He's an interpreter, for the Americans in the group. Listen, Signor Stefani, we have to go. I have your card; if there's anything that comes up that I am able to reveal, I'll call you. Let's go, Riccardo." The man staggered backward as she and Rick got into the back seat and the driver started the engine with an dramatic roar. Rick instinctively looked for a seat belt and found none. "I always have mixed feelings about reporters," said Chiara, "since my father is a journalist. This guy is from ANSA, the news agency, and found out about the murder, but he seems especially sleazy. I remember my father always left the house impeccably dressed when we lived in Washington, saying he had to maintain the Italian image with the Americans. He still never goes out in Rome without a tie, except to the stadium." She had been watching the buildings fly by through the back window. The car jolted to one side, and her shoulder slammed into Rick's, giving him a whiff of her perfume. She made no attempt to return to her side of the seat. "Isn't this more fun than going to church, Riccardo?"

"I'll tell you after we get there. Have you learned anything about this guy Fillipo?"

She sighed and moved to her side of the back seat. "Clean record. Originally from Spello, just over the hill from here. He has a website that shows his work, which isn't too bad, really. Mostly figurative sculpture."

"Garden gnomes and frogs using toadstools for umbrellas?"

"I didn't see any of those."

"And what would you like my contribution to be with this interview?"

She thought for a moment, or at least pretended to think. "You know, Riccardo, since you played the good cop last night, why don't we switch roles and you be bad cop? Do you think you're capable of that?"

The car slowed and pulled up to a metal gate set in a stone wall too tall to see over, even after they stepped to the street. Cut out of the metal were the words *Atelier Fillipo*, next to which hung a chain. Berti pulled the chain, and they heard a bell clang inside, followed by a high-pitched voice announcing that the person with the voice was on his way.

"I've seen enough cop movies, Inspector, that I could probably do it. But when I'm working with the master of the genre, I'd rather just hang back and watch you do your bad cop magic."

He was expecting to see a sculpture garden displaying Fillipo's work on pedestals and to be greeted by a man covered with marble dust. Rick's only similar experience was in Volterra, where workers turned chunks of alabaster into works of art. They were covered with a film of white, giving them a ghostlike and sinister appearance. But the man who opened the gate now was dustless. Arnoldo Fillipo had brown smudges on his smock, and his hands were stained the same color. He was clean shaven, with long hair and a prominent chin that gave the impression— perhaps intentionally—of an artist from the late nineteenth century. Or was it a romantic poet of the same period? Either way, he looked the part. A beret would have completed the image, but that would have covered some of the flowing hair. He smiled and held up his hands.

"Welcome to my workshop. I'm sorry I can't shake hands. I was in the middle of something." He looked from one face to the other. "Please come in. Did someone recommend my work to you?"

"We're not here as art buyers, Signor Fillipo. I am Inspector

Berti and this is Signor Montoya. We are investigating the murder of Ettore Biraldo."

His smile remained. "Oh, yes, of course. I saw the news and should have been expecting you. Please come in."

They stepped through the gate and onto slate pieces set into the grass that surrounded the small stone house. The walkway forked immediately, one row of stones going to the door straight ahead, the other leading around the side. It was to the side that Fillipo led his two visitors. Rick guessed he lived in one part of the house and worked in the other. When they turned the corner, they saw a paved terrace covered by a canvas canopy that stretched from above the open double doors. Inside was the workshop, but on this morning, Fillipo was working outside. Under the canopy, on a tall table, was a lump of brown oily clay starting to take form.

"I'm sorry I can't offer you a place to sit, Inspector; I work standing up. At least you are in the shade." He took a rag from the table and used it without much effect on his clay-covered hands. "The weather is so pleasant today that I moved out here. The fresh air clears my mind."

"We don't mind standing, Signor Fillipo," said the policewoman. "This shouldn't take long."

"As long as you need, Inspector. As you likely already know, I had a business relationship of sorts with Ettore. I suppose you'd like me to explain it?"

"Please." She looked for something to lean on and found nothing.

"A few years ago, we began to run into each other at art openings and other cultural events. He came to a show I had in Perugia, bringing with him a woman who acquired one of my works, and a rather large one at that. So I was grateful to him, and we struck up an acquaintance. I wouldn't say it was a friendship; we were merely in the same social circle, and a wide circle at that. I heard from others that he had a somewhat unsavory reputation, but I assumed it had to do mainly with women. That woman who bought the piece? I found out later she was married to someone other than Ettore. He could be very personable, and not just with women. And also very persuasive, which was what got me into trouble." He paused for a moment. "I should be offering you something to drink. A mineral water, perhaps?" Rick and Chiara politely declined, and he continued. "Shortly before he was to leave for America to take some kind of teaching position, he came to see me. He said he would be living near an arts center, Santa Fe, and wondered if I would be interested in selling some of my work there. It's in the state of New Mexico."

"We've heard of it," said Rick.

Fillipo noticed Rick's cowboy boots and a puzzled look ran quickly across his face before he returned to his story. "He said that he wanted to bring Italian art to America and already had some experience in art sales, though I eventually came to believe he knew nothing about the business. I should have checked around, but as I said, he could be very convincing. I didn't commit to anything at that point, but I gave him some materials and even a small piece that I thought might be of interest to the American market. It was one of those."

He pointed to a shelf just inside the open doors.

"May I?" asked Rick.

"Certainly."

Rick stepped through the doors into the workshop, immediately catching the heavy smell of oil or some chemical he couldn't identify. Some light pushed through a dirty skylight above the center of the room. On the brick floor under it was a relatively clean spot about the size of the table that had been moved outside. A brown-streaked sink took up one corner near a door leading into the house. The space under the sink was taken entirely by two white plastic buckets that held the clay supply. Above hung rows of tools with wooden handles and metal ends. Everything was stained the same brown color as the clay outside except for a few metal figures the sculptor pointed to. Rick walked to the shelf and took a metal bird in his hand. The hooked beak indicated it was a raptor, but its wings were wrapped tightly around itself, giving it a less menacing look. Rick brought it outside and placed it on a relatively clean corner of the table. "Is this the kind of thing you were going to sell in Santa Fe?"

"Precisely, Signor Montoya. I did some research on New Mexico and found that a number of hawk species are found there."

"It's very good," said Rick. "I've been to Santa Fe, and I would guess it would sell well. What's the metal?"

"Brass. I use the lost wax technique, and there is an excellent a foundry in Perugia that does my casting."

"Can we get back to Biraldo?" said Inspector Berti.

"Of course, Inspector. He went off to America, and I had forgotten about our conversation when I got an email from him telling me he'd made contact with an excellent art gallery and was ready to receive a shipment of my work. Naturally, I was pleased. I packaged several pieces similar to this one and dispatched them to the address he gave me. It was not Santa Fe, but a rather strange name."

"Albuquerque," Rick said.

"Yes, that was it. That was where he was living. I didn't hear from him for several weeks but assumed the customs would take a while, as it does here. Finally, I sent him an email asking what was going on. He didn't reply immediately, but when he did, he said there had been some problems with the gallery and he was looking for another place to sell them. I should never have sent them to him."

Berti picked up the hawk and hefted it in her hand. "So you heard that Biraldo was coming back to Assisi and were hoping he was bringing you some kind of payment."

"I would not have known he was in Italy if I hadn't run into Agostino Rucola. I'm guessing Biraldo didn't have any money for me and was avoiding a confrontation."

"Confrontation?"

"Yes, Inspector. I put in many hours of work on those works and had to pay my foundry. This is my livelihood. Let's say our conversation would not have been the most amicable." He looked at the policewoman's face. "To anticipate your next question, I unfortunately never got the chance to have that conversation."

"Tell us your movements two days ago."

"So that was when he was killed, Inspector? Well, let me see." He thought for a moment. "I was here working, except for lunch. I ate a panino down the street; they can vouch for me. A possible buyer came here in the late afternoon. Two of them, actually, a husband and wife. They were Austrian tourists, but they spoke passable Italian. They didn't buy anything."

"What time was that, exactly?"

Fillipo shrugged. "Five? Six? I'm not sure. The sun was still out but starting to set."

"Had you tried to contact Biraldo?" Rick asked the question.

"I was going to track him down today, but Rucola called me and told me he'd been killed."

"When was that?"

"He called me last night. After you talked to him." He noticed the expression on Rick's face and added: "We're not friends, but since we're both part of the arts community here, such as it is, we keep in touch. From what he told me, you were quite hard on him."

Berti ignored the comment. "If you don't mind me asking, how much were the pieces worth that you sent off to America?"

Fillipo picked up the bird and looked at it as he replied. "I sent five, each a different kind of hawk. It could have been sold as a set, but individually I price them here for a bit more than a thousand euros." He carefully placed it back on the table. "A tidy sum, but hardly enough to justify murder. And why would I kill someone who owed me money?"

"It's a fair question," said Rick a few minutes later, as the police car pulled away from the gate. "I would never murder someone who owed me money. How about you, Chiara?"

"Probably not. Work them over a bit, maybe, but not kill them."

The car made a sharp turn and descended through a break in the city wall before stopping at a traffic light. Two tourist buses with the logo of a German tour agency drove past them while they waited for the green.

"But I'm sure you thought of one scenario, Riccardo. If you didn't, you are not your uncle's nephew."

"They meet at the castle, there's an argument that turns ugly, and Fillipo bashes Biraldo in the head. With the bronze hawk, of course."

"*Bravo.*" After more turns on the same street Rick and Zeke had padded up earlier, the car arrived at the hotel. "I'm going to track down Cesare Gallo, the husband of the lovely Letizia. I'll let you know. Where are you off to?"

Rick opened the door and got out before leaning down to answer. "The Basilica of Santa Maria degli Angeli."

"I know it well. Where Francis founded his order, and where he died."

"I'm surprised. I would have thought you were all police business."

"There's much about me you don't know, Riccardo."

CHAPTER EIGHT

Like so many museums in Italy, the one in Pisa where Elio Piombo worked was located in an old structure built for another purpose. Just like the civic museum in Betta's hometown of Bassano del Grappa, this one was originally a convent. The central feature of both buildings was an open cloister, and their walls were a plain white, just as they had been when nuns rather than tourists walked the corridors. The museum in Pisa, however, had a collection far more precious than that of its poor relation in Bassano, a reflection of the wealth that the maritime republic had amassed during its heyday. Perhaps because it was too heavy to have been carted off easily by invaders over the centuries, its collection of sculptures was one of the finest in Italy. Betta and Elio Piombo had finished the sculpture rooms and now contemplated a gilded bust inside a glass case. The man's well-trimmed beard and elegant clothing indicated a nobleman of the fifteenth century, but his eyes, downcast, said something else.

"San Lussorio," said Elio.

Betta had always remembered her friend as dressing well, even back then, when jeans and turtlenecks were the uniform of choice among university students. Today he wore a seersucker suit with a colorful silk tie, making her dark work outfit drab in comparison. She studied the bust, which was in fact a reliquary.

"He's not a saint I'm familiar with. A contemporary of Donatello? The face is so realistic he had to have known him, or at least seen him a few times."

"Lussorio is a rather obscure saint who was martyred by beheading in the third or fourth century. Donatello of course had no idea what someone living a thousand years earlier looked like, so he gave the guy a contemporary look. Why not?" He took on a conspiratorial voice. "There are even some art historians who think that it is a self-portrait of the artist. That would have been pretty cheeky, don't you think, Betta? But I suppose Donatello was already famous enough that he could do what he damn well pleased and get away with it. I hope that was the case. I do like daring in artists."

"Most of the artists in your museum were hardly daring, Elio, but many were geniuses nonetheless. You are fortunate to be surrounded by them."

"Betta, I hope I'm not sensing that you are envious of my work. Remember that I am a bureaucrat not a curator. My usual routine can't hold a candle to the excitement you have of tracking down thieves and international criminals. And all so very hush-hush that you can't share the details with an old friend."

She took him by the arm and they walked toward the entrance to the museum. "Don't get in a huff, Elio. I suppose you can be trusted to keep my latest case to yourself, especially since it's not very exciting."

"Oh, good. My ears are open and my lips are sealed."

"It's the missing *Garden of Eden* pastel from Saint Ursula church."

He stopped short and slapped his head, almost messing

up his perfectly coiffed hair. "That piece of junk? I could have drawn it when I was ten years old."

"Of course, I'd forgotten that you used to work in pastels yourself."

"And I still do, Betta. Perhaps it's because I love the medium that it pains me when people insist on venerating such schlock. Some of his output was passable, but I suspect he did that one after one too many glasses of chianti."

"I'm not very fond of it either, but my orders are to track it down. I'm off now to see someone who might help."

"Really? Some figure from the dark world of international art theft?"

"Hardly. The owner of a local art gallery that specializes in religious art. I had left a message at his shop to call me, and this morning he did. Very nervous sounding, but that often happens when someone is dealing with our office for the first time."

"Are you going to give him the third degree? Some rough stuff?"

"Unfortunately, I forgot to pack my truncheon."

"Where are you meeting him? At his gallery?"

"No, he didn't want to talk with his granddaughter present. He'll be on the Lungarno, directly across from Santa Maria della Spina."

"Is there a bar there? I don't recall one."

"No. He said he'll be standing at the wall, looking down at the river."

"Very mysterious. I can't wait to hear all the details at dinner."

————

"This morning we will be visiting the most sacred site in the life of Francis, as well as the place where he left this earth." A microphone hung near the driver, but Zeke's booming voice needed no amplification. "The Basilica of Saint Mary of the Angels is enormous, but inside it is the tiny church that dates to well before our patron saint's birth. It was there that he renounced worldly things and started his order, and it was there where he spent his final moments of life. We will see the contrast between the simple structure where Francis prayed with his followers and the ornate stone structure that was built to honor him. I think it will be a deep spiritual experience to see it for the first time." He looked to the back of the van where Rick sat with Peter Rael. "Rick, is this your first visit?"

"I was there years ago when I was a kid, Father. I don't remember much." In fact he remembered the little chapel, the Porziuncola, and thought it seemed out of place sitting in the midst of such a cavernous church. He'd asked his mother why they put it there, and she told him that it was there first, and the big church had been built around it. The answer had puzzled him at the time. Why not build the big church somewhere else and leave the little one in the middle of a field?

"How old were you when you came here?" Peter asked, after Zeke had settled back into his seat at the front of the van.

"I think I was in elementary school."

"You were living in Rome?"

"No, at that time my father was working at the embassy in Uruguay, so we must have been in Italy on vacation, to see my mother's family. She always insisted that we come back to Italy once a year when we were assigned somewhere else. Family is important to her, but also to my father."

"The Montoyas go back a long way in New Mexico?"

"Perhaps not as long as the Raels," Rick replied, thinking about what Zeke had told him about Peter's possible *converso* roots.

The comment gave Peter Rael the opening he wanted. "The Raels were one of the original families to settle in the

Rio Grande Valley, bringing with them the Catholic faith. My ancestors worked hard and gave back to the community, and especially to the church. I am not the first Rael to have contributed to the diocese; it is a family tradition. Bishop Lamy could not have built the cathedral in Santa Fe without support from my ancestors."

"Have you studied your family tree? I've done a bit of research on the Montoyas, and it was fascinating, but there are so many of them I got lost about two generations back." Was he pushing too hard? Rael stared out the window for a moment before replying. The bus was on a straight road with fields on both sides, possibly the one Rick and Zeke had jogged down before breakfast.

"There are probably as many Raels in the Albuquerque phone book as Montoyas."

Rick waited for him to answer the question about genealogy, but instead Rael looked out the van window. They were slowing down, and buildings and tall trees began to appear in the place of open land. "This terrain is certainly different from New Mexico, Rick. It reminds me of the times I hired people from back east to work in my company. They either fell in love with the high desert or never got used to its lack of green. Some of them eventually left my company."

"For greener pastures?"

"I guess you… Oh, I see what you did there. Very clever, Rick." He tapped on the window. "It appears we have arrived."

What was surely the largest church in Umbria had been set down in one of the region's smallest towns. The basilica was built in the late sixteenth century in the ponderous style popular in the period, with tall marble side walls and enough classical touches to satisfy the most demanding of Mannerists. Most of all it exuded permanence and stability; but how could it not, sitting as it did surrounded by small buildings and open fields? The town, which before the arrival of the stone masons was a mere bend in the road, had grown to serve the pilgrims. Back then they had arrived on foot, but now they drove up in buses. It was in one of the bus parking lots that Chris had pulled into a space and swung the front door open.

Zeke descended first, followed by the rest of the group. "This is when we should all turn our cell phones off or put them on vibrate," he said. "Also, though I don't think any of us will get lost, please take note of where we are parked in case we get separated." The faces had all been drawn to the basilica. A paved square as large as the footprint of the church itself spread out in front. A row of kiosks, the unavoidable trinket sellers, was visible along the other side of the square through a row of trees. Zeke held up a hand. "Let's walk over to the center of the plaza to get a good view of the facade before going inside."

"Good," Jessica said to Rick. "I wanted to get some shots." Her camera hung from one shoulder and a brown camera bag from the other. No blue jeans and tee today, she was dressed in a flowing skirt and a blouse that covered her arms. Rick noticed that the other women in the group were dressed similarly, no doubt told by Zeke that it was a requirement whenever they were visiting a church. Even Vicki had toned things down. The men kept their standard uniform of short-sleeved shirts and slacks. Zeke set out toward the middle of the square, an imposing figure in black, with his small flock following.

A statue of the Virgin stood at the highest point in the center of the facade, its shimmering gold outlined against the pale green dome behind. At ground level three sets of columns framed three entrances, and above the center doorway was a balcony crowned by an arch decorated with what Rick guessed to be a papal seal in stone. It was probably the family crest of the pope who ordered the basilica built, and was used by him to bless the throngs gathered in the square below. The group had stopped and was taking pictures, mostly with cell phones. Jessica stood next to Rick, staring at the scene like an artist studying a model.

"Can you get the whole church in the shot from here?" he asked.

"Not a problem with this lens." She took the camera in her left hand, steadied it with the elbow pushed against her chest, and squeezed the shutter with her right index finger. After a quick look at the screen on the back of the camera she adjusted the lens and repeated the process.

Rick watched, impressed. "What have you got in the bag?"

She continued to take pictures as she answered. "It looks small, but holds a lot. I've got another lens and a monopod." She noticed the puzzled look on his face. "That's to steady the camera when I need to, like a tripod but just one leg. It folds up small. I've also got a pad to make notes, and the required bottle of water. It would even hold my smartphone and laptop, if my father had allowed me to bring them." She put emphasis on the word *father*.

"Come get in the picture, Jessica," called Zeke. The group had lined up with the church in the background, and he was standing with his own camera in hand. She sighed and walked to the group.

"You get in too, Zeke; I'll take it."

"Great, Rick. Just press the button. This is for the diocese newsletter." Zeke handed over the camera, which was like a toy compared to Jessica's, and got on one side of the lineup, next to Adelaide Chaffee, walking stick in hand. Her niece stood next to her, followed by the Raels, the Alamedas, and finally Chris Carson, whom Rick had to ask to move closer to Vicki, to get everyone in the shot. When she put her arm around his waist to pull him toward her, Rick could see his face blush even through the small camera lens.

"*Formaggio*," Lillian Rael called out, earning a laugh from everyone in the group but Jessica.

Most people in the square were moving toward the right doorway, so that's where Zeke headed with his New Mexicans. Rick found himself walking between Leon Alameda and Peter Rael several steps behind their two wives.

"We didn't see you at dinner last night, Rick," said Leon. "Were you with your police inspector doing more interpreting?" He was pleased with his own humor.

"I'm sorry I missed dinner with the group, Leon. Duty called."

"Duty?" said Peter Rael. "Is that what they call it now?" The two men chuckled.

Was the rift between them just Lillian Rael's alcohol-fueled imagination? These guys were acting suspiciously like friends. "Are you two some kind of comic tag team?"

"We need some levity on this trip, Rick," Leon said. "We're all very pious, but every once in a while, we have to lighten things up."

"Especially after someone in the group gets murdered," Rael added.

The three men reached the columns and found that they led to a portico under the balcony, with the door to the basilica itself a few steps ahead. The jocularity of the previous comments disappeared as they walked into Santa Maria degli Angli, dipped their fingers into a font of holy water, and crossed themselves. Rick had been in many cathedrals, including this one many years ago, but entering one this cavernous always got his attention. There were perhaps a hundred people inside, and their voices melded into a collective murmur, bouncing softly off the tall walls and high ceiling. From the distance an airy soprano voice reached his ears, but he couldn't tell if the words were Italian or some other language. His eyes went upward to check out the decoration on the ceiling, and found it was white, like the massive supportive columns and the outer walls. The architect had not wanted to detract from the bright colors of the saint's rustic little chapel that rested under the cathedral dome. Everyone in the group stood looking at this out-of-place little structure in the distance when Rick felt the vibration of his cell phone. He checked the number and walked quickly outside.

"Yes, Chiara."

"*Buon giorno*, Riccardo. Are you at Santa Maria degli Angeli yet? You should be, according to the tour schedule we found on Biraldo."

"The group just walked in."

"Good. Cesare Gallo's winery is not too far from there, and he's going to be waiting for us. I'll have a car come by to pick you up."

It took Rick a moment to remember who she was talking about. Of course, the husband of the lovely Letizia, the guy who owns the chocolate company and the vineyard. "Why do I need to go along?"

"You were helpful in the two interviews last night, so I thought you should be along. But if you'd prefer—"

"No, no. It is my duty to help the police, and I'm sure Father Zeke would agree." He pictured a police car rolling up to the church, perhaps with a siren. "But give me the address of the winery, and I'll have Chris drive me there."

She gave it to him and got off the line. Rick walked back into the church where the group was still standing in the back taking in the scene and Zeke was explaining that if anyone wished to go to confession, the booths on the other side of the columns were marked with the languages of the priests inside. "Zeke,"

Rick said, "I just had a call from the inspector, and she wants me along to interview another suspect. It's nearby; do you think Chris could drop me there?"

"Of course, Rick. I'm sorry you'll miss spending some time in this wonderful atmosphere, but we have to get to the bottom of Biraldo's murder. You did say that you'd visited it when you were a child, of course. Yes, by all means take the van." Chris Carson was standing next to Jessica, watching her take pictures. "Chris, please take Rick to where he needs to go and drop him off. Rick, can you get back on your own or will you call me? Our next event is a wine talk before lunch in the town of Torgiano. We'll need you for that."

"I'm sure Inspector Berti will arrange to get me there."

Chris blinked. "The policewoman?"

"Don't worry, Chris," said Rick, remembering how nervous the kid had been during the interview at the hotel. "She won't want to talk to you again. Let's go, so you can get back to see the church."

They walked quickly outside and across the plaza to the parking lot. Once inside the van Rick sat in the front passenger seat and gave him the name and address. Chris typed it into the van's GPS and a feminine voice in English ordered him to drive for a quarter mile and turn left. He obeyed. The land quickly turned rural once they crossed Highway 75, but it was mostly olive groves or crops Rick could not identify. Chris stayed silent, his eyes on the road.

"Have you thought of anything else about Biraldo since yesterday?"

Chris looked quickly at Rick, as if just realizing he had a passenger. "Me?"

"You and I are the only ones in the van. Yes, you."

"I have been thinking about it." He paused, and Rick said

nothing, knowing from experience that sometimes it was better to be quiet and wait when the person talking is nervous. It took a few moments. "In the airport, when we were waiting for the plane from Atlanta to Rome, I heard something." More hesitation, but his listener stayed patient. "Biraldo was talking with Leon Alameda. I could only hear bits of their conversation, but from the tone I got the impression that they were somehow conspiring."

"Conspiring?"

"Yeah. They were talking about other people. I heard Mr. Alameda mention his wife, and several times I heard him say Peter."

"Peter Rael."

"I would assume it was Mr. Rael they were talking about. But as I say, I couldn't hear well. They kept announcing flights over the public address, and of course I wasn't trying to eavesdrop."

"Of course."

The voice from the dashboard announced a turn a quarter mile ahead and an arrow appeared on the screen. Grapevines had begun to line the road outside the van, with tiny spring grapes starting to pop out on some of them. Chris slowed the van. The voice told them that their destination was just ahead, and a sign for Dolce Vita winery confirmed that she was correct. They turned in, trading the ample pavement for a narrow lane of gravel. Branches reached out like fingers to touch the side of the van before the lane widened and came to an open area where a police car was already parked. Chiara Berti stood beside it, talking on her cell phone. Chris made a wide looping turn and stopped while watching the inspector.

Rick pulled the door handle. "Thanks, Chris, I'll see you at lunch."

"Are you going to tell her what I said?"

"Don't you want me to?"

"I don't know. Sure, go ahead. It won't matter."

Rick's boots crunched on the gravel when he descended from the van and closed the door. After Chris drove off, he stood in the middle of the lot and looked around. His first thought was that the winery was more of a tax write-off than a moneymaking endeavor. He was certain that Dolce Vita chocolates was a major operation, but unless he was missing something, Dolce Vita winery was not. At the edge of the vines stood a shed that was not much larger than the van. It had one small window, and a pipe protruding from the tin roof indicated that a stove or heater took up some, or perhaps most, of the space inside. An open Quonset hut steps from the shed held a small tractor, metal tools, and stacked wicker baskets. Near the shed sat a shiny new Land Rover, the sign of a gentleman farmer. All that was lacking was Cesare Gallo wearing a tattersall jacket with patched sleeves and sporting an ascot.

"He's out checking his vines," said Chiara while slipping her phone into her jacket pocket. She wore her usual dark pantsuit with a white blouse. "We'll wait for him here, unless you want to walk through the dirt." She looked at the cowboy boots. "I'd rather not."

"You're not a country gal, it would appear."

"It would appear correct. The only dirt I might identify with is what the street sweepers pick up along Via Condotti." She looked toward the fields. "I wonder if he'll have nice boots like you, Riccardo."

"These are my everyday boots. I have fancier ones for dressing up. Did you find out anything about Signor Gallo?"

"He's clean on our records, if that's what you mean. Studied business at the Bocconi in Milan and started at the family company soon after graduating. When his father died, he took over running it, apparently quite successfully. And here he comes."

Cesare Gallo was in fact the image of the gentleman farmer, but Italian rather than English. He wore corduroy pants, a knit shirt, and a lightweight leather jacket. The boots were of dark suede, well scuffed and more practical than fashionable. He wore no hat, perhaps to show off a thick shock of black hair. Aviator sunglasses completed the outfit. He emerged from a row of vines and walked confidently to the two visitors, extending a hand to Chiara as he checked her out.

"You must be Inspector Berti. And this is?"

"Riccardo Montoya," Rick said, taking his turn with the handshake.

"Signor Montoya is assisting in the investigation. Thank you for giving us some of your time, Signor Gallo. This should not take long."

"My time is yours. I'm afraid I have nowhere for us to sit and talk." He tilted his head toward the tiny shed. "It has only one chair and is rather stuffy anyway."

"Out here is fine," Chiara answered. "You tend to your grapes by yourself?"

Gallo smiled. "I have a man who works part-time; he does the pruning and checks on the vines. During harvest, like all the other vineyards, I hire people. It is not a large operation, and I sell all my grapes to others in the valley. I don't make the wine myself."

"Have you had the vineyard long?"

"No, Signor Montoya, only a few years. It's really more of a hobby than anything. I love coming down here a few days a week and walking the rows of vines, watching their progress from tiny buds to clumps of grapes. Even in the winter, when they are scrawny and leafless, it helps clear my head." He pulled at the sleeve of his jacket. "And I don't have to wear a suit and tie. By the way, I like your boots. Are they from Rome? I noticed a bit of a Roman accent."

"From America."

Gallo nodded, thought for a moment, and turned to Chiara. "How can I help you, Inspector?"

"How long did you know Biraldo?"

"We grew up together, going to the same schools. He was always the one getting in trouble and trying to pull his other friends into it with him. A few times my parents told me I shouldn't hang out with him, but I didn't pay much attention to them. We had a bit of a competition in the *liceo* over girls, since he considered himself irresistible. I wouldn't say that Ettore was my closest friend, but we were close enough that he felt he could ask favors of me when we became adults."

"You lent him money."

Gallo folded his arms over his chest and looked her in the eye. "Letizia told me that she'd mentioned that to you. I think she may have overdramatized the facts of the loan; it wasn't really that large an amount. He was going to America, and he wanted some start-up money to import Italian art. Ettore was an old friend, so I couldn't turn him down flat, but I knew him well enough not to lend him too much. When he went so long without paying back anything, I was annoyed with him, but I may have been more annoyed at myself for lending it to him in the first place."

Berti stared back. "Tell us your movements in the late afternoon and evening of the day before yesterday."

"Letizia told me you'd asked her the same thing. I worked late at the office."

"Alone?"

"Alone. It's not much of an alibi, is it? But I had no reason to murder Ettore, certainly not for not paying back a small loan. To state the obvious, now that he's dead, I'll never get that money back."

Rick waited for Chiara's inevitable next question, wondering how delicate she would be in asking it. She stayed true to form.

"You were aware of your wife's relationship with Biraldo, Signor Gallo?"

Apparently Gallo was expecting the question as well. "Letizia feels the need for an occasional indiscretion, so I have come to expect it. She claims that I am only interested in the business and don't give her enough attention." He shrugged. "She may be right. Usually her flings do not end in murder, though. Perhaps this will cure her."

———

Every street that ran along the Arno River was called a *lungarno* rather than a *via*. To make things more confusing for that rare tourist who ventured more than a block from the Leaning Tower, different sections of the *lungarno* had different names. The stretch where Betta was to meet the art dealer was the Lungarno Pacinotti, named for a nineteenth-century physicist and native son. Leave it to Pisa, Galileo's hometown, to name its streets after scientists. She was puzzled by Signor Galilei's insistence on meeting at a deserted section of wall along the river. She'd heard intrigue in the voice of the man when they'd talked, but it might have been the connection. From her experience, most gallery owners enjoyed dealing with the art fraud squad—could the guy have something to hide? Probably not; more likely, he was a fan of spy novels.

The rendezvous point was a short stroll from Elio's museum, which was also right on the river. She started walking on the buildings side of the street, but soon crossed over to the sidewalk that ran along the water. The Arno at this point was about as wide as it was when it flowed through Florence, but unlike the Tuscan capital, here there was no Ponte Vecchio and almost no tourists. Two double sculls zipped along the surface, their young oarsmen reminding her that Pisa was a university town. In the distance on the other side of the river was Santa Maria della Spina, one of the more curious oddities of the city, though not as well-known as the most curious, the Leaning Tower. The church was a miniature bundle of spires, a Gothic doll's house that for some reason had been placed next to the river.

Across the river from the church, as he had promised, stood Massimo Galilei, staring at the water below. At least she assumed it was Galilei, since the age and appearance fit the part. He wore a suit that was a bit heavy for the spring temperatures and looked, even from a distance, to be a touch threadbare. In profile an aquiline nose dominated a face that included bushy white eyebrows, their color matching tufts of white hair that spilled over the ears. She guessed he was mostly bald under a jaunty black beret. The total image, bolstered by the headwear, was that of an aging orchestra conductor. Or an aging art gallery owner. As she got closer, he continued to stare down at the Arno, seemingly oblivious to the click of her heels on the pavement. She took the cue and stopped next to him, leaning on the wall with her elbows. Perhaps there was something interesting floating below.

"Signor Galilei?"

"You're late."

Betta checked her watch. "Actually, I'm a few minutes early."

"Oh. Perhaps you're right." He kept his eyes on the water. "I wasn't expecting a woman."

"Didn't your granddaughter tell you I was a woman?"

"I suppose she did. But still."

"Well, I'm here. What was it you wanted to tell me?"

"I don't like being involved in this kind of thing. I'm a reputable businessman."

"Of that I have no doubt, Signor Galilei." She wanted to add that he appeared to be enjoying it. All he lacked was a cloak and a dagger. "This is a sordid business that goes against every value that we, as lovers of art, hold dear."

For the first time, he looked at Betta. "Yes. Yes, those are my sentiments exactly."

"And you felt it was your civic duty to call me."

"Precisely."

She decided to shake him up and try for a cut to the chase. "Have you got the pastel?"

"Certainly not."

"But you know where it is."

Galilei shook his head, then looked left and right, though it was obvious no one was anywhere near them. For further effect he lowered his voice. "I had a call from someone who said he was in possession of the *Garden of Eden* pastel, and he wanted me to buy it or find him a buyer."

"Now we're getting somewhere. What did you tell him? Or her?"

"It was a man. He had a deep, gruff voice. I almost hung up, thinking it was some crank, but then I thought it was my duty to find out if it was real. I owed it to the art world, and to Oresti."

"Oresti?"

"Father Oresti."

"Of course, the priest. You know him?"

"Saint Ursula's is my parish church. I live nearby."

"I see. But you didn't tell Father Oresti."

"I would have, but then you showed up at the gallery. So I called you."

"You did the right thing." They both watched a rather large

tree trunk float by. "I'm glad you weren't tempted to buy the work yourself."

"And I'm certainly glad he came to me first. What if he had approached some unscrupulous art dealer rather than me? I shudder to think of what would have happened."

"How much do you think the pastel is worth?"

"I'm sure I could have sold it for at least fifty thousand euros. I have a client in Switzerland who loves the work of that artist, and he would have snapped it up, no questions asked."

"Thank goodness you're an honest man, Signor Galilei. How did you leave it with the man who called you?"

"I said I would think about it and call him back."

"Well, we'd better call him now, before he goes to an unscrupulous dealer."

His eyes, which had been in a conspiratorial squint, now widened. "Really? Now?"

"Of course. Tell him you have a wealthy buyer, but she and her husband want to see the pastel before deciding. That's the way these sales work."

"That's smart. Take a real cop along in case there's some violence."

Betta let the slight pass, saying nothing. Galilei pulled a small fold-up phone from his pocket, a model she hadn't seen in years. He extracted from another pocket a wrinkled paper with the number he'd written down, and hit the buttons. The conversation was short, with Betta hearing only a muffled voice on the other end. Galilei scribbled something on the paper, using the top of the wall as a writing surface.

"He wasn't happy with two of you, but I convinced him." He handed her the paper with the address. "And he absolutely forbade me to come along."

Betta heard the disappointment in his voice. "You can wait

outside until we arrest him," she said. "We don't want any witnesses to anything that might happen in there."

Galilei gulped. "I understand."

———

Torgiano was almost a company town, that company being the
various enterprises of the Lungarotti family, beginning with
wine from vineyards that started at the edge of the village. The
company wine museum and olive oil museum brought in tourists, as did the restaurant inside a four-star hotel that looked out
over the fields. On a clear day like today, the view could extend
all the way to Assisi, a tiny swath of white brushed on a green hill
in the distance. It was in front of this hotel, in the space reserved
for arriving guests, that the police car was parked, earning the
silent reproach of the bellhop. Rick and Inspector Berti leaned
against the side of the car.

"Signor Gallo has a point about motive," said Berti. "Why
would he murder someone who owes him money?"

"But that's not his only motive."

She nodded. "True, but he seemed blasé about his wife's
playing around, and the way he said it, I can almost believe him."

"I'm not sure of that, Chiara. He's a smooth talker, and my
sense was that he had his answer ready, and it had been well
rehearsed. He had to be bothered by Letizia's behavior."

"So he lured Biraldo up to the castle and, in a fit of rage,
did him in? He doesn't fit the profile, in my mind. Of course
he could have hired someone." She noticed Rick's puzzlement.
"No, he also doesn't fit the profile for someone staging a hit like
that. And how would he have gotten Biraldo up there, either by
himself or by his assassin? The scene of the crime doesn't make
sense for Gallo."

"Nor for Fillipo or Rucola. Why would they go up there with Biraldo?"

"Good point, Riccardo." She looked up to see the van working its way down Torgiano's narrow main street. "Which means the murderer has to be one of your New Mexican pilgrims. Probably the old lady with the stick."

"Adelaide doesn't pass the scene-of-the-crime test either."

"Why not? She lured him up to a secluded spot in order to seduce him."

"It would have been less trouble to invite him to her room." He thought for a moment. "Though she does like to go hiking."

The van squeezed into what was left of the loading area in front of the hotel, and Chris opened the door. Zeke descended first, followed by the rest of his group. Most avoided looking at the inspector, but Zeke walked right up to her and Rick.

"Inspector, good to see you again. I hope you are getting closer to finding the culprit who killed our guide." He held up his hands and turned to Rick. "Sorry, I forgot. Rick, could you translate?"

"It's all right, Father. I understood."

"Rick, she speaks English." His eyes bounced from Berti to Rick to Berti. "I mean, you speak English, Inspector."

"Better than many of our classmates at UNM," Rick said. "Yesterday was just a police trick to get you all to open up about Biraldo to a fellow New Mexican. Right, Inspector?"

"Not that it helped much," said Berti, sticking with English. "I shall take my leave and return to the drudgery of police work while you both enjoy another Lucullan repast." She opened the back door and got into the car. The driver started the engine and slowly pulled into the street.

"Lucullan repast? She really does speak English better than many of our classmates, Rick." Zeke watched as the car disappeared around a corner in the direction of Assisi. "Were you able to help after you left us? I hope so, since you missed a truly moving visit to the basilica."

"A lot of a police investigation is simply eliminating all possibilities, and we may have eliminated some this morning." It wasn't true, but it sounded good. "I hope you didn't need me at the church."

Zeke gestured to the door and they started toward it. "No, but we will now."

Once inside they were greeted by a hotel employee standing in front of the reception desk who directed them toward the main dining room and said their private room was just beyond it. Even though it was still early by Italian standards, two of the tables in the dining room were occupied by older couples, no doubt foreign tourists. The room was quiet, perhaps forced to be by the elegance of the settings and the decor. Windows along one side looked out over the tiled roofs of buildings to flat, open fields beyond. It was the same view Rick had from his hotel room, but from the opposite direction.

The private room had no view of the valley, but outside its one window was a brick patio packed with overflowing flowerpots. Adelaide and her niece were looking at the flowers when Rick and Zeke came in. The others were chatting in the center of the room. Two tables—a small one with bottles of wine, and a long one lined with place settings—were positioned across from each other. White tablecloths covered both. The chairs and settings were positioned so that all the diners faced the small table.

"This seems to be set for the Last Supper," said Leon Alameda in a loud voice, eliciting a few laughs.

"Not enough places," said Peter Rael.

Bottles of wine stood like two sets of bowling pins on the

small table, two kinds of reds but both with the Lungarotti label. The company logo also lit up the wall behind the wine table from a small projector sitting on it. All very theatrical, including the flourish with which a waiter was starting to open the bottles. Rick was not a wine expert, far from it, and he wondered how esoteric the winery representative would be, as well as how difficult it would be to interpret his words. He pictured a prissy man sporting a goatee and wearing a bow tie and matching pocket handkerchief. At that moment a woman swept into the room, and Rick was happy that his premonition had been incorrect. She looked over the group, spotted Rick, and walked to him.

"I'm guessing you are the interpreter," she said. Her accent was northern, but he couldn't place it. The Veneto?

"I'm Riccardo Montoya. How did you know?"

"Cowboy boots are too bulky to pack for a long trip. You must live in Italy." She extended her hand and introduced herself as Paola Miele. "I am terribly sorry that you'll have to interpret, Riccardo. French and German, I can speak, but not English."

"If all Italians did, I wouldn't have a job." He noticed that the attention of all the men in the room, including Zeke, was on her. Vicki Alameda rolled her eyes. "How would you like to do this?" Rick asked.

"I will talk about Torgiano wines in general and the history of the Lungarotti family in wine making." She held up one of the menu cards. "I'll talk a bit about the two wines you'll have with lunch. Then I'll leave you alone to have your delicious meal, and the waiter will serve you the wines with each course."

"You won't join us for lunch?"

Her charming smile widened. "Thank you, Riccardo, but I have another group coming to our tasting room when I leave here. Perhaps another time." She glanced at the menu card and then at the group milling around. "I can assure you, Riccardo, that the choice of dishes was made to give you a taste of regional specialties. Nothing more."

The comment puzzled Rick, but he let it pass. "Shall we begin?"

At Rick's signal Zeke herded the group toward the long table, and everyone took seats, leaving an end chair for Rick next to Adelaide Chaffee, who had carefully leaned her walking stick on the wall behind her. The opposite end spot was taken by Chris, who had just hurried in after parking the van. At each place, in addition to a full setting of silverware, two wineglasses and a full goblet of mineral water had been carefully arranged. Everyone picked up the card in front of them and read it while the waiter walked along the table and splashed a bit of white wine into one of their glasses.

"All you have to do," Rick said, standing next to Paola, "is stop every couple of sentences so that I can put your words into English."

"I…will…speak…slowly…and…clearly."

"Also, you're not allowed to make fun of the interpreter."

"Sorry."

"All right, everyone," said Rick, "may I introduce Paola Miele, who will be telling us something about the wines we'll be having with lunch today." After pulling out his pad and pen, he nodded to Paola.

Projecting a map on the wall, she began with an explanation of the Italian system of geographic designations for wines, where the Torgiano grapes fit into the map of Umbria, and the types of grapes that went into each of the wines they were tasting. After noting the Lungarotti family's long tradition of wine making, she described the two wines that would accompany their lunch. Likely after much experience with groups like this one, she had sized up the New Mexicans and concluded they were mostly not serious oenologists. As such, she stayed away from wine-speak, sprinkling in just enough words like *delicate, intensity* and *balanced,* to show that she knew her wine, while eschewing others like *nose* and *body.* The whole presentation, including a few questions, took about twenty minutes and earned enthusiastic applause. Rick was impressed.

She was apparently impressed by Rick's work as well. "You must give me a card, Riccardo. On occasion, with large groups, we have the need for an interpreter. Where are you based?"

"I live in Rome," he said while fishing the business card from his wallet. Perhaps on purpose, she held it in her left hand while reading it, and he noticed a shiny gold band on her finger. *No wonder she's all business.* "I would enjoy coming back, Paola. Just give me as much lead time as possible."

With a wave and a *"Ciao, grazie"* to the group, she departed. Rick took his seat next to Adelaide just as the antipasto, mushroom crostini, began arriving at the other end of the table.

"A lovely girl," she said. "And so knowledgeable about wine." She held up her glass of wine, which had been filled by the waiter, and Rick took the cue, tapping his against it. He noticed that her outfit was more subdued than the previous evening, no doubt due to the visit to the basilica. A silver bracelet was her only turquoise bangle. "And you did very well with the interpreting, Rick. This was a bit different from when you helped that policewoman at the hotel."

"Certainly wine is a more pleasant topic than homicide."

Dishes were placed in front of them and Adelaide peered at hers before picking up the menu card. *"Crostini,"* she said. "Is that like bruschetta?"

"They are almost the same." He didn't feel that he knew Adelaide well enough to correct her pronunciation of *bruschetta,* even though it was a pet peeve. He also looked at the menu card and stifled a laugh. Now he understood Paola's comment about the choice of dishes.

"What? Something funny on the menu? You mustn't keep it from everyone."

"I promise to explain before the pasta arrives."

Each plate had only one slice of toast covered with a dark mushroom paste. But everyone soon realized that given the strong earthy flavor, one slice was more than enough. Also two courses would follow, not counting dessert. After finishing his appetizer, Rick noticed that Leon Alameda, sitting on the other side of Adelaide, was deep in discussion with Zeke. He recalled what his mother had told him once before a dinner with his father's embassy contacts. That night a guest had canceled at the last minute, and Rick, then a high school junior, was properly suited up to fill in the seating chart. He knew by then what fork to use and other basics, but she had stressed one point considered crucial. "Be sure that you keep up conversation with the women sitting next to you." Remembering his mother's order, he turned to Adelaide.

"I'm sorry I missed the visit to the basilica. Tell me about it."

"Very moving, Rick. The tiny chapel in the center is worth the visit by itself, and we spent several minutes inside it in prayer. How could we not, knowing that Francis had done the same all those centuries ago? The painting on the walls, inside and out, are beautiful, but for me they only added to the sacred atmosphere. If the artists are famous, that's fine, but you don't go to a place like that to look at art."

Rick had his wineglass almost to his lips, but he put it back down while he listened. For the past twenty-four hours, he had been thinking of the group as suspects in a murder investigation and little else. What he was hearing now were the words of someone searching for, and finding, a deep spiritual experience.

Perhaps he'd been in Italy too long and become as cynical as the
Romans, especially when it came to the papacy. Was being surrounded by the natural beauty of New Mexico better for one's
faith than living in the shadow of the Vatican? He wondered
if his New Mexican father and Roman mother had ever had a
debate on the issue.

"I will have to get in there myself. Perhaps when I leave to
drive back to Rome."

"That little car parked at the hotel is yours?"

"It's my uncle's."

"What does he do?"

"He's a policeman."

"Oh, my. So that's why that woman brought you in so quickly
to the investigation. And I thought it was because she had other
designs on you." She smiled and took a sip of wine.

"Adelaide, I'm shocked."

She leaned toward him. "No, you're not. Now tell me how
the investigation is going." She cut another slice of the toast and
waited for his reply. A few mushrooms fell off, and she replaced
them with her fork.

"I'm not privy to all of the details of Inspector Berti's work,
of course, but I know she is exploring every possibility and has
interviewed several Italians who knew Biraldo. But even if she
was homing in on a suspect, I doubt if she would inform me. I
am not a policeman."

"But you work for the police."

"Occasionally. But just as an interpreter."

She swallowed and took a sip of water. "But if you have any
suspicions about this group you would tell her, I trust?"

"Is there something you want me to pass on to her, Adelaide?"

They watched as their empty plates were whisked away
and glasses refilled. At the other end of the table, the pasta was

starting to arrive. The noise level in the room had increased slightly, no doubt the effect of the wine.

"You were going to tell me what you found humorous on the menu."

"Yes, of course." Rick got to his feet, holding the glass of wine. With the other hand, he tapped his remaining empty glass, getting everyone's attention. "As your resident interpreter, I must point out a curiosity about the dish you are now being served. You'll notice that it is a handmade pasta in the form of twisted strips. Its name, *strozzapreti*, is said to go back to a period in the history of Umbria when many priests were not held in the same high esteem as we hold our Father Zeke." He paused for dramatic effect. "The word can be translated as 'priest choker.'" Everyone burst out laughing, including Zeke. "Signora Miele," Rick continued, "assured me that the dish was put on the menu only because it is a traditional pasta, but nonetheless, I would urge Father Zeke to chew very carefully. *Buon appetito.*"

Everyone clapped, and Rick sat down. Jessica pulled out her camera and snapped a picture of Zeke tucking into his pasta.

"Is that true, Rick? Priest choker?"

"Or priest strangler. Perhaps I shouldn't have said anything, given what's happened, but I couldn't resist." He tried some of the pasta, which was coated with a simple sauce of oil and garlic, spiced up with a bit of red pepper and sprinkled with chopped parsley. "Adelaide, you were about to tell me something that would interest Inspector Berti."

"Was I? With my memory these days, it's a miracle that I remember my own name. I doubt if it was anything of consequence."

"What is nothing of consequence?" It was Leon Alameda, who had turned toward Adelaide.

"I was trying to think of something Rick could tell that woman to help her investigation."

"Is it not going well?" Leon asked, with a probing look for Rick. "What's the problem?"

"It hasn't even been twenty-four hours since they found the body, Leon. Cut her some slack. And as I told Adelaide, she doesn't tell me everything she's doing."

"If there's something that involves any of us," said Leon, "you have an obligation to let us know."

"I didn't realize that. Is it in the fine print of my contract?"

Adelaide patted Rick's arm. "Leon is just as curious as the rest of us, Rick. But we all understand what an awkward position you have been put in. Don't we, Leon?"

"Of course." He returned to his pasta.

Rick took a large gulp of his wine. "If there is something I can share with all of you, Adelaide, I will. And when you remember what it was you wanted to tell me, you know where to find me."

They finished their *strozzapreti* while talking about the art scene in Santa Fe, something Rick was familiar with from visits there from Albuquerque. He asked her specifically about one gallery in the city, without mentioning that it cooperated in one of Rick's early cases with the Italian art police. As they talked, the pasta dishes were cleared and the main course appeared. It was a hearty *stracotta di manzo al Rubesco*, beef simmered for hours in the very same Rubesco wine that accompanied it at the table. Knives had been provided at each place setting, but they weren't needed to cut the succulent meat into bite-sized pieces. It bore no resemblance to the coriaceous pot roast Rick remembered eating at his fraternity house in college. Perhaps in deference to the Americans, or just to sop up the rich sauce, the chef had placed thin slices of roasted potato next to the meat on each plate. It was not until her dish was almost empty, and after her third glass of wine, that Adelaide returned to the subject of Biraldo's murder. She leaned closer to Rick.

"I probably shouldn't say this, but I have been concerned about Chris."

Without thinking, Rick looked at the driver, who sat directly opposite him at the other end of the table. Chris was staring at his plate, concentrating on getting the last bits of sauce with a piece of crusty bread. His wineglasses had been removed before the first course, indicating he took his designated driver role seriously.

"What do you mean by 'concerned'?" Rick asked.

"He's been very different ever since we were all called in to be interviewed by your policewoman. He seems preoccupied. Up until then he was excited to be in Italy, smiling a lot, especially when he was with my niece. Of course we were all shaken by the terrible news, me included. I knew Biraldo better than anyone in the group, after all." She looked at the driver, who was staring blankly at a now empty plate. "But Chris has taken it harder than anyone. He has almost closed up."

CHAPTER NINE

The wines' effects were obvious on the ride back to the hotel. As Chris piloted the van along the stretch of highway lined with industrial buildings, only Rick and Zeke had not nodded off. They sat together in the last row, watching the landscape fly past the windows.

"Are you happy, Rick?"

"Is that a question from Father Zeke or Zeke my old friend?"

"I can't separate the two. Does it make a difference?"

"Probably not. I assume you are referring to my lot in life, my spiritual well-being, my hopes and dreams, my relationships with others, especially the opposite sex?"

"All that."

"Well, my business is doing so well that my next decision may be whether to open an office and hire a secretary, or continue to work out of my apartment by myself. I have a pleasant circle of friends, including many classmates from my high school days in Rome, some Italians, some expat foreigners. It has certainly been wonderful getting to know my uncle better. I can talk to him about almost anything, and he also confides in me. And I'm learning more about the city, not that you can ever know it well, even after a lifetime. I do try to go to mass once a week, and most weeks I succeed. I have to, since my mother grills me about it every time we talk. That cover it?"

"Your mother is a wise woman, Rick." The van looped off the highway onto a two-lane road, the same one Rick had used to drive into Assisi the previous day. "You have not mentioned anyone special who you are seeing. You're not getting any younger, Rick."

"You sound like my mother, Zeke. There is someone, her name is Betta Innocenti, and she works for the art fraud squad. She's in Pisa at the moment, on a case involving art stolen out of a church."

"Doing the Lord's work, then. Is there any chance I might meet her?"

"If she's back in Rome when you go through again, I'll try to arrange it. She doesn't speak much English, though."

"Perhaps we can find someone to interpret."

Rick chuckled. "And you, Zeke? You seem to be at peace with yourself. Is my impression a correct one?"

"It is, my friend. But I will tell you that when I entered the seminary, I went through a period of doubt, wondering if I'd made the right choice. Early on I was assigned a mentor, Father Ingemar, who could have been from another planet. Picture a skinny, aging Swede from Minnesota in deep conversation with a young Black man who outweighed him by a hundred pounds. We cut quite a figure. At first I was very skeptical that someone so different could ever be of help to me, but over time it worked. It turned out one thing we did have in common was an initial period of questioning whether the life of a priest was the right one for us. He got me through that by, as much as anything, just listening to me. He was a great listener, which I came to realize is an important skill for a priest. But he also told me inspiring stories of his own work through the years."

"Sounds like quite a guy."

Zeke nodded while looking up at the bell tower over the basilica of Saint Francis.

Ten minutes later the bus pulled into the lot in front of the hotel. Chris got out on his side and ran around to open the passenger door with a bang, waking up anyone who was still napping. They slowly descended to the pavement, some rubbing their eyes. Zeke reminded them that what was left of the afternoon had been set aside for shopping, and they had until seven thirty to work up an appetite for dinner at the hotel.

"We'll do our best," said Peter Rael and began trudging up the steps.

Jessica pulled out her camera and began snapping pictures of the groggy group, despite their protestations. While Leon Alameda headed to the front desk to pick up their key, his wife walked to where Rick and Zeke were standing. "I think you're avoiding me, Rick," she said.

"I need to send an email back to the diocese," Zeke said, excusing himself and walking quickly to the hotel steps.

"I am definitely not avoiding you, Vicki, any more than I'm avoiding anyone else."

"I'm the only one in the group who is an old friend."

"Except Zeke."

"Not the same, and you know it."

Her look reminded him of that point when he'd realized that their relationship had become all about her, and it was time to end it. Vicki hadn't changed, except perhaps to get more self-centered. "I'll make a point to sit with you and your husband at dinner."

It was not the answer she wanted. She stared at him for a moment before turning on her heel and walking into the hotel.

Five minutes later Rick was in his room looking out at the

countryside. Small clouds puffed like smoke signals over the hills, their shadows throwing dark dots onto the landscape. He walked to the desk, turned on his laptop, and typed in the hotel password. A few emails appeared and he scrolled through them quickly. Two were requests for translations but nothing urgent. Another was from the embassy public affairs office, an interpreter gig for an American writer coming through Rome the following month. He typed a short reply; it was the kind of job he loved. As he hit Send, his phone rang.

"Commissario Fontana, it is an honor to speak with you."

"The honor is all mine, dear nephew."

"If you are calling for an update on the murder investigation, there is not much to report. Inspector Berti and I interviewed Italian suspects, but nothing came of it."

"I know; I've read her reports. That was not the main reason I was calling."

It was never easy to read anything into Piero's tone of voice, especially over the phone, but Rick sensed something. "What was it?"

"Not the best news from Sicily. The Mafia lawyer in New York has been told about the transcript, and he alerted the boss back in Palermo. Inspector Cribari's sources tell him that the family found out about the translation and are not happy. The don apparently flew into a rage."

Rick's chest tightened as his uncle continued.

"They've already made a visit to the other translator in Palermo, the one who turned down the job. She denied she had done it, and they believed her."

"So now they are trying to find who did the work. Do you think they will?"

"They can be very persistent. It's probably good that you are not in Rome, in case they start going through a list of translators working in Italy. There is such a thing, I suppose?"

"There is an association, and the members are listed on its website."

"What worries me more is that your name will leak some other way. But there's more troubling news. Our *penitente* has gone missing."

Rick remembered vividly the screen image of an exhausted Mafioso. "Isn't that the idea behind the witness protection program?"

"Not when his police handler can't locate him. He may have gotten scared and taken off to somewhere else on his own, but it could also mean his location was compromised. But that's our problem, not yours."

Rick stood by the window. What he saw was very different from the scruffy landscape of Sicily he'd seen while driving between the airport and Palermo.

"Riccardo, I'm going to ask Inspector Berti to assign a body-guard to you."

"Do you really think that's necessary, Uncle? This is Assisi, the most tranquil place in Italy. And I can certainly take care of myself."

"The Mafia likes tranquility. I've got to go. Be careful."

Rick slipped the phone into his pocket. Outside his window, the green central valley of Umbria did not seem quite as peace-ful. He gazed at the landscape for a moment, pulled his phone back out, and pressed the screen. The call was answered after the third ring.

"*Ciao*, Rick. How goes it in the town of saints?"

"As tranquil as it has been for centuries, Betta. Nothing new on my case; I was wondering if you've had more success finding your work of art."

"Well, the short answer is yes. It's all set up, and we'll be mov-ing in on the art thief this evening."

"You've certainly worked fast. I'm very impressed. And for a work of art that you don't particularly like."

"But there are those who do like it, Rick. The art dealer here says he could get fifty thousand euros for it in a heartbeat from some collector in Switzerland."

"There's no accounting for taste. But anyway, I'm glad you're not going alone. Those art thieves can play rough. Have you gotten along well with your local police contact?"

"Detective Pisani and I get along fine, but don't worry, I can take care of myself."

Eerily, it was exactly what he had said to his uncle moments earlier. "But the detective will go with you, won't he?"

"No, he won't, but I'm taking Elio along. He's got some kind of martial arts rating, if that makes you feel better, but mainly I want him there to verify the work of art. He really knows his pastels. There's one here in his office that he did himself. It's fabulous."

Rick heard a muffled laugh in the background. It made no sense, but he was starting to get annoyed with Elio. "Betta, be careful," he said, echoing the words of his uncle.

—

Following their conversation, Rick realized he would be seriously remiss if he failed to bring Betta something from Assisi. Perhaps some earrings. His mother always said that no woman has enough earrings. Also, Zeke had said that the afternoon had been reserved for shopping, so it was his duty as a member of the group to browse the shops. Better to do it now before Berti assigned some annoying cop to dog his every step. He turned off his computer and left the room.

After dropping his key at the reception desk, he turned to

leave but was stopped by a man who had jumped up from a chair near the door.

"Can I speak with you? I am Angelo Stefani, with ANSA. You are the interpreter for the group of Americans, am I correct?" The stubble on his face had darkened since the morning.

"You are correct, Signor Stefani, but I can't talk to you now."

"It will only take a moment. I have just a few questions about how the Americans are dealing with the murder of Biraldo. My English is insufficient to ask them directly, so your help would be greatly appreciated." He pulled out a small pad and stubby pen. Hollow eyes blinked at Rick.

"I'm sorry, I have no comment."

"We could meet later, for coffee."

"I don't think so, Signor Stefani. If you'll excuse me." Rick brushed past and pushed open the door while the journalist stared at his back with no change in the blank expression on his face.

When he got to the city gate above the hotel, Rick tried to recall any pleasant encounters he'd had with reporters, and couldn't. Certainly not the one in Urbino who was annoyingly persistent, but at least she was better than the guy in Orvieto who had almost gotten Rick shot. Stefani, like the others, was just trying to do his job, but that didn't make him any more pleasant to be around.

Rick turned sharply and climbed the narrow Via Frate Elia, named for one of the first followers of Francis. Instead of reflecting the asceticism so important to Brother Elia, the street was filled with souvenir shops filled with religious trinkets. Not tempted, Rick passed them all and found himself in a wide rectangular square striped by colored stone and surrounded by a scalloped colonnade. Past it sat the massive bulk of the cathedral.

Like many other buildings he'd seen in Italy, it was a

mixture of architectures, each reflecting the style popular at the moment when funds were found to build and then expand. The exterior of the original cathedral, now the lower church, was all but hidden by later additions, most notably the Gothic upper cathedral, reachable by climbing an outdoor stairway and crossing the grass in front. To the left began a complex of buildings that extended to the crest of the hill. The stone of the newer structure had hidden the buttresses of the upper cathedral but not the arched doors that led into the lower church. Rick stopped and watched the crowds coming and going through the entrance, many led by priests. It had been this church, with the tomb of Francis in its crypt, that he had visited all those years back with his parents, and now he realized he'd better go in. Mama would not be pleased if she found out he'd spent a couple days in Assisi and not visited the most holy shrine in the city.

On walking through the arched doorway, the change was total. Outside people chatted and laughed, but in here the mood was quiet and serious. The rich fragrance of incense replaced the fresh breeze floating through the piazza from the countryside below. Most noticeable was the difference in light. It went from bright sun bouncing off the stone pavement outside to a half light from a few dim bulbs, the flickering flames of votive candles, and a distant stained-glass window. He was barely able to find the font of holy water. Slowly his eyes adjusted to the point where he could take in the plan put in place by Elia and other Franciscan brothers mere days after the death of the saint. A series of flattened arches supported the low ceiling and divided the apse into ribbed vaults. Every inch of wall, ceiling, and floor was decorated, either with geometric or religious designs. He walked forward, passing small side chapels and a long line of people waiting to descend the narrow stone stairway to the crypt.

He reached the sanctuary, on the floor plan the top of a Tau, the Greek cross carried by Francis. It was here, Rick knew, that some of the most famous frescoes were found, including one ceiling composition by Cimabue. After peering upward, he sat at one of the pews, said a silent prayer, and started back toward the door. People were praying and meditating, either singularly or in pairs, in each of the side chapels he passed. One couple caused Rick to stop to be sure he was seeing correctly in the dim lighting. Yes, it was Jessica and Chris. She had her head bowed, and he knelt next to her, his clasped hands resting on the pew in front of him.

Zeke would be pleased to know that the two had taken the time to pray, though it would not be Rick's place to tell him. Finding that the younger generation wasn't totally obsessed with the material world was heartening, but it also made him feel old.

Outside again, he climbed the stairs up to the expanse of grass in front of the upper cathedral and glanced back at the rose window above its double doors before continuing toward the town's main square. Via San Francesco was a street of small shops, religious organizations, and anonymous buildings, some in rough stone, others covered in the yellow stucco found in every Italian city. Rick was still not tempted by the shops he passed, nor were most of the other people trudging along, enjoying the good weather and the lack of cars. Most of the city was pedestrian only, especially welcome here since the street narrowed as it climbed. He stopped, as he always did in Rome, to read a historical plaque, this one commemorating a Franciscan scholar who had toiled inside the building until his death. A few steps ahead, a break opened between the buildings on the right where a stairway led down to another street below. In the distance was the green valley, seen at a different angle than from his hotel room view but equally beautiful.

The street narrowed more, or perhaps it just seemed that way because of increased foot traffic closer to the Piazza del Comune. Still no shops caught his eye, and he was beginning to wonder if anything besides religious souvenirs was sold in this town. At that moment a store appeared on his left that had promise. Its door opened onto a paved niche large enough to display pieces of sculpture in both stone and wood. A woman sat on a bench with her dog, both surveying the wares positioned around them. He went inside where a woman behind a glass display case was talking in English while removing jewelry to show an older couple. Rick guessed them to be British. The shoes were always the giveaway, and these two wore sensible leather footwear rather than the running shoes that seemed to be a requirement for Americans on holiday. The salesperson smiled at Rick with a silent "I'll help you next" before turning her attention back to the couple. Rick nodded and walked to a shelf lined with small figures, most of them animals of one species or another. They reminded him that Saint Francis was the patron saint of animals. One was a sleeping cat, its body rounded with an almost Oriental face, not at all like the one who showed up occasionally at his apartment window in Rome. He replaced it on the shelf and moved to another piece, which he picked up and held it in his hand.

"You are looking for sculpture?" The woman had left the other customers and stood next to Rick. Her English was accented but reasonably fluent.

"I can speak Italian, if you'd like."

Her eyes darted to his cowboy boots. "But I thought…"

"They fool everyone." He turned the piece in his hand. "This hawk is very nice; it's a Fillipo, isn't it?"

"You are familiar with our Assisi artists. Now I am very confused. You have a Roman accent so you cannot be from here." She looked over her shoulder. "Excuse me a moment, these people appear to have made a decision." She hurried back to the counter, wrapped their item, and put it in a small paper bag marked with the name of the store. When the credit card transaction was complete, she thanked them and came back to Rick.

"What I'm looking for is a gift for a friend," he said. "But not sculpture. I noticed that you had a few earrings."

"Of course, come to the counter." She took her place behind, opened the glass, and pulled a row of earrings from the shelf below. "Something large and dangly? Something small?"

"Small, so that she can wear them to work but also evenings. She wears her hair very short." He pointed. "Perhaps those."

As he tried to make a decision, the woman helped by pulling back her hair and holding them next to her empty earlobe. He eventually decided on tiny loops from which hung a drop of gold. As she was wrapping them in cotton and placing them in a tiny box, Rick noticed something else under the glass. "Those boxes are interesting."

She reached again and took out two miniature ceramic boxes of similarly bright floral design, one slightly larger than the other. "These are by an artist based in Tuscany." She turned over one of the boxes where the name Innocenti was written in script.

"I think you've made another sale; that is my friend's name. Those earrings should fit nicely in that smaller one."

The woman smiled. "She must be a very special friend."

In front of the shop, Rick held the small bag and tried to decide whether to go back by the same route or continue up the hill before dropping back to the hotel on another street. He opted for the latter and set out again in the direction of the former Roman forum. The late afternoon pedestrian traffic had increased, including even those who could be taken for locals. They strode resolutely, talking on their phones and keeping eyes straight ahead. Religious professionals dressed in black, sometimes in pairs, mixed in with the others.

He came to where the street was joined by another, two small tributaries forming a larger river of people. Where the streets intersected sat a triangular corner patio into which five umbrella-shaded tables were squeezed. At one table sat Adelaide Chaffee and Arnoldo Fillipo, each with a glass of white wine. Adelaide had changed from her somber outfit into Santa Fe regalia, including a broomstick skirt and a silver bracelet. Her gray hair was done into a bun with a silver and turquoise clip. The sculptor had cleaned himself up since meeting Rick and the inspector that morning. His hands were clean, and the lack of clay revealed perfectly manicured fingernails. A linen shirt was open one button too many, and he wore no socks with his loafers. Mr. Casual. Adelaide spotted Rick and waved him over. Her wide smile contrasted with the suspicious look on the face of her table companion.

"Rick, won't you join us? I'd like you to meet Arnoldo, a talented local sculptor."

"We have met already," said Fillipo with only a slight accent tacked on his English.

"It is a pleasure to see you again, Signor Fillipo. I was just admiring one of your pieces in a store just down the street from here."

"From the size of your sack, I am guessing you did not buy it."

"You would guess correctly." He turned to Adelaide. "I didn't realize you knew Signor Fillipo."

"We finally managed to make the connection. Won't you have a glass with us, Rick?"

"Thank you, but I really must get back to the hotel." He

detected a look of relief on the sculptor's face. "And I'm sure you have business to discuss."

"We certainly do," she answered, patting Fillipo's hand and giving Rick a wink. "I'll see you at dinner."

Rick made the near U-turn and started down the hill in the direction of the hotel, considering what he'd just seen. It would make sense that Adelaide knew Arnoldo Fillipo, or at least knew of him, because Biraldo had shown her pictures of his work before she agreed to buy them for her gallery. And she had to have known that he worked in Assisi. But telling Rick that she'd "finally made the connection" was a bit odd, unless Biraldo had purposely kept the information from her. Why would he do that?

The chance encounter with Adelaide and Fillipo raised questions without any answers in return. He was going nowhere. His cell phone ring snapped him out of his thoughts. It was the call he'd been expecting.

"Yes, Inspector."

"Riccardo, where are you? I sent Rossi to the hotel, and they said you had gone out. Didn't you get a call from your uncle?"

He ducked into a doorway away from the ears of other pedestrians. "I did, which is why I went out. After all, it was my last chance to enjoy the city without being tailed by a flatfoot." He threw in the last word in English, to see if she got it. Apparently she did. "And why Rossi? Isn't it a bit of overkill to put a detective on a job that could be handled by a regular cop?"

"Do I need remind you that you are the nephew of a very high-level policeman?"

He laughed. "Of course. Why didn't I think of that? So Rossi will be my alter ego until I leave Assisi."

"At which point you'll have a police escort all the way back to Rome. You'll have to drive the speed limit."

"I always do."

"But I'm giving Rossi the night off, and you'll have another bodyguard."

"At least a sergeant, I would hope."

"Even better than that. An inspector. You and I need to review the case, and we can do it over dinner. I'll be at the hotel at eight."

She ended the call and he slipped the *telefonino* back in his pocket. He tried to convince himself that it would be good to talk about the case with Berti, and why not do it over dinner? They both had to eat, didn't they? And he had things to share with her, like running into Fillipo with Adelaide, and what Adelaide had said about Chris Carson at lunch. So it would definitely be just police business. He remembered the bag in his hand and thought how much Betta was going to enjoy her gifts.

A few minutes later, walking through the gate of the hotel parking lot, Rick noticed someone crouching next to his uncle's car, peering at the undercarriage. When the man heard Rick's footsteps on the gravel, he got up and brushed off his pants.

"Detective Rossi, are you thinking of buying a Spider?"

"It would be my dream, Signor Montoya, but on a simple policeman's salary, not likely. No, I was checking your vehicle. I trust that Inspector has told you that it will be my pleasure to keep an eye on you while you are here."

"She did. But I don't plan on going anywhere until dinner, and I'll be safe inside the hotel until then. If you'd like, you—"

"I would, Signor Montoya." He looked at his watch and started toward the gate. After two steps he stopped and turned around. "Be sure to stay in your room. I will see you tomorrow, though you may not see me." He smiled and walked away.

As Rick bounded up the hotel steps, he noticed a silver Ferrari parked next to his uncle's Alfa. This was a nice hotel, but anyone who could afford that car should be staying in one with more stars. Walking to the reception desk, he heard his name called and turned to see Aunt Filomena. She wore a flowing dress and silver-strapped sandals, and was sitting next to a man of indeterminate age, but much more in her range than Rick's. The man wore brown linen slacks, a print shirt open at the collar, and loafers with beige socks. A few tufts of gray hair above the ears graced an otherwise bald and very tan head. Rick walked to his aunt and bent to kiss her on both cheeks.

"What a nice surprise, Zia."

"I hoped it would be," she replied. "Riccardo, I'd like you to meet my friend Eduardo dei Paschi. I managed to drag him away for work, and we thought we'd zip down to Assisi and invite you to dinner."

Rick extended a greeting and shook hands with Signor dei Paschi—who immediately insisted he be called Eduardo—before taking a seat next to his aunt. "I would have loved to have dined with you this evening, but unfortunately I have a dinner engagement I just can't break." He neglected to mention that it was with a police inspector.

"Then you will at least have a drink with us. Filomena has told me so many good things about her nephew that I must insist on spending a few minutes with him." Decades of smiles had worn wrinkles in just the right places on Eduardo's face, making it obvious to Rick why his aunt enjoyed the man's company. Being driven around in a Ferrari likely added to the fun. "Does this hotel have a terrace bar, Riccardo? If we're going to have a drink in Assisi, we have to have a view."

"It's a very nice bar, but no view."

"In that case, there is a hotel around the corner that does." He stood up. "Shall we take a short stroll, Filomena? I need it after being cramped in that car."

Rick was relieved that Rossi had decided to leave him alone. It would have been awkward if they had noticed they were being followed by a policeman.

The other hotel was not far, and as they walked, Rick was peppered with questions about living in Rome and his translating and interpreting business. From the way the man listened, Rick was sure Eduardo was sincerely interested in the answers. When they entered the hotel, dei Paschi was set upon by the man behind the counter who rushed out to shake their hands. Introductions were made.

"Eduardo, you didn't tell me you were coming. I am mortified that I have no free rooms, but we will work something out."

"No, no, Rino. Filomena and I have driven down just for the evening, to have dinner with Riccardo. But I wanted to show him the wonderful view from your terrace. Is there a table free?"

"Do you really need to ask?"

The view lived up to Eduardo's billing. It was the same as from Rick's hotel room, though at a slightly different angle, and the sun was still high enough to need the shade of the large umbrella over their table. After ordering drinks, the three sat in silence admiring the Umbrian countryside. It was Rick's turn to ask Eduardo about his work.

"I've mostly pulled back from the daily operations of the bank." The comment elicited a light cough from Filomena. "Yes, my dear, I know you don't think I've pulled back enough, but one cannot suddenly walk away after so many years. It wouldn't be healthy for me, and it certainly would not be good for the bank."

Eduardo had ordered a bottle of Colli Perugini Bianco, and it arrived in an ice bucket with three glasses and a plate of pâtè crostini. When the glasses were filled, he raised his and toasted the soon-to-arrive sunset. "It is the most precious part of the day," he said after they took tastes. "And the view is essentially the same as that witnessed by Saint Francis." He studied the straw-colored liquid. "Francis may well have had this wine before he rejected worldly things."

"In the category of worldly things," said Filomena, "I saw on the news that there was a murder involving someone connected to an American tour group. Would that have been your group, Riccardo?"

"I'm afraid so."

"An American was killed?" Eduardo asked.

"No," Rick answered. "An Italian from Perugia, named Biraldo."

His eyebrows crimped in thought. "Biraldo. I think I met a man by that name, Filomena. A friend of Cesare Gallo. I might even have met him during a party at Cesare's."

"He was the man you were asked to fill in for, wasn't he, Riccardo? The interpreter?"

"That's right, Zia. And my first interpreting duties turned out to be for the inspector in the interviews with the Americans in the group."

"Do the police think one of the Americans killed the man?"

"I had the sense during the interviews that the police inspector was going through the motions with the Americans. Of course they're also talking with Italians who knew Biraldo."

Eduardo tapped a finger to his lips, indicating he was trying to remember. "I only met him that once. He made an impression, but not a positive one. If I remember right, Cesare Gallo knew him from childhood, which would explain why he was there that night, since Cesare calculates everything based on how it can benefit him, including his guest lists."

"Everyone does that, Eduardo."

"Not like Cesare, Filomena. He also carries a grudge like no one I've ever encountered in business. I recall once when one of his managers was thinking of taking a job with another chocolate company. He found out, fired him on the spot, and made sure no one in Perugia hired him. Most people would have realized the man's worth and offered him a raise to stay, but that's not the way Cesare operates."

Filomena patted Eduardo's hand. "We're not here to talk about such things as vengeance and murder. Let's let Riccardo tell us more about his lady friend. Her name is Betta, and she works at the culture ministry." She smiled at Rick. "That sounds so fascinating, Riccardo. She must meet some very interesting people."

———

The address the pastel thief had given Galilei was in a part of Pisa that had never been seen by the tourists, nor by most locals. A spur of track ran parallel to the street, its aging wood ties obscured by weeds and broken bottles. Had any American tourists wandered here by accident, they would have realized immediately that they were on the wrong side of the tracks, though the other side didn't look much better. On the opposite side of the street, the walls of a line of warehouses served as the canvases for local graffiti artists. Rusted bars covered the windows, but not enough to have kept most of the panes intact. Shadows were beginning to creep over the broken pavement, but of the four streetlights along this stretch, only one had blinked on. Betta and Signor Galilei stood surveying the scene while Elio was taking care of the taxi.

"I'm glad you brought this policeman along," Galilei whispered to Betta. "He looks like he can handle anything."

"We're in good hands," said Betta.

Elio strode up to them, returning his wallet to his jeans. "The taxi driver didn't want to wait."

"I can't imagine why not," said Betta. "All right. The building should be that one." She pointed to a warehouse whose address number was faded and barely visible. Outside the door a vintage motor scooter was parked. "He seems to have arrived, and like he promised, alone. As we discussed, Signor Galilei, you will stay outside until we call you in. I probably shouldn't have brought you along, but since you've been instrumental in setting this up, you have earned it."

The old man beamed. "I'll be in that alley."

"Don't talk to strangers," said Betta. "Let's go, Elio."

After they were out of Galilei's hearing, Elio said: "Don't you think you should have brought a real policeman along? You said you have a local contact."

"The guy would be worthless, and if this is all a hoax, I wouldn't want my boss to get word of it. If it's real, I'll call a police car to get us all." She patted his arm. "We'll be fine. Dear."

"Oh that's right, we're married. Do I look like a good husband?"

"You're fine, Elio. I hope our thief doesn't notice that neither of us is wearing a ring." They were close to the doorway. "Remember that besides providing the muscle if needed, I want you to confirm the authenticity of the pastel."

"Not to worry. Dear." He pushed the metal door and it swung open, banging against the inside wall. "Hello?"

"I'm in here."

The voice sounded very much like that of the man they'd left outside, surprising Betta. In her mind she had created an image of a cat burglar, like in the movies, dressed in a black turtleneck sweater and wearing fingerprint-avoiding gloves. She should have known that suave cat burglars don't drive old motorbikes. What she and Elio found instead, when they followed the sound of the voice, was an old guy in overalls and work shirt, sitting at a wooden table. Not even any gloves. His white hair flew out at all angles, and he squinted like he'd forgotten his glasses. The faint light of a single bulb hanging over the table picked up a gleam of perspiration on his high forehead. Something wrapped in brown paper sat on the table in front of him. He waved a calloused hand at two chairs.

"I didn't want to have more than one of you," he said, his voice almost cracking.

"We always make our major decisions together," answered Betta.

Elio nodded in agreement. "Can we see it now?"

It took a moment for the man to understand. "Oh, of course." He carefully tore the tape from the corners of the package, unwrapped its contents, and placed it in front of them. Elio picked up the frame and moved it to catch as much of the weak light as he could. He studied it for a full two minutes before giving Betta a nod.

"That's it. Just as bad as I remember."

Betta sighed. "Well, let's get this over with so we can have dinner." She reached into her bag and pulled out a leather case.

"You have the money now?"

"Not exactly, Signor…what is your name?"

"I'd rather we didn't use names."

Betta pulled a laminated card from the case. "You'll have to give your name eventually." She showed him the card. "I'm with the art fraud police."

The man looked like he had been punched in the stomach. "Police? I don't understand."

"You stole a valuable work of art. I caught you. It's not that complicated." She pulled out a notepad and pen as Elio got up and started toward the door. "Now, give me your identity card so I can copy down the information." He did as asked and she began writing. "Nando Toricella from Pisa. I was hoping for an international criminal to boost my resume."

"You must listen to me. This is not what it seems."

She kept on writing. "What am I missing?"

Elio and Signor Galilei appeared out of the darkness and walked toward the table.

Galilei stopped suddenly. "Nando! You?"

"Massimo, you weren't supposed to be here."

Betta waved a hand. "Wait, wait. You two know each other?"

The art dealer ignored her question. "Nando, how could you? Stealing from your own church? What will Father Oresti say?"

"He wouldn't have known anything if you hadn't gone to the cops."

"What would you expect? I'm an honest art dealer."

The two old men stood facing each other while Betta and Elio sat like spectators at a tennis match.

"Massimo, it was our only chance to get the roof fixed. Our campaign had raised only a hundred euros. Now you've blown it."

"You did this for the roof fund?"

"Of course. Do you think I'm a common criminal?" He waved a hand over the pastel. "And you have to agree that nobody in the parish would have missed it."

"No one but Father Oresti."

"Oresti can't fix the roof."

Betta finally intervened. "Signori, we're getting nowhere." She closed her notepad and put away the pen. "Signor Toricella, we know where to find you, and I don't expect you to flee the country, so I won't call a police car to take you away. You can go."

"That's all?" He got to his feet slowly, like his back hurt.

"For now."

They watched as Nando shuffled slowly out of the room after giving Galilei a final scowl. A moment later the muffled rattle of the motorbike engine seeped through the walls and then disappeared slowly. Nobody said anything for several minutes until Galilei broke the silence.

"I should have just sold it to that buyer in Zurich."

Another extended period of silence followed, but this time it was Betta who spoke.

"I think I see a way out of this. But I'll need help from both of you."

CHAPTER TEN

The police car had turned down the hill from the hotel rather than up toward Assisi itself. Gathering speed, it dropped quickly to the flat plain below the city, taking the route that Rick and Zeke had used that morning on their run.

"I know police like to drive fast, Chiara, but isn't this a bit too much?"

"We can't be too careful when guarding the nephew of a high-level policeman."

Rick switched into English. "Enough with the nephew stuff. And you know very well that around here nobody could follow us without it being obvious." He turned and looked out the back window. "The only ones behind us are other drivers cursing at your car under their breath. I should have stayed at the hotel and had a quiet dinner with the group, rather than risking death in a car accident."

"I'll get you back to your hotel in one piece. Don't forget that we have to discuss the investigation. This is a business dinner."

He would not have guessed that from the way she was dressed. Unlike the previous evening, she had changed out of her work clothes, fixed her hair, and added more eye makeup than he'd seen before. As she spoke, an invisible cloud of perfume hit his senses, and he was sure it was different from what she was wearing the night before. Tonight she had given herself a very liberal dose, but he couldn't place it. Either it was something very new or he was losing his touch.

The car slowed slightly as it went through Santa Maria degli Angeli, but sped up again after getting on Highway 75. There was little traffic, but what there was their driver passed easily, flashing his high beams to force cars into the right lane before roaring past them.

"Where are we going?"

"A nice little restaurant in Spello, about ten minutes away. This time I actually did reserve a table. Have you been to Spello?"

"I don't think so."

"An interesting town. Roman, like Assisi, but somewhat smaller. It managed to preserve more of its Roman heritage, like city gates and an amphitheater, though the general atmosphere is definitely medieval. Its most famous attraction is a chapel in one of its churches decorated by Pinturicchio. We could drive by, but it won't be open at this hour."

"I didn't realize you were a lover of fine art, Inspector Berti."

"How could one not be? Art is all around us, Signor Montoya."

The Spello exit was upon them, and the driver reluctantly slowed as the car descended the ramp, then rolled through a stop sign to go under the highway toward the town. Twilight was beginning to paint shadows between buildings that started to appear on both sides of the road, and a few streetlights had flickered on. The buildings of Spello, arranged along the lower spine of Monte Subasio, were visible until their lines were blocked by the city wall. After some sharp turns, the car passed a stone tower and entered the old city through an arched opening in the wall. Either in deference to the signs indicating the start of a pedestrian zone, or because the street became steep and narrow, the car was reduced to a steady crawl. Evening strollers moved aside to let it through, some only after the driver tapped on his horn. Rick decided that Berti was correct; Spello inside its walls had a definite medieval feel, perhaps more so than Assisi. It also was also not crowded with tourists, if he accurately read the clothing and faces of the people they passed. Some carried cloth grocery bags; others had the air of enjoying a stroll.

The car took a sharp bend, then climbed what turned out to be a final incline and rolled up in front of a low stone building. Across the street, at what had to be the highest point of the town, benches lined the edge of a large patch of grass. It was what Italians call a *belvedere*, offering a panoramic view of the countryside below. While children played on the grass behind them, their parents chatted and watched the evening roll in over the valley. Rick and the inspector stepped to the pavement, while the driver stood next to the car eyeing everyone in the vicinity. The bulge in his jacket was all too visible, at least to Rick.

"I will be much more relaxed at dinner knowing he's out here," said Rick as they walked to the restaurant door. He added, with a smile: "Naturally, I would feel even safer if you were packing as well."

"But I am armed, Riccardo."

He opened the door and glanced at her tight-fitting slacks and clinging silk blouse. "Chiara, you have taken the art of concealed carry to a new level."

The door closed behind them; they strode toward the entrance.

"Riccardo, your uncle did not suggest it, but you might want to consider wearing a vest. I have one in the trunk, and it's very lightweight."

He stopped and held up his hands. "Please, Chiara. My police escort will be more than enough to keep me safe. I have complete confidence in Rossi."

She shrugged.

Inside, they were taken through the main dining room and out to a terrace where tables were set up under umbrellas strung with tiny lights. Their table was next to the railing, giving them an unobstructed view of the valley, where shadows were bringing the night into the dips and hollows. Rick surveyed the scene and wondered where Betta was having dinner, and with whom. No doubt her friend Elio, but they wouldn't have a view like this. Menus appeared in front of them, along with a basket of bread and a bottle of mineral water, and he turned to his dinner companion.

"What's good here, Inspector?"

She picked up her menu. "They have an excellent chef, so everything is good. The roast pigeon is one of his specialties."

"That sounds perfect for a *secondo*." After the ample lunch he wasn't very hungry, but it would be bad manners to say so. He began looking over the list of pasta dishes and was surprised to feel a tinge of hunger. Perhaps he could be sociable after all and order two courses. He settled on *minestra di farro*. Chiara decided against pasta and ordered an *antipasto, cuori di carciofi*. Artichoke hearts? It didn't sound like anything special to Rick, and he was glad he'd ordered the soup. They both chose the pigeon for the second course, and she ordered the house red. It was from a vineyard between Spello and Montefalco, possibly one of the lights that now twinkled far below the restaurant terrace. The wine arrived in a glass carafe and was poured by the waiter.

Chiara looked around to see how close they were to the other diners before raising her glass. "Here's to solving this murder."

Sitting in such a setting with an attractive woman, he was not expecting her to propose that kind of toast. Just what was he expecting? "I'll drink to that," he said.

After they both took a taste, she settled into her chair. "I interviewed Fillipo and Rucola again this afternoon. They stuck to their stories. Fillipo wouldn't tell me how much Biraldo owed him for the works sent to the States, and Rucola wouldn't tell me how much he owed Biraldo from that loan he got. I thought if the two amounts were similar, it could mean something, though for the life of me I couldn't say what. I'm starting to...what's the phrase?"

"You're grasping at straws?"

"That's it. I really need more opportunities to practice my English. Anyway, Rucola again said I should be looking at Biraldo's female conquests, and their husbands or boyfriends. He said the guy was shameless in his attempts at female conquest, most of them successful. He might have a point, but right now the only one we know about is the lovely Letizia Gallo, and her husband doesn't seem bothered in the least by her extramarital activities."

"Which reminds me, I heard something about Cesare Gallo." He told her about meeting Aunt Filomena and her friend for a drink, and recounted what he'd heard from dei Paschi about Gallo.

Chiara peered at the wine in her glass. "Interesting. It tells us something about Gallo's personality but unfortunately doesn't allow me to put handcuffs on the man."

The first courses arrived at the table. They wished each other *buon appetito* and the conversation inevitably turned to food. Chiara's artichoke hearts turned out to be grilled in the oven after being topped with chopped prosciutto and cheese, which she said was one of the specialties of the chef. Rick was somewhat chagrined that he hadn't ordered it as well, but he was not bold enough to ask for a bite. Discussion moved on to his soup, and she surprised him by launching into a mini-lecture on cooking traditions. Its main ingredient was spelt, a grain cultivated widely in ancient times and a staple for the Roman legions. With the popularity of wheat, it fell out of style for centuries, but now was appearing on menus thanks to cooks who were interested in local culinary history. But the farro really needed the right mixture of herbs to overcome a naturally bland taste. Rick was impressed with her knowledge and decided he was glad he'd ordered the soup after all.

"What have you gotten from your Americans?" she asked, suddenly returning to the investigation.

He spooned the last of his *minestra* into his mouth and patted his lips with the napkin. "I don't have much to report except observations and conjecture volunteered to me by some of the people. Adelaide, the woman with the walking stick, thinks that Chris, our driver, has been acting suspiciously, and I must say he seemed very nervous when he drove me to meet you at the vineyard this morning. But he may just be a moody kid."

The waiter refreshed their wineglasses and cleared the empty dishes.

"What about the others?"

"I don't think I mentioned Peter Rael and the *converso* issue."

She frowned. "Whatever that is, the answer is no, you didn't."

Rick gave her a quick history of the *conversos* in New Mexico and how Peter Rael could have been angered that someone would doubt his Catholic faith. "If Biraldo found out and merely said something to Rael about it, that wouldn't seem to be enough of a motive. If Biraldo had threatened to expose the man, then we're into a possible blackmail scenario. From what we've heard about our murder victim, blackmail wouldn't surprise me."

"If Rael is such a pious man, he should have heard about the commandment not to kill. No, Riccardo, I just don't see that one. What else have you got?"

"I saw Adelaide with Fillipo this afternoon."

She raised a thumb. "Now that's something. What happened?"

"They were sitting outside at a bar, having a glass of wine, and I was walking by. It's not like they were being furtive about it; she even waved me over and asked me to join them, which I didn't. When you think about it, it would make sense that she would try to track down the artist whose work Biraldo was selling to her gallery. They were clearly talking business."

"Which means now there is no middleman to pay, so both can benefit more from sales." She stared at her wineglass. "But unless they sell a lot of sculpture, it's still pretty weak as a murder motive."

The aroma of the roasted pigeons, strong and flavorful, arrived before the dish itself. Each was arranged carefully on the plate, with the two small drumsticks leaned against the body. Next to the bird were slices of fennel that had been cooked in the same roasting pan. Drippings had been drizzled over everything, with sprigs of rosemary completing the plate. It was not, by any measurement, a large portion of food, which was fine with Rick.

"I'm glad we're having this dish here in Spello. Every statue I've seen of Saint Francis has him surrounded by birds about this size, so I'd feel uncomfortable eating a pigeon in Assisi."

"He's the patron saint of all animals," she said. "You'd have to go on a vegetarian diet."

They took bites and marveled at the flavor of the meat, especially when combined with a bit of the crisp skin. They made a point of eating slowly, given the naturally small portions. Soon only bones were left on her plate, and Chiara pushed it away before taking a long drink of the wine.

"We're nowhere on this case, Riccardo, and we're almost into our third day. Nothing at the crime scene implicated any of our suspects, including your Americans. Not a footprint, not a fingerprint, nothing. What are we missing? Maybe there was someone in Biraldo's past who reappeared, someone who is not on our radar at all but had a serious grudge against him. Tomorrow I'll dig more into his past to find earlier acquaintances and see what might turn up. Somebody met him up there and hit him with something hard enough to send him over the railing to his death. If it wasn't any of your religious group, or the Italians we've interviewed so far, it has to be someone else. It wasn't a suicide."

"Something will turn up." It was a feeble comment, but the best he could muster.

She shook her head. "Dessert?"

"After all that meat? I'm stuffed."

"Don't say that around anyone from Australia, like I did once. Apparently it has another meaning down under."

"I will tuck that bit of knowledge away into my translator's memory. It could come in very handy someday. How about a coffee?"

"Yes, perfect."

Rick signaled the waiter just as a tall man wearing a long white apron and a shirt with rolled-up sleeves appeared on the terrace. The stylish stubble on his face framed a smile with a perfect set of teeth, and his long black hair was combed back over his ears. He chatted with people at two other tables before approaching theirs, coming up behind Chiara.

"*Ciao, bella.*"

Her face lit up and she turned to accept kisses on both cheeks. "Riccardo, this is Gianni, the chef of this wonderful restaurant."

They shook hands. "I hope you enjoyed your meal. I understand you had the *minestra di farro.*"

"It was excellent, and Chiara gave me a lesson on grain."

"She is very good at giving lessons."

"Riccardo has been assisting me on a case, Gianni, but we have hit a dead end."

"I'm sure you'll work it out. If you'll excuse me, I must get back to the kitchen." He bent down and repeated the double kiss. "It was a pleasure to meet you, Riccardo."

She turned to watch him walk toward the door. The coffee arrived and they downed it quickly.

"This has been a wonderful dinner, Chiara. I'm sorry we weren't able to discover the murderer over the pigeon, but we'll hope for a breakthrough tomorrow."

Her face again took on the look of a police inspector on a case. "That would be helpful."

"And thank you for guarding me this evening."

"It was my duty, you being the nephew of a prominent police commissioner. But Sergeant Capanga will take over now and get you back to your hotel." She noticed the puzzled look on his face and added: "I'm going to stay here and have a grappa with Gianni. I'm sure you won't mind, Riccardo. After all, I haven't seen my fiancé in four days."

———

Ten minutes later, as Sergeant Capanga pulled onto the highway and shifted into fifth gear, Rick was still smiling. It all made sense now: the heavy perfume, the makeup, the sexy outfit, even the insider knowledge about ancient grains. Not to mention the emphasis on discussion of the case over their meal. Well, good for Chiara. She needed someone, just like everyone does, and who better than a good-looking guy who knows how to cook? They both work terrible hours, so that should not be an issue. No, it was a match made in heaven, and Umbria was closer to heaven than most places in the world. He watched the shadows shoot past the car window and settled back into the seat. True, his ego was bruised, but only slightly, and that was nothing new.

The policeman left the car parked directly in front of the hotel and began surveying the building's perimeter in preparation for his night shift. When Rick wished him a good evening, he didn't mention the morning run. Judging by the girth of Sergeant Capanga, he had difficulty picturing the man jogging behind him and Zeke. Since Rick didn't relish the idea of being followed by a police car, he thought it might be better if he slept in the next day and let Zeke jog alone.

The lobby was silent and empty when Rick walked through the door and picked up his key from the night shift clerk. As he waited for the elevator, the sound of glasses being washed in a sink came from the bar. Minutes later, when he turned on the lights of his room, he saw that his bed had been turned down and the shirt he'd left on it had been folded and placed on the dresser. This was a quietly classy hotel. He pulled out his phone and called Betta.

"*Ciao*, Rick. I was just going to call you."

He sat down on the bed. "How did your encounter with the art thief go?"

"Not like we expected." She told him about the meeting in the abandoned warehouse, the surprise art thief, and the man's noble intentions.

"Things are never simple, Betta. Sometimes the bad guys turn out to be not so bad."

"I suppose you're right. But what about you? Anything new on your investigation?"

"I'm afraid not. Inspector Berti and I went over it all over dinner and couldn't come up with anything promising. She thinks we're at a dead end."

"She? You didn't tell me she was a she."

"Didn't I? Probably because it wasn't important."

"Or you were feeling guilty. What's she like? Young and attractive, I suppose."

"Not that young; she's an inspector, after all. But I suppose she could be described as attractive." He was trying to decide how long to string it out.

"You're going to tell me that you only talked about the investigation over dinner?"

"Pretty much. Well, except for the food. We had to talk about what we were eating."

"And why is that, Signor Montoya?"

"She's engaged to the chef, and he came out from the kitchen when we were almost finished. Very nice guy, and good-looking, too. He didn't seem at all upset that his fiancée was having a working dinner with some American from Rome." He put an emphasis on the word *working*.

"You're a good cook too, Rick. I'm sure he has nothing on you."

"I don't know about that. His spelt soup was pretty tasty."

After the call ended, Rick realized he hadn't mentioned that he now had a bodyguard. Just as well. He had barely pulled off his boots when someone knocked softly on the door. He glanced at the clock next to his bed and padded over to see who could be there at this late hour. His hand reached for the door but stopped just inches from the knob when he remembered his earlier conversation with his uncle. He peeked through the spy hole and recognized the person standing on the other side. It was most definitely not a Mafia hit man, and he eased it open.

"Couldn't sleep, Vicki?"

She was dressed in sneakers, jeans, and a baggy sweatshirt,

with her hair brushed back. The casual outfit, as well as the perfume, pulled him years into the past.

"I need to talk to you, Rick."

"Of course, but not here. Why don't I buy you a nightcap in the bar downstairs?"

It was not the welcome she was expecting. "You don't have a minibar in your room?"

"I'll be down in five minutes, Vicki."

"Yeah, you're right. I'll see you there."

She turned and disappeared down the hall. Rick closed the door, leaned back against it, and took a deep breath. Maybe she really did just need to talk. And maybe she had something else in mind, and because of that, when he got to the bar, she wouldn't be there. He walked to the bed and pulled his boots back on.

Vicki was sitting in the bar when he walked in a few minutes later. She was at a table in a corner and gave him a sheepish grin, causing Rick the translator to wonder about the phrase. Do sheep really grin? He would try to remember to look up the etymology of the phrase.

"Red wine, Vicki?"

"Please. The one you brought me the last time was very good."

The bartender awaited him from his place behind the long counter. Rick ordered a red for her and pointed to one of the bottles on the shelf for himself. He waited while the man did the pours, and walked back to the table with a large glass in one hand and a very small one in the other.

"What's that?" she asked, pointing at his drink.

"It's what they call a *digestivo*, which as the name indicates helps you digest your meal, and I had a large meal."

They tapped glasses. Religious pilgrims—at least not those staying in this hotel—apparently did not stay up late drinking, so the clink of the glass was the only sound in the otherwise empty room. With no more glasses or cups to be washed, the barman had gone back to reading a magazine.

"I had a big meal too. That's all we seem to do on this trip is eat. Not that the food isn't good. By the way, you said you were going to have dinner with the group."

"Something came up. Sorry. I wasn't avoiding you."

"I didn't say you were."

This was not going well, and he sensed it could get worse. "Vicki, you said upstairs you needed to talk, so let's talk. Like the two old friends we are."

She blinked, which he knew from experience often preceded tears. Instead she took a long drink of the wine. "Rick, this murder has me on edge. I've never been involved in anything like this before, and the fact that they could suspect my husband. Well, it's just…"

So she really did need to talk. "I understand. But the inspector has to suspect everyone; that's how the police work. As the investigation progresses, she'll cross people off the list"

"Has she crossed Leon off the list?"

He took a drink from his glass to give him time to decide on an answer. "She hasn't told me one way or the other about any of you, but I know she was initially skeptical that the murderer could come from a religious group."

"A religious group. That's a laugh."

"Meaning?"

"You'd expect rich people like those in our group to have big closets at home. But some of their closets are filled with skeletons."

Was the wine having its usual effect on Vicki? Rick suspected that she was referring to the *converso* controversy with Peter Rael, since it was her husband who had prodded the man about it. At least according to Lillian Rael, he had.

"Vicki, everyone, but especially wealthy people, have something in their past that they may not be proud of. What kind of skeletons have you heard about?"

"I'm not a gossip. But I'll mention just one person, and that's Lillian Rael."

"Lillian?" Except perhaps for Jessica Chaffee, Lillian's was the last name he expected to hear.

"Yes, Lillian, the perfect wife. She drinks too much, of course, but that's not her skeleton. It has to do with her first husband, who years ago died a very mysterious death just after they were married. Not many people know that, but Leon does, and he told me. It was a hiking accident, and poor Lillian was distraught. So, so distraught. Fortunately for her, Peter Rael, a family friend, comforted her, and the rest is history. Did I mention that her first husband was extremely wealthy and she inherited it all? Did I also mention that it was her fortune that launched Peter Rael's business? Is that enough of a skeleton for you, Rick?"

"More than enough." He tried to think what, if anything, this tale could have to do with Biraldo's murder, and all he could come up with was a convoluted blackmail scenario. Instead he decided that Vicki, contrary to her disclaimer, was just gossiping. "Why don't we talk about you, Vicki? Apart from this investigation, I hope you are taking advantage of the trip. I remember I used to bore you talking about Italy. Is the real thing better than my descriptions?"

"You never bored me, Rick. I like it here. But I'm getting a little sick of churches. That's all we seem to visit, one after another." She drained her glass and glanced toward the bar. Rick signaled the waiter for another.

"That's the way I used to feel when I was a kid; they all started looking the same after a while. Now they don't, and

I'm glad my parents dragged me through them. But didn't you expect churches on this trip? It was organized by the archdiocese, after all."

She thanked the waiter, who had brought a new glass and taken her empty. "Yes, I guess you're right. And Zeke is so good at making it all very meaningful. He's a real dear."

"That would not have been the way those who played football against him would have described Zeke, but I agree with you."

She stared at her glass, and again, he remembered that it meant she was getting ready to say something important.

"I didn't want to talk to you to gossip or talk about churches, Rick. There was something else, and you're the only one who can help me."

He braced himself with another drink, wishing he had ordered something stronger. "What is it, Vicki?"

"Well, you remember that I used to sell perfume."

He tried not to show surprise. "How could I not?"

"Well, I recall that you got quite good at identifying scents when you were waiting for me to get off work. I was very impressed. I need your help now."

"I don't understand."

"Don't you get it? I'm here in Italy, Rick, and I don't know what perfume to buy."

"That's it?"

"Isn't that enough? You do know something about Italian perfumes, don't you?"

"I suppose you could say that."

She leaned forward. "Well, let's have it."

He gathered his thoughts. "Obviously Italian women use a lot of French perfume, but there are two big perfume makers in Italy. One is Acqua di Parma, which of course comes from Parma, or at least it did originally. My favorite scent by them is Peonia Nobile, which as the name—the noble peony—indicates, has a strong floral scent. You might like that one."

"I knew you would help me, Rick. Go on."

"The other one you should certainly try is Acqua di Santa Maria Novella, by a company of the same name in Florence. They make numerous scents, but that is perhaps their most famous, and certainly their oldest. It was created in the sixteenth century for Caterina di Medici before she went off to France to get married. That one is heavy on the citrus."

"What about the ones made by the Italian fashion houses?" She had forgotten her wine.

"They're all made in France. If you want Italian, try those two brands. What you need to do is go into a perfume shop. I passed one yesterday when I was walking around Assisi. I'm sure the hotel can find a good one for you and point you in the right direction." Thinking she might ask him to go along, he added: "All these shops are used to the tourists and will speak English. Otherwise wait until you're back in Rome."

She reached across the small table and squeezed his hand. "Rick, you're a lifesaver. Could you write those two names down?"

"Of course. I'll leave it at the desk." He pointed to the clock on the wall. "Vicki, we could chat all night, but it's getting late."

"Leon won't miss me; he's snoring away like he does every night."

"But I need my sleep. I was up early." He signed the bill and they walked to the elevator. "You go on up, I need to check something at the reception desk."

She gave him a kiss on the cheek, and he was hit with her perfume. "Thanks for listening to me."

He walked to the desk after the elevator doors shut. "I need to leave a message for Padre Zeke with the American group. He'll be down very early in the morning." The clerk said he would still be on duty the next morning and would be sure the priest got the message. Rick took the paper and pen passed to him and wrote a short note saying that he would be passing on the morning run. Then he wrote the perfume names on another sheet and asked the clerk to put it in the box for Signor Alameda's room.

He walked to the door and looked outside at the police car, still parked in the same place. He could see the figure of Sergeant Capanga in the front seat, but it was too dark to tell if he was awake or asleep. He toyed with the idea of going out and pounding on the hood, but instead turned and walked to the elevator.

CHAPTER ELEVEN

Rick woke at his usual early hour and immediately regretted having to pass on the morning run. The regret only grew when he threw open the shutters to see the sun starting to spread weak light over the fields below the window. Fresh air wafting into the room added salt to the wound. He sighed and wondered if Zeke had taken the same route as the previous day or cut up through the stone streets of the town. After a shave and shower, he dressed for the day. According to the schedule, the morning activity was a visit to the Eremo delle Carceri, in the forested hills east of town where Saint Francis and his followers went for prayer and contemplation. When he got to the breakfast room, he was surprised to find Zeke sitting alone at one of the tables, tucking into eggs and bacon. Only a few other hotel guests were dining at the early hours, and since the caffeine had not yet kicked in, there was little conversation. Rick signaled to the waitress for coffee and hot milk and took a seat with his friend.

"You must have been up early, unless you too skipped your run, Padre."

"Good morning, Rick. No, I did my run, though perhaps a bit abbreviated from yesterday's. What happened to you?"

A silver pot of black coffee and another of hot milk arrived at the table. Rick thanked the waitress and poured equal amounts into his large cup. After adding sugar he took a long drink. "That's good. What happened to me? Well, I didn't think you'd want a police car following us, so I skipped the run." Without going into detail, he explained that he was temporarily being given a guard for something that had nothing to do with the events in Assisi.

"That's why the police car is parked in front of the hotel?"

"Correct." He got up out of the chair. "If you'll excuse me, I'm going to check out the buffet table before the rest of the group comes down and grabs all the best items." He returned a few minutes later with a roll, packets of butter and jelly, a yogurt, and an orange.

"How did your dinner go with the inspector? Case solved?"

"Not exactly." Rick broke the roll in two and started to apply butter and jelly. "She has made no breakthroughs with her Italian suspects, and she was hoping that I had something to report about the Americans. I gave her as much as I could, but it was thin gruel."

Zeke grinned. "Wait a minute; she really did want to have dinner to discuss the investigation?"

"Yes, that was the purpose. Well, she also wanted to introduce me to her fiancé, who is the chef at the restaurant."

Zeke roared with laughter.

"The night wasn't over, Padre. I know we are not in confessional, but I trust anything I tell you will be held in complete confidence?"

"You have my word." He placed his fork down on the empty plate. "Go on."

"Vicki came by my room when I got back to the hotel. She said she needed to talk."

"Oh, dear."

"Oh, dear indeed. You will be pleased to know that I insisted on meeting her in the hotel bar rather than inviting her into my room."

"I would expect nothing less from you, Rick."

"As it turned out, her interest in talking with me had to do with perfume."

"You just lost me."

Rick explained, and Zeke once again was consumed by laughter, but he quickly got himself under control. "Were you able to help her?"

"Of course."

"I'm glad to hear that. Your expertise in perfume is something that I must have missed during our friendship at UNM." He poured more coffee into his cup and drank it without adding milk or sugar. "After what you told me about your lady friend in Rome, I imagine you are relieved that you didn't have to fight these women off."

"Absolutely, Zeke. Very perceptive on your part."

The priest stirred his coffee, even though nothing had been added to need stirring. "Then why is this bothering you?"

"I'm not at all bothered."

Zeke chuckled a deep chuckle. "Come now, Rick. We are good friends; we know each other well. And now I'm a priest, so I see these things."

"I said I'm fine."

"Good. It's sounds crazy, but it had occurred to me that two women scorning you on the same night may not have been the best thing for your self-esteem. So I'm pleased to have been mistaken."

Rick smiled as he began to peel his orange. "Maybe my meeting up with an old friend in Assisi was a big mistake." He pulled off an orange section and offered it to Zeke, who popped it in his mouth.

"That's very good."

"Sicilian blood oranges, Zeke. They're the best."

"Have you spent much time there?"

"A bit. I don't get many calls to work in Sicily. What's on the agenda this morning for the group?" He finished the orange and started to spread jam on his roll.

"We're going to one of the most hallowed sites connected to the life of Francis, a spot in the hills outside of town where he and his followers would often go to pray and meditate."

"Of course, Eremo delle Carceri. My parents took me there during a visit to Assisi when I was in high school, and I remember it vividly. It was a cold day and got even colder when we hiked through the woods to get to it. *Rustic* is too benign a term to describe it. When I saw where Francis voluntarily spent so much time, despite the conditions, my view of the saint changed. He must have been one tough hombre."

"His strength came from the Lord."

They finished their breakfasts in pious silence. On the way out of the dining room, Rick tapped Zeke on the shoulder. "I'll see you on the bus. I need to say hello to someone." Zeke continued to the door while Rick walked to a corner table where a couple were in quiet conversation. The coffee had not yet done its work.

"*Buon giorno,* Zia, *buon giorno,* Eduardo."

Filomena looked up with a wide smile. "*Buon giorno,* Riccardo. You are certainly up early. We were just talking about you." She waved at one of the empty chairs at the table, and Rick sat down. "We had a lovely dinner, but it went quite late since Eduardo ran into an old friend. Your hotel had a room so we decided to stay over."

"We were greeted by a lovely view when we got up," said Eduardo. "We were trying to decide if the panorama of the valley is more striking in the afternoon, like we saw from the terrace, or the morning. The light is quite different. Another coffee, Riccardo?"

"Thank you, Eduardo; one was enough to hold me for the morning. Did you come to any conclusions on the view?"

"We decided the morning has an advantage," said Filomena. "Everything is fresh, and there is a certain natural optimism about the morning hours. Sunsets don't stand a chance against that kind of comparison."

It was a brief yet brilliant explanation of why Rick enjoyed his early morning runs, even through the dirty streets of Rome. He would have to remember to tell Betta—who enjoyed sleeping in when she could—what his aunt had said.

"Riccardo," said Eduardo, "I was thinking about something we talked about last evening."

"What was that?"

"You'll remember that I recalled meeting this man Biraldo, the murder victim, one evening at Cesare Gallo's apartment in Perugia. Last night during dinner, I remembered more about that evening. As Filomena will tell you, at the restaurant there was a young couple sitting near us who were having an argument. I don't know if the two were married, but it was clear that one of them thought that their relationship had some issues."

"We strained out ears, but couldn't really tell who was being the naughty one," said Filomena.

Eduardo chuckled. "Anyway, later it made me think again of that event at Cesare's apartment. It was a party with lots of people, and his wife, who I recall is named Letizia, had too much to drink. At a certain point Cesare pulled her aside, rather roughly as I recall, and talked with her. Everyone pretended not to notice, of course. I thought that would be the end of things, but later I heard Cesare's voice coming from the terrace. He has a penthouse, and the terrace is quite vast, with a great view of the city. I stood at the open doorway, admiring the blinking lights, and could see Cesare talking with Biraldo at the other end of the terrace. Perhaps talking at him would be a better way to describe it. He was jabbing his finger at the man's chest as he made whatever point he was trying to get across. Biraldo was passive, perhaps because he was a guest in Cesare's home and didn't want to make a scene. Of course it could have been that he deserved to be dressed down, whatever the issue was." He tapped his hand on the table. "That's all I recall; I must have become involved in another conversation at that point."

"Can we conclude," Rick asked, "that you think the altercation had something to do with Gallo's wife?"

"I thought so at the time, since Cesare's chat with his wife, if you can call it that, and his chat with Biraldo were not that far apart. But I could have been mistaken, and the first had nothing to do with the second."

"How long ago was it?" Filomena asked.

"Not more than a year ago. When I thought about it last night, I couldn't help but wonder if the police are talking to Cesare."

"It would seem logical that they would," said Rick, staying neutral. "When I see the inspector again, I'll mention your recollection of the party, if you don't mind."

"Please do. You never know what could be helpful." A look of concern spread over Eduardo's face. "Don't get the idea I think Cesare Gallo could be involved in the man's murder. I wouldn't want the police to think I'm accusing him of such a crime."

"I will say that to the inspector as well." Rick pushed back his chair. "I must get up to the room to check my email before the group heads out for the day. Aunt Filomena, I'm sorry that I got sidetracked on this; I was looking forward to spending some time with you."

"I understand, Riccardo. Perhaps you could stop in on your way back to Rome. We can have a glass of wine on my terrace, and you can tell me everything. Let's hope the murderer is found by then."

Rick stood, shook hands with Eduardo, and kissed his aunt's cheeks. "I hope so. Eduardo, it was my pleasure to meet you, and I hope to see you both again very soon."

Back up in his room, he thought about the two sides of his family. There were many more Montoyas, spread across New Mexico, but those few he knew on the Italian side were certainly an interesting group. He promised himself to seek out more on the Fontana side, and to spend more time with Filomena. Pondering about his family and reading the few emails that had landed in his in-box had temporarily taken his mind off the murder of Biraldo. Now, as he stared out the window of his room, he tried to sift through his thoughts. Nothing new came to mind, even the incident Eduardo had recounted didn't add much to the case. Cesare Gallo's jealousy, or lack of it, had already been hashed over with the inspector, without any firm conclusions. Perhaps Chiara would have something new to tell him the next time they talked.

For now, it was off to the forest primeval east of Assisi.

———

Rick turned around in his seat and saw that the unmarked police car was keeping a discreet distance between it and the van. He was tempted to wave at Detective Rossi, who was behind the wheel, but decided against it. Adelaide Chaffee, sitting next to Rick in the back row of the van, might find it strange. She was dressed for the great outdoors: brand new hiking shoes, a long-sleeved blouse, and a sweater tied around her waist. The skirt was the usual length, falling just below the knee, but the material was a blue denim, ready for walking through brush. After trudging through churches and along cobblestoned streets, dirt paths would be a welcome change for someone used to hiking the trails of northern New Mexico. She had leaned her walking stick against the window next to her and was studying the screen of her phone, not paying attention to Rick. Just as well, since his mind was still stuck on the investigation. The van left the walls of Assisi behind and headed east. Rick glanced at Adelaide, who was now scrolling images across the cell's screen with her finger.

"I didn't know you were taking photos, Adelaide. I thought you left that to your niece."

She took her eyes off the phone. "Oh, no, I don't use the phone for photos. These are all Jessica's." She noticed the look of incomprehension on his face. "Let me explain. When I agreed to bring Jessica on this trip, my only stipulation to my brother was that she leave her cell phone at home. Fortunately, he backed me up. It is something that drives me crazy about her generation; those phones are almost another appendage of their bodies. When I would have lunch with my brother and Jessica, she would be looking at it during most of the meal. Don't these children understand the value of human interaction? Lord knows what she was consulting it about or to whom she was sending messages. Not that she's any different from the others of her generation. When I go shopping, I see their eyes glued to the screen as they walk around like zombies a few steps behind their parents. I suppose it's just as much the parents' fault. I want to go over and shake them."

"But you restrain yourself."

"Barely."

"You were saying about Jessica's pictures?"

She picked up the phone, which had dropped to her lap. "Oh, yes. Sorry for the rant. I promised my brother we would send back pictures of the trip, so every day Jessica downloads photographs from her camera into my cell phone. Then I send them off to him. She's really very good, I have to say, and not just because she's my niece. Have you seen any of her pictures?"

Rick shook his head. "I've only watched her taking them."

Adelaide tapped on the screen with a finger that held a silver and turquoise ring. "I'm not very savvy with these things, but I think I just brought it back to the beginning of the roll. Of course it's not a roll, but you know what I mean." She passed the phone to Rick. "Just push it to the left with your finger—it's called scrolling." She passed him the phone.

He could see immediately that Adelaide was correct about her niece's skill with the camera. Even the group pictures were well done, showing the faces at just the right distance. There were many pictures of the group, many taken in airport waiting rooms, and they included Biraldo. It was the first time Rick had seen the man other than as a crumpled body, and he tried to read something from the man's features. What came across was someone with a high opinion of himself, a handsome, well-dressed Italian with a facial expression that fell somewhere between a smile and a smirk. It was understandable that Letizia Gallo would be attracted to that face.

Shots that would be considered more artistic appeared after the group had arrived in Rome. Jessica must have ventured out immediately with her camera and begun taking photographs of those small details that fascinate visitors to the city: ancient doors, metalwork, small fountains, sewer covers marked with the SPQR of the municipal government. Leaving the big city, panoramic views became a frequent subject, along with more shots of the group members. Some of the New Mexicans were obviously not happy with being photographed, possibly because the fatigue from the jet lag was catching up with them, and it showed. In one frame, both subjects were giving the camera an annoyed look. Distance shots and street details returned with the arrival in Assisi, and Rick recognized some quaint shops he had passed near the hotel. She had included some locals to add color, but they were oblivious to the camera. A number of photographs were devoted to the visit to Santa Maria degli Angeli, including those taken outside when Rick had talked with her about her equipment. He was in some of them, and in many more taken at the restaurant after he'd rejoined the group for lunch.

Adelaide had been looking at the screen as he scrolled. "She's quite proficient, don't you think, Rick?"

"Absolutely. She has an eye for capturing whatever the scene requires, whether it's a group shot or a more artistic subject."

When he said it, something clicked. He returned his finger to the screen and pushed the roll back until he found what he was looking for. He studied the photograph for a moment to be sure, then scrolled back to the beginning and passed the phone to Adelaide.

"Thanks for letting me see them," he said, trying to keep his voice normal. He put his hand around his own cell phone in his pocket, but decided to wait until the van stopped to make the call.

———

The final kilometers of winding road had weaved through dense forest made sinister by intervals of fog that floated out of the trees, engulfed the van, and moved on. Rays of morning sunshine tried to fight their way through branches overhanging the pavement, but the van, as well as the car behind it, kept their headlights on low beam. Chris slowed down the van and pulled into a parking area marked for the Eremo delle Carceri on the right side of the road. Five cars were parked together on the far side of the lot, and Rossi drove in past the van and parked next to them. Nearby was a sign with an arrow, indicating the route to the Eremo. Chris Carson pulled over at the opposite end from the cars, turned off the engine, and opened the door. Zeke, who was sitting next to him, stood and faced the group.

"I'm glad we brought our sweaters," he said. "It looks like it will be chilly."

Rick had not gotten the sweater memo, but his shirt was long-sleeved and of a thick material. He waited for everyone to disembark, including Adelaide, and then worked his way down the aisle to the door. He stepped onto the gravel and noticed the change in temperature; a good ten degrees cooler than in the sun outside the hotel. He looked around and saw Rossi leaning against his car trying to look like just another religious pilgrim, which was hard to do in a suit and tie covered by a raincoat. Nobody in the group appeared to notice the policeman; they were too busy talking about the chill or chatting excitedly about what they were about to see. The priest was starting to herd them toward the path when Rick pulled him aside.

"Zeke, I need to make a phone call, and I'm not sure of the signal once we get out of this clearing. I'll catch up with the group in a bit."

"Sure, Rick. I'm not sure if we'll need you to interpret anyway." Anxious to see the site of Francis's hermitage, he turned and started toward the trail with his New Mexicans in tow. Only Vicki noticed that Rick was hanging back, and after a puzzled look, she continued on with the group. In a moment they all were out of sight, and the parking area became silent.

Rick pulled out his phone, hit a number, and Inspector Berti answered on the third ring. He explained what he had seen, and she listened without comment until he was finished.

"You're right; there can be no other explanation. Stay with the group, Riccardo; I'll be there as soon as I can." The call ended.

Rick put the phone in his pocket and looked around the parking lot to be sure no one had been close enough to overhear what he'd said. He needn't have worried; no new vehicles had driven up, and the lot was still mostly empty. Even Detective Rossi had vanished. Perhaps the cop had decided to head up the path ahead of Rick, thinking one of the Americans could be a Mafia hit man. The thought brought a quick smile to Rick's face, but it went away when he returned to the matter at hand. He turned over in his mind the interviews of the last two days, trying to recall everyone's alibi, if they had one. Nothing contradicted what he'd just seen on Adelaide's phone. He started toward the trail, the gravel crunching under the heels of his boots. At the edge of the parking lot, a sign in four languages indicated that it was twelve hundred meters to the Eremo and that visitors should stay on the path. He stepped onto it from the parking lot, finding well-trodden dirt rather than gravel. Small holes from Adelaide's walking stick ran along the right side.

The overhanging branches immediately cut down on the light like a dimmer switch, but at least the patches of fog had not penetrated the forest. A light wind blew through the branches, causing a rustle not unlike that of aspen trees in the Sandia Mountains, where Rick had hiked so many times. There would be no views on this hike like in New Mexico, despite the hills. Tall trees covered any chance of that. The path cut back and forth, avoiding steep stretches but adding to the length of the hike. For those in a hurry, a set of steps ran directly up the hill, crossing the path in the middle of each switchback. Rick considered taking the steps, but decided to stay on the path. He was enjoying the tranquility of the forest and being able to run things over in his head. He had just made a turn and was starting up a relatively benign incline when he saw someone entering the path from the steps. Rick stopped when he recognized the reporter who had been begging him for an interview. The man's chin had more stubble, and he wore a heavier shirt, but otherwise, except for a small backpack, he looked the same.

Stopping to catch his breath, Angelo Stefani spotted Rick and smiled. "Well, this is perfect. We have no one to interrupt us when I ask you a few questions. Certainly you will oblige me after I came all this way."

Rick did not try to hide his annoyance. "How did you find out the group was coming here this morning?"

"An anonymous tip. I would tell you, but you know how it is. We journalists have to protect our sources." He slipped his pack off his shoulder and held it by one strap. "I'll just get out my pen and notepad." The zipper stuck. He looked up at Rick, smiling, before jerking it open. His hand slipped into the bag and rummaged around inside.

"Listen, Signor Stefani, I'm not going to answer any questions, and I really must—"

Rick was interrupted by a gunshot behind him that sounded like it was next to his ear. Stefani's face showed total surprise as he stared down at the red spot on his shirt. He looked back at Rick and slowly crumpled to the ground. The open backpack fell next to him.

Rick spun around to see Detective Rossi; arms stiff, hands firmly gripping a pistol. He lowered it and inserted it somewhere inside his jacket. "Stay where you are, Signor Montoya." The policeman moved past Rick and knelt next to the body of the reporter before looking back. "He was about to shoot you, you know." He pulled on a pair of rubber crime-scene gloves from his pocket and pushed them over his fingers.

Rick was frozen in place. "I don't see any weapon."

Rossi smiled. "It must be in here." He lifted the backpack with his gloved hand and peered inside. "No, not there." He looked at Rick and shrugged before reaching into the pocket of his own raincoat and pulling out a dark pistol with a stubby silencer screwed to its barrel. "Oh, here it is." He lifted it and pointed it directly at Rick. "I may have misspoken, Signor Montoya. I said he was about to shoot you, but unfortunately he already did." He looked at the gun in his hand, still pointed at Rick. "And with this silencer, he would likely have gotten away with it. No one would have heard the shot that killed the famous translator. Thank goodness I came upon the crime scene, but what a shame that I got here a moment too late to prevent it." His eyes looked over the top of the pistol. "Well, at least I was able to kill your murderer. It will look very good on my record that I took out a Mafia hit man."

Rick stared at the end of the weapon, cursing himself for not accepting Chiara's offer of a bulletproof vest. How could he get out of this? Stall for time. Keep him busy. Don't mention that Berti is on her way, since that would rush him to finish the job sooner. "So when you worked in Palermo, Detective, it wasn't just for the police."

"The family can be very persuasive."

"Did you work for Inspector Cribari?"

"Ah, the good inspector. A model policeman. But unfortunately for you, we have no time to chat. Someone may have heard the shot." He raised the pistol higher and steadied his aim.

"Aren't you supposed to use a *lupara*? I've always heard it is the preferred weapon of the *Mafiosi* when getting revenge."

"Much too messy. And too bulky to carry easily."

Rick's eyes moved past Rossi. "A very large man is about to attack you."

Rossi laughed and looked at Rick's boots before turning his attention back to his aim. "That may work in your American cowboy movies, but not—"

The blow caught him squarely in the neck, and he was unconscious before he hit the ground. The pistol landed on the dirt with a thump.

"Lord, forgive me," said Zeke as he knelt next to the policeman. "Who is this guy, Rick?"

"Someone who doesn't like translators."

"And this one?"

"A journalist who found himself in the wrong place at the wrong time."

Zeke crossed himself and knelt over Stefani's body. He put his fingers to the journalist's neck, then quickly pulled a handkerchief from his pocket. "He's still alive." He pressed the cloth to the wound.

The sound of police sirens floated over the trees.

———

When Inspector Berti came around the bend in the path, she quickened her pace. The three uniformed cops with her did the same while pulling out their revolvers. What they saw was the priest kneeling next to a body, while Rick bent over the unconscious policeman, trying to extract his service revolver. The gun with the silencer lay on the ground beside them. Rick heard the approaching trio and looked up to see two guns trained on him.

"Are you all right?" Berti asked.

"Why wouldn't I be? I just saw a man nearly murdered, was almost killed myself, and more cops are aiming their guns at me. I'm fine."

"All right, I understand that sarcasm is your way of dealing with stress, Riccardo. Now tell me what this is all about." She glanced at the cops and switched languages. "You'd better do it in English."

"So there are no witnesses if this turns out to be as bad as it looks? You need not worry."

Zeke held his position, his hand still pressed to Stefani's shoulder. "This man needs medical attention. I've seen worse gunshot wounds, but he should get to a hospital."

She turned and barked orders to the uniformed men. One immediately ran down the path while pulling out his cell phone. The other rushed to the fallen journalist and took Zeke's place.

Rick explained what had happened on the trail, from the time the journalist had appeared until Zeke's mighty blow to the neck of Rossi.

"I can confirm what Rick said," said Zeke. "I had heard the shot and left the group to come back down the trail. I was able to come up behind the man when he was pointing his weapon at Rick. They were talking, but of course I couldn't understand what they were saying."

Berti told the third policemen to handcuff Rossi. She looked down at the still unconscious man on the path. "You did that, Father? You're a large man, but still…"

"Zeke was in the Marines before he took his vows," Rick said.

"That would explain it. The ambulance should be here soon, but I'll have them take care of Rossi second." She pulled out her cell phone and stepped away.

"Are you in trouble, Rick?"

"No, Zeke, but thanks for your concern. And thanks for saving my life."

"You can buy me a beer at the hotel."

After her calls, Berti turned back to Rick and spoke in English. "Your uncle will not be pleased with this, Riccardo. He was taking a personal interest in the Mafia case because you were involved. There will have to be a full investigation of the *questura* in Palermo, of course, and to say that it will be extremely messy would be an understatement. And to think that Rossi was working for me. You have to wonder how many other dirty cops there are around, waiting for orders from their Mafia bosses."

"Perhaps Rossi can shed some light on that."

"If he ever wakes up. You did a number on him, Padre."

Zeke asked if it was all right for him to rejoin the group, since they had to be wondering what had become of him.

"Of course. We'll get a formal statement from you later. Semper fi."

Zeke turned and trotted up the path.

Semper fi? Again Rick was impressed by her familiarity with popular American idioms but decided to test it again. Perhaps such word games were another of his defense mechanism with stress. "Well, Chiara, this was the undercard; now it's time for the main event." She was looking down at Rossi, who was starting to regain consciousness, and Rick was sure he'd stumped her.

"Let's hope it doesn't also end in a knockout."

"Rats."

"What?"

"Nothing. Listen, I think this next arrest should be handled rather delicately. I don't believe either of us is expecting any resistance, and I would prefer to not get the rest of the group more upset than they will be anyway. Could we keep your policemen out of sight?"

"I'm not as confident as you about a lack of resistance. We'll take two of my men; the other can wait here with Rossi. When we get up there, I'll have to check the lay of the land before deciding how to proceed. Let's hope the group stayed together; there are too many hiding places up there if they didn't." She went over to the policeman and gave them orders before returning to Rick. "Let's go. It should only take about ten minutes to get there."

"You sound like you've been here before."

"Many times. It is one of Gianni's favorite places. He loves its tranquility after the chaos of the kitchen, and he's also a very pious man."

"Pious and a good cook, the perfect combination for a husband."

"My thoughts exactly."

The trail continued to climb, but now it stayed straight, and low stone walls lined both sides of the path. Through the light mist that still clung to the forest, they could see a stone arch in the distance marking the entrance to the complex itself.

"The Eremo of today wouldn't be recognized by Francis," said Chiara. "It's still quite rustic by modern standards, but when he and his followers came up here, they slept in caves or on the bare ground. All the present structures were built well after his death."

When they passed through the arch and the buildings came into view, it was impossible to tell which had been the original stone structure. Over the centuries a jumble of additions had been tacked on at various angles, all clinging to the side of a ravine. Dense forest crowded in from above and below, as if trying to reclaim its space from the interloper in its midst. The thick green of the trees contrasted with the raw stone surfaces that were high enough to catch rays of sunlight.

A monk in brown Franciscan robes stood just inside the

arch and maintained a smile, despite the arrival of a group that included two uniformed policeman. "May I be of assistance?"

Inspector Berti answered, "We're looking for the group of Americans. They should have arrived here about twenty minutes ago."

"Oh, yes. With the tall priest. If they took the regular route, they would be somewhere near the chapel about now. I gave him a map, so I would expect they will follow it. Would you like one?"

"Thank you. I think I know the way."

"Is there something wrong?"

"No, Brother," she answered. "Thank you for your help."

With Rick and the two policemen in tow, the inspector walked quickly down a walkway that ran along the edge of the ravine. At the end they passed through a doorway into one of the buildings and were back in semidarkness. A narrow stairway took them up to another level where they came out onto a small patio before entering another inside corridor. Everything was stone, but the slabs that were exposed to the sun radiated warmth, while the walls inside held tightly to the chill. The maze continued.

"You really do know your way around this place," said Rick. Thanks to his daily runs, he was keeping up well, but he could hear the policemen behind him gasping for breath.

"We're almost there," Berti said. "I hope the brother was right."

He was. Rick and the inspector passed out of the dim light onto an open terrace where Zeke was addressing the group. Berti told the two policemen to watch from the doorway, out of sight, and they quickly pulled back into the shadows. Two other doorways opened onto the terrace: one directly across from where the new arrivals stood; the other was the entrance to the chapel. Opposite the chapel, and above the gaping ravine, ran a low wall topped by a metal rail for protection and flowerpots for decoration. The red of the geraniums stood out against the drab gray of the stone and the somber darkness of the forest below.

Zeke noticed Rick and Chiara, finished what he was saying to the group, and walked over to them with a look of concern on his face. "I suppose you are here to arrest me for assaulting a police officer," he said to Chiara, remembering that she spoke English.

"No, Father. We're here for another reason, I'm afraid. Thanks to Rick, we know the identity of the person who killed Biraldo. I regret to say that it is someone in your group."

Zeke clasped his hands together. "Dear God. That isn't possible." He looked behind him, where the others were now grouped in a line with their backs to the wall while Jessica snapped pictures. Everyone was mugging for the camera except Leon Alameda and Peter Rael, who had spotted Rick and the inspector, losing interest in photographs. Alameda said something to his wife, and she shot a glance at the new arrivals.

"What are you going to do?" Zeke asked.

"I need to talk to the photographer," said Chiara. "In order to be sure." She inclined her head toward the door of the chapel. "Let's do it over there, away from the others. Perhaps you should be present."

"Of course, Inspector."

By now everyone was aware that something was up, and they were talking in low voices and glancing at the policewoman. Jessica's camera hung from a strap around her neck as she stood next to Chris Carson. Zeke went to her, said something in her ear, and they walked together to the far side of the terrace where Rick and Berti were now standing.

"Jessica," said the inspector, "you remember who I am?"

"Of course." The girl's eyes darted between the faces of the three people standing with her. "What do you want? I answered all your questions at the hotel. Why didn't you speak English then?"

Berti ignored the second question and continued, her voice uncharacteristically soothing. "Jessica, you have become the unofficial photographer of the group, haven't you?"

"I suppose you could say that." She gripped her camera.

"You've taken photographs of everyone several times, and probably other pictures that could be described as more artistic, I suppose?"

"That's what I want to do. Become a professional photographer."

"Rick tells me your aunt is very proud of your skills with the camera. She was showing him your photographs on her cell phone before sending them back to you father. He also told me that you have a real knack for photography."

The girl swallowed hard and looked at Rick. "You saw all of them?"

"Yes, but there are three in particular that I'd like to show the inspector."

Jessica turned and looked back at Chris Carson. Fear covered his face.

Clutching her camera, she suddenly turned and ran toward the door but immediately saw the two policeman. With the rest of the group frozen in place and staring at her, she ran past everyone to the low wall and started to climb. Rick and Zeke took off in her direction.

"Jessica, no!" yelled Chris Carson, and he too rushed toward her.

She swung her knee over the metal rail, dislodging one of the flowerpots. It teetered before falling from the wall and crashing onto the rocks below. She was almost to the edge

220 DAVID P. WAGNER

when her camera became lodged between the rail and the wall, its strap tugging on her neck and holding her in place. She was struggling to get herself free when Zeke reached the wall. With one arm he grabbed her by her jacket collar and pulled her back down to the stone pavement. Rick took the camera and passed it to the inspector.

Jessica sat on the cold stone, staring but not seeing. Chris, sobbing, was next to her, stroking her hair. He looked up at Zeke, defiance showing through the tears.

"He deserved it, Father."

CHAPTER TWELVE

As he often did when deep in thought, Commissario Piero Fontana swirled the wine in his glass, watching the deep red liquid climb the sides and flow back to the center. He had ordered an excellent Barolo, an indication to Rick that his uncle was feeling some guilt at having recently put his nephew into danger. Since Betta was also at the lunch, it would mean two bottles, costing more than their food, even in a high-end Rome restaurant like this one where only Piero, the host, had been given a menu with prices. Rick and Betta waited while Piero pondered.

"I recall cases when a camera was used to commit blackmail, but never when it was a murder weapon."

"Not directly, Zio. The blow she gave Biraldo with her camera stunned him enough to cause him to lose balance and fall. When he hit, his neck was broken, causing death."

"She didn't intend to kill the man," Betta said, more as a statement than a question.

"I'm sure not," said Rick, "but she was certainly trying to hurt him. She said Biraldo was aggressively groping while trying to kiss her, and she became enraged and swung the camera.

Chris Carson had followed her and witnessed the whole scene from a distance. Then they concocted their alibis."

"Making him an accomplice," said Betta.

"Not exactly," said the *commissario*. "But close enough." He sighed like he had heard such stories before and they were never pleasant. "However, I think the jury will be lenient with her. With both of them, in fact, given the circumstances and the odious nature of the murder victim."

"It's Perugia, Zio, but I hope you are correct. Zeke told me her father hired a top trial attorney recommended by the embassy, so that should help. Which is likely what the girl expected, since her father had on more than one occasion stepped in when she'd gotten into trouble. Zeke thought it might have influenced her thinking."

"She thought, *Maybe I can get away with this, and if not, my father will get me off the hook.*"

"Exactly, Betta," said Rick.

"That would never happen in Italy," she said with a sly smile.

All three had ordered *risotto alla Milanese*, which the menu had specified would take a minimum of fifteen minutes to prepare. That was about the time Rick had needed to recount the story of the investigation into Biraldo's murder.

"I'm surprised that she was lured up there by the man," said Betta. "An Italian girl her age would never have done it."

"He promised to show her a spectacular sunset, Betta, which as a photographer she couldn't resist. And the pictures she took of it before the attack were excellent."

"It was her misfortune that you recognized the view from seeing it out of your hotel room window," said the *commissario*. "They could have gotten away with it."

A steaming bowl of risotto arrived at the table, and the waiter deftly divided it among three plates before placing one in front of each of the diners. He glanced at the almost empty wine bottle and received a nod from Piero in response. They exchanged wishes of *buon appetito*, sprinkled cheese over the golden grains, and had their first tastes.

"Close your eyes and you're a few steps from the Duomo," said Piero. He turned to Betta, who was seated between the two men. "We'll get back to Riccardo's adventures later. Now you must tell me about your investigation in Pisa."

She glanced at Rick, who was enjoying another forkful of rice. "Well, Piero, I was certainly not optimistic when I arrived there. Thefts from small churches happen all the time, and there's not much hope to get the stolen works back. But in this case, thanks to some extremely good fortune, it all turned out for the best. There was an anonymous tip, and the pastel was found without any noticeable damage. We didn't catch the thief, but what was important was returning this precious work of art to its rightful place in the church. The parish priest was beside himself with joy."

"I would imagine he would be. The stolen art was probably a steady source of visitors to the church."

Rick made a gesture like he was putting coins in a slot. "And revenue. The coins needed to turn on the spotlight can add up. I would imagine that the theft and recovery isn't hurting the tourist traffic either. People can be more interested in crime than a work of art."

Betta nodded. "Especially that work of art—it's not exactly Leonardo's *Last Supper*. So it all ended well for the parish. And something else I haven't told you yet, Rick. There was even more good news for the parish. A few days ago, the priest got an anonymous donation of fifty thousand euros to fix the church's leaking roof."

Rick coughed and took a sip of mineral water. "Sorry,

something went down wrong." He patted his lips with the linen napkin. "That is indeed good news."

For a minute they enjoyed their *risotti*, and the air was filled with the aroma of saffron, rather than with conversation.

"Has any progress been made in the case of Detective Rossi?" Rick knew crooked cops were a sore point with his uncle, but he felt that after what he'd gone through in Assisi, he could raise the issue.

The policeman thought for a moment before answering. "He's a hard nut to crack, as you would expect, with the Mafia waiting in the wings. If he revealed anything, he would be a dead man, so he may go to jail without giving up any information. That would be the safest for him in the long run. With the mob looking after him inside, nobody would dare touch him, even if he was a cop."

"What about the Palermo *questura*? Is my friend Cribari a suspect?"

"They're still investigating." Piero did not appear eager to share details, which Rick could understand. Perhaps at a later time, when they were alone, he would be more forthcoming.

Rick tugged at his shirt. "Something else, Zio. Will I be wearing this vest for the rest of my life? It's starting to chafe, even over an undershirt."

Piero smiled for the first time in many minutes. "That was a bit of good news I almost forgot to tell you. The Mafia family boss who had sworn revenge on you was found yesterday, and apparently he was not wearing a bulletproof vest himself. The rival family finally settled things in a manner typical of the Mafia. The new syndicate has no issues with you. In fact they might even want to thank you for the work you did. So you can drop the vest."

"Since it's police property, I'll bring it by your office tomorrow."

His uncle changed the subject. "I'm glad you had a chance to see your great-aunt, Riccardo."

"You did not tell me what a delight she would be, Zio."

"Filomena is on the Fontana side of your family, Riccardo. You should not have expected anything less." He placed his fork down on his empty dish. "And now to the decision on what to have next. Perhaps a *costoletta* to make it a completely Milanese meal?"

———

Outside the restaurant, after they thanked Piero and he had headed back to work, Rick and Betta began walking in the direction of her office. She slipped her arm under his as they walked.

"Your earrings are very becoming, Betta."

"Some guy I know brought them to me from Umbria." She touched the gold with her fingers before replacing her arm inside his. "You didn't tell me anything more about the inspector you worked with in Assisi."

"Nothing more to tell, really. As far as I know they haven't set a date for the wedding. Maybe we'll get an invitation."

"If he's catering the reception, we'll have to go." They walked a half block before Betta spoke again. "Was there anyone in this group from America that you knew? Besides the priest, I mean."

"One person, someone I remembered from when I was going to school."

"One of the men?"

"No, one of the wives."

"Uh huh." She gestured with her free hand to indicate that she was expecting more detail.

"She wanted my advice on what kind of Italian perfume to buy."

"Of course."

"No, really. As you would imagine, I was flattered that she remembered my interest in perfume."

"Likely it was the only thing she remembered about you. But I can understand that; your knowledge of scents was what attracted me to you when we first met."

"That was all?"

"Pretty much."

She had been staring down at the cobblestones, and now she looked up. "After all that wine, I think I could use another coffee."

"Good idea; there's a bar on the next corner." They walked another half block in silence before Rick was the one to break it. "Betta, that was quite a coincidence that the church got a donation that was just about the same as the value of the stolen artwork."

Betta was staring at the cobblestones as they walked. "Yes, that was indeed a coincidence."

They took more steps. "Betta, now I'm curious about something."

"What would that be?"

"Which one got your friend Elio's forgery—the church or the anonymous Swiss buyer?"

She was still looking down at the cobblestones, but Rick noticed the hint of a smile on her face.

"The next time you're in Pisa, you can visit the church and see for yourself what a beautiful pastel it is."

"You haven't answered my question."

"No, Rick, I suppose I haven't."

FOOD AND WINE

As his fans have come to expect, Rick again manages to eat well and does his best to sample as many local specialties as he can. Though most of the action on these pages takes place in Umbria, it all starts in Palermo, where he enjoys an excellent meal after a day's hard work. Seafood is ubiquitous on the island of Sicily, and the rolled-up swordfish filets are a delicious local specialty. After fish, eggplant may be the most popular food staple other than pasta for Sicilians, and his first course is appropriately gnocchi tossed with a tomato and eggplant sauce. The wine he has, a straw-yellow Bianco d'Alcamo, is named for the zone just southwest of Palermo where its grapes are grown. You probably won't find it in your local wine store unless you live in Italy.

Then Rick is off to Umbria. My wife was wary about him being served *vitello tonnato* during the lunch on his great-aunt's terrace. "David," she said, "that is a warm-weather dish, and it's early spring in the book." I managed to convince her it worked, mainly because it is one of my favorites, but also the lunch takes place on a warm day. Thin slices of veal served cold with a slather of tuna caper sauce sounds like it shouldn't work, but it does. At Rick's lunch the veal was preceded by what could be

called pasta primavera, and it is very easy to make: ripe tomatoes, capers, and fresh basil tossed in olive oil with the pasta of
your choice. After the required bottle of Prosecco to celebrate
the family reunion, they move to an unnamed white served in a
ceramic pitcher. It could be almost any local wine, perhaps one
produced for Filomena by a friend. All good wine does not have
to come out of a bottle with a fancy label, and if you are self-
confident about such things, like Filomena, you don't worry
about it.

The cuisine of Assisi is like that of the rest of Umbria, with
an emphasis on basic local ingredients such as mushrooms,
pork, game, and truffles. At Rick's first meal with the comely
inspector, they have two local specialties. Their pasta show-
cases the local olives, which in this dish have been turned into
a dark paste. Every region in Italy south of the Alps thinks
their olives are the best, but the black ones from Umbria are
especially tasty. Their second course is not what one might
think of as Italian food, but in fact chicken in a piquant sauce
is an Umbrian dish. Rick, after years in New Mexico, may have
found it bland.

Lunch the next day is at a more upscale restaurant, in fact a
real one where I have dined on a few occasions. The Hotel Le
Tre Vaselle sits in the middle of tiny Torgiano, almost a company
town, since everything seems to be owned by the Lungarotti
family, including the hotel. They also run both a wine museum
and an olive oil museum, and I have to say that I found the latter
more interesting. The Lungarottis are best known as a producers
of fine wine, and rows of their grapes spread out from Torgiano
to the east toward Assisi. Torgiano wines—that is a legal geo-
graphical denomination—along with those from Montefalco to
the east are rated among the finest in Umbria. So it would make
sense that a representative of the vineyard would talk to a group

of wealthy American visitors, especially since their labels can be found in wine shops in the States.

I had some fun with the lunch menu in Torgiano. *Strozzapreti* are a pasta popular in Umbria but also in other parts of Italy where they are sometimes called *strangolapreti*, but the idea is the same: they are so good that priests gorge themselves on them and choke. Since Umbria and especially Perugia were traditional bastions of Ghibelline (anti-papal) sentiment over the centuries, the dish was a natural to be served to the group. Also logical was the second course of beef cooked in the local wine. *Stracotto di manzo* sounds so much more exotic than "pot roast," which is essentially what it is. Of course the right cut of beef and an excellent wine make all the difference. In this case the wine was a Lungarotti Rubesco, which also accompanied the meal.

At the interlude with his aunt and friend on the hotel terrace, it is natural that they are served a bottle of Colli Perugini, since, as the name indicates, it comes from the hills around Perugia, in this case just south of town about equidistant between the Umbrian capital and Assisi.

After that lunch in Torgiano, it might be surprising that Rick has any appetite at dinnertime. But it is strange how hunger always seems to appear close to mealtime in Italy, despite what has been consumed earlier. He and the inspector dine on a hotel restaurant terrace in Spello, and again I had a place in mind for this one: the Hotel La Bastiglia. It has a commanding position at the top of the narrow hill on which Spello sits. I don't need to describe his spelt soup, since that is covered well in that scene. Inspector Berti's artichoke hearts are another example of how Italian chefs can take simple ingredients—in this case artichoke hearts, chopped ham, and cheese—to make an elegant and delicious dish. Their second course, roast pigeon, is something that I enjoyed on my first trip to Assisi many years ago.

Coincidentally, Rick has the same thoughts I did at the time about the irony of such a dish in the hometown of St. Francis. Their wine is again an unnamed local red, reminding us that all but the most elegant restaurants in Italy have a house wine, and in my experience it is always good.

All the books in this series end with Rick having lunch with his uncle, and in this one they are joined by Betta. I did not have a specific Roman eatery in mind for this repast, but it is a high-end place. The meal is very Milanese, starting with *risotto alla Milanese*. In Italy, at least in the good restaurants, menus warn that *risotto* will take time to cook correctly and diners should be prepared for the wait. This is because when it is done correctly, broth must be slowly added to the rice and stirred in until it is absorbed. Then more broth is added until the correct crunchy consistency is finally reached. Often restaurants will also specify that a minimum of two people must order the dish, since it's such a production to prepare it. *Risotto alla Milanese* is made with saffron, giving it a strong flavor and golden color. According to tradition—which probably means it isn't true—chefs in Renaissance Milan sprinkled gold dust on the dish to add to the golden color and demonstrate the wealth of the host. Their second course is a *costoletta alla Milanese*, a breaded veal cutlet always served with the bone in. In Milan the meat is pounded thin, lightly breaded, and served with a lemon wedge. To accompany the meal, and their discussion of the investigation, Piero has ordered a bottle of Barolo from the hills near the town of Asti, southeast of Torino. Rick's uncle could have ordered a wine from Lombardia, whose capital is Milan, to go with the Milanese food, but neither Rick nor Betta complained about drinking one of Italy's most famous reds.

AUTHOR'S NOTE

Rick unconsciously follows the title of book four in this series—*Return to Umbria*—to venture into the northern part of this most peaceful of Italian regions for number eight. Umbria is famous for its tranquility, helped by being land-locked and just far enough from neighboring Tuscany not to have been completely overrun by tourists. Being the birthplace of numerous saints also adds to the image. The regional capi-tal, Perugia, is known for chocolates, including the wonderful drops of hazelnut and dark chocolate called Baci. On one visit, my wife and I found ourselves in the midst of the annual choc-olate festival, with the main street, Corso Venucci, lined with vendors. Fortunately, no one had warned us, and since we had confirmed hotel reservations, it was a pleasant surprise. We ate a lot of chocolate.

While Perugia is large and bustling, as would be expected for a regional capital, once you drop off its hill into the rest of Umbria, everything becomes more peaceful. That is certainly the case in Assisi, even with the number of tourists who seek it out. To a great extent it draws a different kind of tourist: the religious pilgrim. I always tell people that because of Francis and Saint Clare, Assisi has a serenity you won't find in Italian towns of similar size. Not that it doesn't have art and other draws for the average tourist. Most famous is the thirteenth-century cycle of frescoes on the life of Francis by Giotto, in the Gothic upper cathedral.

Some of the action in this book takes place in Pisa, which is on the western edge of Tuscany. I always tell people that Pisa gets a bum rap because everyone thinks it is stuffed with tourists. It is, but only around the leaning tower. Back when Pisa was fabulously wealthy and one of the four great maritime powers of the Mediterranean, the city fathers decided to build their cathedral not in the center, like in most Italian cities, but far from the river. (It was likely because the ground was more stable there, but we know how that worked out with the tower.) As a consequence, nowadays tourist buses park just outside the north wall; visitors go in to see the tower and then leave to get back in their buses. If you go to Pisa, of course you have to see the cathedral, baptistery, and tower. The cathedral alone is one of the marvels of early Renaissance architecture. But if you venture a few blocks away from the tower, toward the river, the number of tourists drops significantly, and you find yourself in a relatively normal town. The Museo Nazionale di San Matteo (where Betta's friend Elio works) has a wonder-ful collection, including the Donatello bust described in the story, but it gets few visitors. The river that the museum faces is as impressive as when it flows through Florence. Pisa is also a college town, boasting one of the country's top universities, and that adds a nice atmosphere to the place. So be sure to see the rest of the city. Pisa has a fascinating history, and I would also urge you to read up on it before you go to make your visit more meaningful. Of course that's the advice I give if you're going anywhere in Italy.

And while you're doing research, you might look into the *conversos*, a fascinating subject I learned about when I lived in New Mexico. There are several scholarly books on the subject.

As always, I got help from others to get this book to press in addition to the great folks at Poisoned Pen Press and Sourcebooks. Kallene Faris was kind enough to provide needed support materials during the research and editing process. Bryan Kelsen graciously let me pick his brain about cameras and photographic equipment. My brother helped me to get details correct regarding the Marine Corps. When trying to decide what kind of car Rick should drive to Assisi, I naturally consulted my son, who is knowledgeable about all things automotive. Thanks again, Max. And as always my wife was instrumental in getting things right on these pages. In all my books, she checks the art references, food descriptions, and fashion, but this time she was there when I needed more than the usual help on perfume. She really deserved much more than a small bottle of Acqua di Santa Maria Novella perfume out of the deal.

Read on for an excerpt from

COLD TUSCAN STONE

another exciting
Rick Montoya Italian Mystery

CHAPTER ONE

Fall's coldest day brought a damp chill that seeped through clothing and skin, but the bearded man was oblivious to the temperature. He crossed his arms over his chest, bent forward slightly, and focused on the figures before him. His breath came in small clouds of vapor, obscuring the scene that held his gaze. He could not tear his eyes away from the drama before him.

The funeral procession he watched followed the ancient traditions of Etruria, but timeless sorrow was etched deeply into the faces of the family. Two powerful horses pulled the covered cart, heads bowed as if to honor the dead man inside. Their waving manes and pulsing muscles, so full of life, contrasted with the flat, tomb-shaped stones of the wall behind them. The wife, or perhaps an older daughter, followed on foot behind the cart with two children in tow, their eyes questioning her in silence. Behind their round faces, her robe dragged on the ground, covering sandaled feet. She gripped the tiny hands and stared ahead, her face stiff with grief. The observer guessed the two small figures were the grandchildren of the deceased, not quite aware of what was going on but sensing something dark. A lone male rider, cloak flowing behind him, sat on a saddled horse at

DAVID P. WAGNER

the head of the cortege. The steed strained forward against the reins, but the man's head was turned back toward the cart, his face reflecting the sadness of the woman. Was he her brother and now the reluctant head of the family?

The watcher would never know. He breathed deeply and pulled at his carefully trimmed beard, hoping the gesture didn't betray his nervousness to the two men with him.

"Spectacular," he said. One arm reached out to touch the cold alabaster, its fingers running across the smooth faces of the two draft horses, down through the curled grooves of the milky manes, and pausing for a moment at the muscles of their shanks. His hand and eyes continued to caress the stone as he spoke. He almost whispered, as if he were standing before an altar in a church. "It looks like it was carved yesterday."

The two other men exchanged glances, and one of them spoke.

"The urn was discovered only recently, and it has been professionally cleaned with great care." The voice was clipped and businesslike. "Had it been exposed to the elements for more than two millennia instead of buried in a tomb all that time, it would never have survived in this condition."

The three men stood in a half-lit basement room around the only piece of furniture in the space—a table on which the rectangular stone box sat. A heavy black cloth, which had covered the piece when they entered the room, was now folded neatly on the side of the table. The damp chill of the Milanese streets outside had seeped into the house; only the lack of wind kept the temperature bearable. All three men kept on their heavy coats, not that there was anywhere to hang them. A musty smell, maybe of something stored there in the past, permeated the room, but the man intently inspecting the funerary urn was oblivious to all but the stone box before him.

"Volterra? Fourth century BC?" His eyes stayed on the urn, examining the sides where the carving continued.

"Precisely." The two returned to silence as their visitor circled the box. The collector had made his desires known weeks earlier—put in his order, as it were—and they had delivered. Now it was time to let the Etruscan urn itself make the final sale.

Minutes passed before the man turned from the ancient stone to the two men who had been waiting patiently. "The cover?"

"This is the way it came to us. The lid must have been lost or destroyed at some point."

The first man ran his hand along the top edge and peered inside. "That makes it considerably less desirable."

"The price reflects that."

"Your price does seem reasonable...but I should like a few days to decide. It is not a small sum. Perhaps I could take a few photographs to help me—?"

When the potential buyer lifted a small camera from his coat pocket, the larger of the other two stepped forward and held up his hand.

"No." He spoke a touch too firmly. Then he added, in a less menacing tone, "I'm sure you will understand that photographing this piece is impossible. Under the circumstances."

"Yes, I understand completely." He slipped the camera back into his pocket. "As to the tomb where it was found...where was it located?"

The two associates exchanged glances, as if to decide who would reply. The shorter one finally said, "I'm afraid we can only say that it was in Tuscany, in the area around Volterra." He glanced again at his companion. "We are not told the exact location."

The man pretended that the answer satisfied him. "Yes, of course."

After a few more minutes of examination, the urn was covered with the cloth again and the three walked to the door. The buyer opened it and headed up the shadowed stairs toward the street. The larger man turned to his colleague and shook his head quickly. The other nodded agreement before following their visitor up the stairs. At the top, a metal door creaked open. The three stepped outside into a fog that almost obscured the building across the narrow alley. The short man pulled out a key and noisily closed the dead bolt on the door before turning to the client. Thirty meters away, where the alley began, cars crept slowly through the fog, their lights on but dimmed. The Milanese knew fog well and treated it with respect. The three walked in silence out to the street where they stopped.

"I will be in contact by the end of the week. I know you need an answer."

The dealers smiled stiffly and nodded. No handshake was offered, so the buyer hurried off toward the center of town while a tram rumbled past him on its tracks, making the sidewalk vibrate under his feet. They watched him until one tapped the other on the arm and jerked his head back toward the passage. By the time the tram was passing the alley, the key was back in its metal door.

ABOUT THE AUTHOR

David P. Wagner is a retired foreign service officer who spent nine years in Italy, learning to love all things Italian. Other diplomatic assignments included Brazil, Ecuador, and Uruguay, as well as two hardship postings to Washington, DC. He and his wife, Mary, live in Pueblo, Colorado. Visit his website at davidpwagnerauthor.com.